Tales From The Forest Lands

Traditional tales, fables and sagas from Finland & the Baltic...

Compiled & Edited by Clive Gilson

"Tales from the World's Firesides"

Book 10 in Part 1 of the series: Europe

Tales From The Forest Lands,

edited by Clive Gilson, Solitude, Bath, UK

www.clivegilson.com

First published as an eBook in 2018

2nd edition © 2019 Clive Gilson

3rd edition © 2023 Clive Gilson

Printed by IngramSpark

ISBN 978-1-913500-10-8

I have edited Clive Gilson's books for over a decade now – he's prolific and can turn his hand to many genres. poetry, short fiction, contemporary novels, folklore and science fiction – and the common theme is that none of them ever fails to take my breath away. There's something in each story that is either memorably poignant, hauntingly unnerving or sidesplittingly funny.

Lorna Howarth, *The Write Factor*

Tales From The World's Firesides is a grand project. I've collected '000's of traditional texts as part of other projects, and while many of the original texts are available through channels like Project Gutenberg, some of the narratives can be hard to read by modern readers, & so the Fireside project was born. Put simply, I collect, collate & adapt traditional tales from around the world & publish them for free as a modern archive. *Part 1* covers a host of nations & regions across Europe. I'm not laying any claim to insight or specialist knowledge, but these collections are born out of my love of story-telling & I hope that you'll share my affection for traditional tales, myths & legends.

Image by Chil Vera from Pixabay

ORIGINAL FICTION BY CLIVE GILSON

- Songs of Bliss
- Out of the Walled Garden
- The Mechanic's Curse
- The Insomniac Booth
- A Solitude of Stars

AS EDITOR – *FIRESIDE TALES – Part 1, Europe*

- Tales From the Land of Dragons
- Tales From the Land of The Brave
- Tales From the Land of Saints And Scholars
- Tales From the Land of Hope And Glory
- Tales From Lands of Snow and Ice
- Tales From the Viking Isles
- Tales From the Forest Lands
- Tales From the Old Norse
- More Tales About Saints and Scholars
- More Tales About Hope and Glory
- More Tales About Snow and Ice
- Tales From the Land of Rabbits
- Tales Told by Bulls and Wolves
- Tales of Fire and Bronze
- Tales From the Land of the Strigoi
- Tales Told by the Wind Mother
- Tales from Gallia
- Tales from Germania

EDITOR – *FIRESIDE TALES* – *Part 2, North America*

- Okaraxta - Tales from The Great Plains
- Tibik-Kìzis – Tales from The Great Lakes & Canada
- Jóhonaa'éí –Tales from America's Southwest
- Qugaaĝix̂ - First Nation Tales from Alaska & The Arctic
- Karahkwa - First Nation Tales from America's Eastern States
- Pot-Likker - Folklore, Fairy Tales, and Settler Stories from America

EDITOR – *FIRESIDE TALES* – *Part 3, Africa*

- Arokin Tales – Folklore & Fairy Tales from West Africa
- Hadithi Tales – Folklore & Fairy Tales from East Africa
- Inkathaso Tales – Folklore & Fairy Tales from Southern Africa
- Tarubadur Tales – Folklore & Fairy Tales from North Africa
- Elephant And Frog – Folklore from Central Africa

Preface

I've been collecting and telling stories for a couple of decades now, having had several of my own works published in recent years. My particular focus is on short story writing in the realms of magical realities and science fiction fantasies.

I've always drawn heavily on traditional folk and fairy tales, and in so doing have amassed a collection of many thousands of these tales from around the world. It has been one of my long-standing ambitions to gather these stories together and to create a library of tales that tell the stories of places and peoples from the four corners of our world.

One of the main motivations for me in undertaking the project is to collect and tell stories that otherwise might be lost or, at best forgotten. Given that a lot of my sources are from early collectors, particularly covering works produced in the late eighteenth century, throughout the nineteenth century, and in the early years of the twentieth century, I do make every effort to adapt stories for a modern reader. Early collectors had a different world view to many of us today, and often expressed views about race and gender, for example, that we find difficult to reconcile in the early years of the twenty-first century. I try, although with varying degrees of success, to update these stories with sensitivity while trying to stay as true to the original spirit of each story as I can.

I also want to assure readers that I try hard not to comment on or appropriate originating cultures. It is almost certainly true that the early collectors of these tales, with their then prevalent world views, have made assumptions about the originating cultures that have given us these tales. I hope that you'll accept my mission to preserve these tales, however and wherever I find them, as just that. I have, therefore, made sure that every story has a full attribution, covering both the original collector / writer and the collection title that this version has been adapted from, as well as having notes about publishers and other relevant and, I hope, interesting source data. Wherever possible I have added a cultural or indigenous attribution as well, although for some of the tiles, the country-based theme is obvious.

This volume, *Tales from the Forest Lands* is part of a set of collections covering the Scandinavian story-telling tradition. This volume of tales from the north concentrates on Finland. Many of these stories have their roots in the folklore of Finnish paganism, and they have many features shared with fellow Finnic Estonian mythology and other Uralic fables. Finnish folklore also shares some similarities with neighbouring Baltic, Slavic and to a lesser extent, Norse mythologies.

Much of Finnish mythology survived within an oral tradition of mythical poem-singing and folklore well into the 19th century. One of my favourite aspects of Finnish mythology is the wonderful sense of darkness at its heart.

These stories come from collectors such as Andrew Lang and his *Coloured Fairy Books*, the elusive R. Eivind's *Finnish Legends for*

English Children and Zacharias Topelius and *The Birch and the Star, and Other Stories*. Most derive from legendary cycles such as the *Song of the Kalevala* and earlier collections such as the *Lapplandische Märchen*.

These titles will grow over coming years to tell lost and forgotten tales from every continent, and even then, I'll just be scratching the surface of the world's lore and love. That's the great gift in storytelling. Since the first of our ancestors sat around in a cave, contemplating an ape's place in the world, we have, as a species, told each other stories of magic and cunning and caution and love. When I began to read through tales from the Celts, tales from Indonesia, tales from Africa and the Far East, tales from everywhere, one of the things that struck me clearly was just how similar are our roots. We share characters and characteristics. The nature of these tales is so similar underneath the local camouflage. Human beings clearly share a storytelling heritage so much deeper than the world that we see superficially as always having been just as it is now.

These tales were originally told by firelight as a way of preserving histories and educating both adult and child. These tales form part of our shared heritage, witches, warts, fantastic beasts, and all. They can be dark and violent. They can be sweet and loving. They are we and we are they in so many ways. I've loved reading and re-reading these stories. I hope you do too.

Clive

Bath, 2023

Andras Baive

Adapted by Andrew Lang in his Orange Fairy Book from an original by Josef Calasanz Poestion in Lapplandische Märche. The Orange Fairy Book was published by Longman, Green & Co in 1906.

ONCE UPON A TIME THERE LIVED in Lapland a man who was so very strong and swift of foot that nobody in his native town of Vadso could catch him if they were running races in the summer evenings. The people of Vadso were very proud of their champion, and thought that there was no one like him in the world, till, by-and-by, it came to their ears that there dwelt among the mountains a Lapp, Andras Baive by name, who was said by his friends to be even stronger and swifter than the bailiff. Of course not a creature in Vadso believed that, and declared that if it made the mountaineers happier to talk such nonsense, why, let them!

The winter was long and cold, and the thoughts of the villagers were much busier with wolves than with Andras Baive, when suddenly, on a frosty day, he made his appearance in the little town of Vadso. The bailiff was delighted at this chance of trying his strength, and at once went out to seek Andras and to coax him into giving proof of his vigour. As he walked along his eyes fell upon a big eight-oared boat that lay upon the shore, and his face shone with pleasure. "That is the very thing," laughed he, "I will make him jump over that boat." Andras was quite ready to accept the challenge, and they soon settled the terms of the wager. He who could jump over the boat without so much as touching it with his heel was to be the winner, and would get a large sum of money as the prize. So, followed by many of the villagers, the two men walked down to the sea.

An old fisherman was chosen to stand near the boat to watch fair play, and to hold the stakes, and Andras, as the stranger was told to jump first. Going back to the flag which had been stuck into the sand to mark the starting place, he ran forward, with his head well thrown back, and cleared the boat with a mighty bound. The lookers-on cheered him, and indeed he well deserve it; but they waited anxiously all the same to see what the bailiff would do. On he came, taller than Andras by several inches, but heavier of build. He too sprang high and well, but as he came down his heel just grazed the edge of the boat. Dead silence reigned amidst the townsfolk, but Andras only laughed and said carelessly, "Just a little too short, bailiff; next time you must do better than that."

The bailiff turned red with anger at his rival's scornful words, and answered quickly, "Next time you will have something harder to do." And turning his back on his friends, he went sulkily home. Andras, putting the money he had earned in his pocket, went home also.

The following spring Andras happened to be driving his reindeer along a great fiord to the west of Vadso. A boy who had met him hastened to tell the bailiff that his enemy was only a few miles off; and the bailiff, disguising himself as a Stalo, or ogre, called his son and his dog and rowed away across the fiord to the place where the boy had met Andras.

Now the mountaineer was lazily walking along the sands, thinking of the new hut that he was building with the money that he had won on the day of his lucky jump. He wandered on, his eyes fixed on the sands, so that he did not see the bailiff drive his boat behind a rock, while he changed himself into a heap of wreckage which floated in on the waves. A stumble over a stone recalled Andras to himself, and looking up he beheld the mass of wreckage. "Dear me! I may find some use for that," he said, and hastened down to the sea, waiting till he could lay hold of some stray rope which might float towards him. Suddenly - he could not have told why - a nameless fear seized upon him, and he fled away from the shore as if for his life. As he ran he heard the sound of a pipe, such as only ogres of the Stalo kind were wont to use; and there flashed into his mind what the bailiff had said when they jumped the boat, "Next time you will have something harder to do." So it was no wreckage after all that he had seen, but the bailiff himself.

It happened that in the long summer nights up in the mountain, where the sun never set, and it was very difficult to get to sleep, Andras had spent many hours in the study of magic, and this stood him in good stead now. The instant he heard the Stalo music he wished himself to become the feet of a reindeer, and in this guise he galloped like the wind for several miles. Then he stopped to take breath and find out what his enemy was doing. Nothing he could see, but to his ears the notes of a pipe floated over the plain, and ever, as he listened, it drew nearer.

A cold shiver shook Andras, and this time he wished himself the feet of a reindeer calf. For when a reindeer calf has reached the age at which he begins first to lose his hair he is so swift that neither beast nor bird can come near him. A reindeer calf is the swiftest of all things living. Yes; but not so swift as a Stalo, as Andras found out when he stopped to rest, and heard the pipe playing!

For a moment his heart sank, and he gave himself up for dead, till he remembered that, not far off, were two little lakes joined together by a short though very broad river. In the middle of the river lay a stone that was always covered by water, except in dry seasons, and as the winter rains had been very heavy, he felt quite sure that not even the top of it could be seen. The next minute, if anyone had been looking that way, he would have beheld a small reindeer calf speeding northwards, and by-and-by giving a great spring, which landed him in the midst of the stream. But, instead of sinking to the bottom, he paused a second to steady himself, then gave a second spring which landed him on the further shore. He next ran on to a little hill where he saw down and began to neigh loudly, so that the Stalo might know exactly where he was.

"Ah! There you are," cried the Stalo, appearing on the opposite bank, "for a moment I really thought I had lost you."

"No such luck," answered Andras, shaking his head sorrowfully. By this time he had taken his own shape again.

"Well, but I don't see how I am to get to you," said the Stalo, looking up and down.

"Jump over, as I did," answered Andras, "it is quite easy."

"But I could not jump this river; and I don't know how you did," replied the Stalo.

"I should be ashamed to say such things," exclaimed Andras. "Do you mean to tell me that a jump, which the weakest Lapp boy would make nothing of, is beyond your strength?"

The Stalo grew red and angry when he heard these words, just as Andras meant him to do. He bounded into the air and fell straight into the river. Not that that would have mattered, for he was a good swimmer; but Andras drew out the bow and arrows which every Lapp carries, and took aim at him. His aim was good, but the Stalo sprang so high into the air that the arrow flew between his feet. A second shot, directed at his forehead, fared no better, for this time the Stalo jumped so high to the other side that the arrow passed between his finger and thumb. Then Andras aimed his third arrow a little over the Stalo"s head, and when he sprang up, just an instant too soon, it hit him between the ribs.

Mortally wounded as he was, the Stalo was not yet dead, and managed to swim to the shore.

Stretching himself on the sand, he said slowly to Andras, "Promise that you will give me an honourable burial, and when my body is in the grave go in my boat across the fiord, and take whatever you find in my house. Kill my dog, but spare my son, Andras."

Then he died; and Andras sailed in his boat away across the fiord and found the dog and boy. The dog, a fierce, wicked-looking creature, he slew with one blow from his fist, for it is well known that if a Stalo"s dog licks the blood that flows from his dead master's wounds the Stalo comes to life again. That is why no REAL Stalo is ever seen without his dog; but the bailiff, being only half a Stalo, had forgotten him, when he went to the little lakes in search of Andras. Next, Andras put all the gold and jewels which he found in the boat into his pockets, and bidding the boy get in, pushed it off from the shore, leaving the little craft to drift as it would, while he himself ran home. With the treasure he possessed he was able to buy a great herd of reindeer; and he soon married a rich wife, whose parents would not have him as a son-in-law when he was poor, and the two lived happy for ever after.

The World's Creation And The Birth Of Wainamoinen

Adapted by R. Eivind in Finnish Legends for English Children, from the original Song of the Kervala. Finnish Legends for English Children was published in 1893 by T. fisher Unwin, London.

LONG, LONG AGO, BEFORE THIS WORLD was made, there lived a lovely maiden called Ilmatar, the daughter of the Ether. She lived in the air - there were only air and water then - but at length she grew tired of always being in the air, and came down and floated on the surface of the water. Suddenly, as she lay there, there came a mighty storm-wind, and poor Ilmatar was tossed about helplessly on the waves, until at length the wind died down and the waves became still, and Ilmatar, worn out by the violence of the tempest, sank beneath the waters.

Then a magic spell overpowered her, and she swam on and on vainly seeking to rise above the waters, but always unable to do so. Seven hundred long weary years she swam thus, until one day she could not bear it any longer, and cried out, "Woe is me that I have fallen from my happy home in the air, and cannot now rise above the surface of the waters. Oh great Ukko, ruler of the skies, come and aid me in my sorrow!"

No sooner had she ended her appeal to Ukko than a lovely duck flew down out of the sky, and hovered over the waters looking for a place to alight; but it found none. Then Ilmatar raised her knees above the water, so that the duck might rest upon them; and no sooner did the duck spy them than it flew towards them and, without even stopping to rest, began to build a nest upon them.

When the nest was finished, the duck laid in it six golden eggs, and a seventh of iron, and sat upon them to hatch them. Three days the duck sat on the eggs, and all the while the water around Ilmatar's knees grew hotter and hotter, and her knees began to burn as if they were on fire. The pain was so great that it caused her to tremble all over, and her quivering shook the nest off her knees, and the eggs all fell to the bottom of the ocean and broke in pieces. But these pieces came together into two parts and grew to a huge size, and the upper one became the arched heavens above us, and the lower one our world itself. From the white part of the egg came the moonbeams, and from the yolk the bright sunshine.

At last the unfortunate Ilmatar was able to raise her head out of the waters, and she then began to create the land. Wherever she put her hand there arose a lovely hill, and where she stepped she made a lake. Where she dived below the surface are the deep places of the ocean, where she turned her head towards the land there grew deep bays and inlets, and where she floated on her back she made the hidden rocks and reefs where so many ships and lives have been lost. Thus the islands and the rocks and the firm land were created.

After the land was made Wainamoinen was born, but he was not born a child, but a full-grown man, full of wisdom and magic power. For seven whole years he swam about in the ocean, and in the eighth he left the water and stepped upon the dry land. Thus was the birth of Wainamoinen, the wonderful magician.

Tales From The Forest Lands

The Planting Of The Trees

Adapted by R. Eivind in Finnish Legends for English Children, from the original Song of the Kervala. Finnish Legends for English Children was published in 1893 by T. fisher Unwin, London.

WAINAMOINEN LIVED FOR MANY YEARS UPON the island on which he had first landed from the sea, pondering how he should plant the trees and make the mighty forests grow. At length he thought of Sampsa, the first-born son of the plains, and he sent for him to do the sowing. So Sampsa came and scattered abroad the seeds of all the trees and plants that are now on the earth; firs and pine-trees on the hills, alders, lindens, and willows in the lowlands, and bushes and hawthorn in the secluded nooks.

Soon all the trees had grown up and become great forests, and the hawthorns were covered with berries. Only the acorn lay quiet in the ground and refused to sprout. Wainamoinen watched seven days and nights to see if it would begin to grow, but it lay perfectly still. Just then he saw ocean maidens on the shore, cutting grass and raking it into heaps. And as he watched them there came a great giant out of the sea and pressed the heaps into such tight bundles that the grass caught fire and burnt to ashes. Then the giant took an acorn and planted it in the ashes, and almost instantly it began to sprout, and a tree shot up and grew and grew until it became a mighty oak, whose top was far above the clouds, and whose branches shut out the light of the Sun and the Moon and the stars.

When Wainamoinen saw how the oak had shut off all the light from the earth, he was as deeply perplexed how to get rid of it, as he had been before to make it grow. So he prayed to his mother Ilmatar to grant him power to overthrow this mighty tree, so that the sun might shine once more on the plains of Kalevala.

No sooner had he asked Ilmatar for help than there stepped out of the sea a tiny man no bigger than one's finger, dressed in cap, gloves, and clothes of copper, and carrying a small copper hatchet in his belt. Wainamoinen asked him who he was, and the tiny man replied, "I am a mighty ocean-hero, and am come to cut down the oak-tree.' But Wainamoinen began to laugh at the idea of so little a man being able to cut down so huge a tree.

But even while Wainamoinen was laughing, the dwarf grew all at once into a great giant, whose head was higher than the clouds, and whose long beard fell down to his knees. The giant began to whet his axe on a huge piece of rock, and before he had finished he had worn out six blocks of the hardest rock and seven of the softest sandstone. Then he strode up to the tree and began to cut it down. When the third blow had fallen the fire flew from his axe and from the tree; and before he had time to strike a fourth blow, the tree tottered and fell, covering the whole earth, north, south, east, and west, with broken fragments. And those who picked up pieces of the branches received good fortune; those who found pieces of the top became mighty magicians; and those who found the leaves gained lasting happiness.

And then the sunlight came once more to Kalevala, and all things grew and flourished, only the barley had not yet been planted. Now Wainamoinen had found seven magic barley-grains as he was wandering on the seashore one day, and he took these and was about to plant them; but the titmouse stopped him, saying, "The magic barley will not grow unless you first cut down and burn the forest, and then plant the seeds in the wood-ashes.'

So Wainamoinen cut down the trees as the titmouse had said, only he left the birch-trees standing. After all the rest were cut down an eagle flew down, and, alighting on a birch-tree, asked why all the others had been destroyed, but the birches left. And Wainamoinen answered that he had left them for the birds to build their nests on, and for the eagle to rest on, and for the sacred cuckoo to sit in and sing. The eagle was so pleased at this that he kindled a fire amongst the other trees for Wainamoinen, and they were all burnt except the birches.

Wainamoinen then brought forth the seven magic barley-seeds from his skin-pouch, and sowed them in the ashes, and as he sowed he prayed to great Ukko to send warm rains from the south to make the seeds sprout. And the rain came, and the barley grew so fast that in seven days the crop was almost ripe.

How Some Wild Animals Became Tame Ones

Adapted by Andrew Lang in his Brown Fairy Book from an original in Lapplandische Märchen. The Brown Fairy Book was published by Longman, Green & Co in 1904.

ONCE UPON A TIME THERE LIVED a miller who was so rich that, when he was going to be married, he asked to the feast not only his own friends but also the wild animals who dwelt in the hills and woods round about. The chief of the bears, the wolves, the foxes, the horses, the cows, the goats, the sheep, and the reindeer, all received invitations; and as they were not accustomed to weddings they were greatly pleased and flattered, and sent back messages in the politest language that they would certainly be there.

The first to start on the morning of the wedding-day was the bear, who always liked to be punctual; and, besides, he had a long way to go, and his hair, being so thick and rough, needed a good brushing before it was fit to be seen at a party. However, he took care to awaken very early, and set off down the road with a light heart. Before he had walked very far he met a boy who came whistling along, hitting at the tops of the flowers with a stick.

"Where are you going?" said he, looking at the bear in surprise, for he was an old acquaintance, and not generally so smart.

"Oh , just to the miller's marriage," answered the bear carelessly. "Of course, I would much rather stay at home, but the miller was so anxious I should be there that I really could not refuse."

"Don't go, don't go!" cried the boy. "If you do you will never come back! You have got the most beautiful skin in the world - just the kind that everyone is wanting, and they will be sure to kill you and strip you of it."

"I had not thought of that," said the bear, whose face turned white, only nobody could see it. "If you are certain that they would be so wicked - but perhaps you are jealous because nobody has invited you?"

"Oh , nonsense!" replied the boy angrily, "do as you see. It is your skin, and not mine; I don't care what becomes of it!" And he walked quickly on with his head in the air.

The bear waited until he was out of sight, and then followed him slowly, for he felt in his heart that the boy's advice was good, though he was too proud to say so.

The boy soon grew tired of walking along the road, and turned off into the woods, where there were bushes he could jump and streams he could wade; but he had not gone far before he met the wolf.

"Where are you going?" asked he, for it was not the first time he had seen him.

"Oh , just to the miller's marriage," answered the wolf, as the bear had done before him. "It is rather tiresome, of course - weddings are always so stupid; but still one must be good-natured!"

"Don't go!" said the boy again. "Your skin is so thick and warm, and winter is not far off now. They will kill you, and strip it from you."

The wolf's jaw dropped in astonishment and terror. "Do you really think that would happen?" he gasped.

"Yes, to be sure, I do," answered the boy. "But it is your affair, not mine. So good-morning," and on he went. The wolf stood still for a few minutes, for he was trembling all over, and then crept quietly back to his cave.

Next the boy met the fox, whose lovely coat of silvery grey was shining in the sun.

"You look very fine!" said the boy, stopping to admire him, "are you going to the miller's wedding too?"

"Yes," answered the fox, "it is a long journey to take for such a thing as that, but you know what the miller's friends are like - so dull and heavy! It is only kind to go and amuse them a little."

"You poor fellow," said the boy pityingly. "Take my advice and stay at home. If you once enter the miller's gate his dogs will tear you in pieces."

"Ah, well, such things have occurred, I know," replied the fox gravely. And without saying any more he trotted off the way he had come.

His tail had scarcely disappeared, when a great noise of crashing branches was heard, and up bounded the horse, his black skin glistening like satin.

"Good-morning," he called to the boy as he galloped past, "I can't wait to talk to you now. I have promised the miller to be present at his wedding-feast, and they won't sit down till I come."

"Stop! stop!" cried the boy after him, and there was something in his voice that made the horse pull up. "What is the matter?" asked he.

"You don't know what you are doing," said the boy. "If once you go there you will never gallop through these woods anymore. You are stronger than many men, but they will catch you and put ropes round you, and you will have to work and to serve them all the days of your life."

The horse threw back his head at these words, and laughed scornfully.

"Yes, I am stronger than many men," answered he, "and all the ropes in the world would not hold me. Let them bind me as fast as they will, I can always break loose, and return to the forest and freedom."

And with this proud speech he gave a whisk of his long tail, and galloped away faster than before.

But when he reached the miller's house everything happened as the boy had said. While he was looking at the guests and thinking how much handsomer and stronger he was than any of them, a rope was suddenly flung over his head, and he was thrown down and a bit thrust between his teeth. Then, in spite of his struggles, he was dragged to a stable, and shut up for several days without any food, till his spirit was broken and his coat had lost its gloss. After that he was harnessed to a plough, and had plenty of time to remember all he had lost through not listening to the counsel of the boy.

When the horse had turned a deaf ear to his words the boy wandered idly along, sometimes gathering wild strawberries from a bank, and sometimes plucking wild cherries from a tree, till he reached a clearing in the middle of the forest. Crossing this open space was a beautiful milk-white cow with a wreath of flowers round her neck.

"Good-morning," she said pleasantly, as she came up to the place where the boy was standing.

"Good-morning," he returned. "Where are you going in such a hurry?"

"To the miller's wedding; I am rather late already, for the wreath took such a long time to make, so I can't stop."

"Don't go," said the boy earnestly;" when once they have tasted your milk they will never let you leave them, and you will have to serve them all the days of your life."

"Oh , nonsense; what do you know about it?" answered the cow, who always thought she was wiser than other people. "Why, I can run twice as fast as any of them! I should like to see anybody try to keep me against my will." And, without even a polite bow, she went on her way, feeling very much offended.

But everything turned out just as the boy had said. The company had all heard of the fame of the cow's milk, and persuaded her to give them some, and then her doom was sealed. A crowd gathered round her, and held her horns so that she could not use them, and, like the horse, she was shut in the stable, and only let out in the mornings, when a long rope was tied round her head, and she was fastened to a stake in a grassy meadow.

And so it happened to the goat and to the sheep.

Last of all came the reindeer, looking as he always did, as if some serious business was on hand.

"Where are you going?" asked the boy, who by this time was tired of wild cherries, and was thinking of his dinner.

"I am invited to the wedding," answered the reindeer, "and the miller has begged me on no account to fail him."

"Oh , fool!" cried the boy, "have you no sense at all? Don't you know that when you get there they will hold you fast, for neither beast nor bird is as strong or as swift as you?"

"That is exactly why I am quite safe," replied the reindeer. "I am so strong that no one can bind me, and so swift that not even an arrow can catch me. So, goodbye for the present, you will soon see me back."

But none of the animals that went to the miller's wedding ever came back. And because they were self-willed and conceited, and would not listen to good advice, they and their children have been the servants of men to this very day.

Wainamoinen And Youkahainen

Adapted by R. Eivind in Finnish Legends for English Children, from the original Song of the Kervala. Finnish Legends for English Children was published in 1893 by T. fisher Unwin, London.

THUS WAINAMOINEN FINISHED HIS LABOURS AND began to lead a happy life on the plains of Kalevala. He passed his evenings singing of the deeds of days gone by and stories of the creation, until his fame as a great singer spread far and wide in all directions.

At this time, far off in the dismal Northland, there lived a young and famous singer and magician named You kahainen. He was sitting one day at a feast with his friends, when someone came and told about the famous singer Wainamoinen, and how he was a sweeter singer and a more powerful magician than anyone else in the world. This filled You kahainen's heart with envy, and he vowed to hasten off to the south and to enter into a contest with Wainamoinen to see if he could not beat him.

His mother tried to persuade him not to go, but in vain, and he made ready for the journey, declaring that he would sing such magic songs as would turn old Wainamoinen into stone. Then he brought out his noble steed and harnessed him to a golden sledge, and then jumping in, he gave the steed a cut with his pearl-handled whip, and dashed off towards Kalevala. On the evening of the third day he drew near to Wainamoinen's home, and there he met Wainamoinen himself driving along the highway.

Now You kahainen was too proud to turn out of the road for anyone, and so their sledges dashed together and were smashed to pieces, and the harnesses became all twisted up together. Then Wainamoinen said, "Who are you, oh foolish youth, that you drive so badly that you have run into my sledge and broken it to pieces?"

And You kahainen answered proudly, "I am You kahainen, and have come here to beat the old magician Wainamoinen in singing and in magic."

Wainamoinen then told him who he was, and accepted the challenge, and so the contest began. But You kahainen soon found that he was no match for his opponent, and at length he cried out in anger, "If I cannot beat you at singing and in magic, at least I can conquer you with my bright sword."

Wainamoinen answered that he would not fight so weak an opponent, and then You kahainen declared that he was a coward and afraid to fight. At last these taunts made Wainamoinen so angry that he could not restrain himself any longer, and he began to sing. He sang such wondrous spells that the mountains and the rocks began to tremble, and the sea was upheaved as if by a great storm. You kahainen stood transfixed, and as Wainamoinen went on singing his sledge was changed to brushwood and the reins to willow branches, the pearl-handled whip became a reed, and his steed was transformed into a rock in the water, and all the harness into seaweed. And still the old magician sang his magic spells, and

You kahainen's gaily-painted bow became a rainbow in the sky, his feathered arrows flew away as hawks and eagles, and his dog was turned to a stone at his feet. His cap turned into a curling mist, his clothing into white clouds, and his jewel-set girdle into stars.

At length the spell began to take effect on You kahainen himself. Slowly, slowly he felt himself sinking into a quicksand, and all his struggles to escape were in vain. When he had sunk up to his waist he began to beg for mercy, and cried out, "Oh great Wainamoinen, you are the greatest of all magicians. Release me, I beg, from this quicksand, and I will give you two magic bows. One is so strong that only the very strongest men can draw it, and the other a child can shoot.'

But Wainamoinen refused the bows and sank You kahainen still deeper. And as he sank, You kahainen kept begging for mercy, and offering first two magic boats, and then two magic steeds that could carry any burden, and finally all his gold and silver and his harvests, but Wainamoinen would not even listen to him. At length You kahainen had sunk so far that his mouth began to be filled with water and mud, and he cried out as a last hope, "Oh mighty Wainamoinen, if you release me I will give you my sister Aino as your bride."

This was the ransom that Wainamoinen had been waiting for, for Aino was famous for her beauty and loveliness of character, and so he released poor You kahainen and gave him back his sledge and everything just as it had been before. And when it was ready You kahainen jumped into it and drove off home without saying a word.

When he reached home he drove so carelessly that his sledge was broken to pieces against the gate-posts, and he left the broken sledge there and walked straight into the house with hanging head, and at first would not answer any of his family's questions.

At length he said, "Dearest mother, there is cause enough for my grief, for I have had to promise the aged Wainamoinen my dear sister Aino as his bride."

But his mother arose joyfully and clapped her hands and said, "That is no reason to be sad, my dear son, for I have longed for many years that this very thing should happen - that Aino should have so brave and wise a husband as Wainamoinen."

So the mother told the news to Aino, but when she heard it she wept for three whole days and nights and refused to be comforted, saying to her mother, "Why should this great sorrow come to me, dear mother, for now I shall no longer be able to adorn my golden hair with jewels, but must hide it all beneath the ugly cap that wives have to wear. All the golden sunshine and the silver moonlight will go from my life."

 But her mother tried to comfort her by telling her that the sun and moon would shine even more brightly in her new home than in her old, and that Kalevala was a land of flowers.

Aino's Fate

Adapted by R. Eivind in Finnish Legends for English Children, from the original Song of the Kervala. Finnish Legends for English Children was published in 1893 by T. fisher Unwin, London.

THE NEXT MORNING THE LOVELY AINO went early to the forest to gather birch shoots and tassels. After she had finished gathering them she hastened off towards home, but as she was going along the path near the border of the woods she met Wainamoinen, who began to speak, "Aino, fairest maid of the north, do not wear your gold and pearls for others, but only for me; wear for me alone your golden tresses."

"Not for you," Aino replied, "nor for others either, will I wear my jewels. I need them no longer; I would rather wear the plainest clothing and live upon a crust of bread, if only I might live for ever with my mother."

And as she said this she tore off her jewels and the ribbons from her hair, and threw them from her into the bushes, and then she hurried home, weeping. At the door of the dairy sat her mother, skimming milk. When she saw Aino weeping she asked her what it was that troubled her. Aino, in reply, told her all that had happened in the forest, and how she had thrown away from her all her ornaments.

Her mother, to comfort her, told her to go to a hill-top nearby and open the storehouse there, and there in the largest room, in the largest box in that room, she would find six golden girdles and seven rainbow-tinted dresses, made by the daughters of the Moon and of the Sun. "When I was young," her mother said, "I was out upon the hills one day seeking berries. And by chance I overheard the daughters of the Sun and Moon as they were weaving and spinning upon the borders of the clouds above the fir-forest. I went nearer to them, and crept up on a hill within speaking distance of them. Then I began to beseech them, saying, "Give some of your silver, lovely daughters of the Moon, to a poor but worthy maid; and I beg you, daughters of the Sun, give me some of your gold.' And then the Moon's daughters gave me silver from their treasure, and the Sun's daughters gave me gold that I might adorn my hair and forehead. I hastened joyfully home with my treasures to my mother's house, and for three days I wore them. Then I took them off and laid them in boxes, and I have never seen them since. But now, my daughter, go and adorn yourself with gold and silk ribbons; put a necklace of pearls around your neck, and a golden cross upon your bosom; dress yourself in pure white linen; put on the richest frock that is there and tie it with a belt of gold; put silk stockings on your feet and the finest of shoes. Then come back to us that we may admire you, for you will be more beautiful than the sunlight, more lovely than the moonbeams."

But Aino would not be consoled, and kept on weeping. "How happy I was in my childhood," she sang, "when I used to roam the fields and gather flowers, but now my heart is full of grief and all my life is filled with darkness. It would have been better for me if I had died a child; then my mother would have wept a little, and my father and sisters and brothers mourned a little while, and then all their sorrow would have been ended."

Aino wept for three days more, and then her mother once more asked her why she wept so, and Aino replied, "I weep, Oh mother, because you have promised me to the aged Wainamoinen, to be his comforter and caretaker in his old age. Far better if you had sent me to the bottom of the sea, to live with the fishes and to become a mermaid and ride on the waves. This had been far better than to be an old man's slave and darling.'

When she had said this she left her mother and hastened to the storehouse on the hill. There she opened the largest box and took off six lids, and at the bottom found six golden belts and seven silk dresses. She chose the best of all the treasures there and adorned herself like a queen, with rings and jewels and gold ornaments of every sort.

When she was fully arrayed she left the storehouse and wandered over fields and meadows and on through the dim and gloomy fir-forest, singing as she went:

"Woe is me, poor broken-hearted Aino!

My grief is so heavy that I can no longer live.

I must leave this earth and go to Manala,

the country of departed spirits.

Father, mother, brothers, sisters,

weep for me no longer,

for I am going to live beneath the sea,

in the lovely grottos,

on a couch of sea-moss."

For three long weary days Aino wandered, and as the cold night came on she at last reached the seashore. There she sank down, weary, on a rock, and sat there alone in the black night, listening to the solemn music of the wind and the waves, as they sang her funeral melody.

When at last the day dawned Aino beheld three water-maidens sitting on a rock by the sea. She hastened to them, weeping, and then began to take off all her ornaments and lay them carefully away. When at length she had laid all her gold and silver decorations on the ground, she took the ribbons from her hair and hung them in a tree, and then laid her silken dress over one of the branches and plunged into the sea.

At a distance she saw a lovely rock of all the colours of the rainbow, shining in the golden sunlight. She swam up and climbed upon it to rest. But suddenly the rock began to sway, and with a loud crash it fell to the bottom of the sea, carrying with it the unhappy Aino. And as she sank down she sang a last sad farewell to all her dear ones at home, a song that was so sweet and mournful that the wild beasts heard it, and were so touched by it that they resolved to send a messenger to tell her parents what had happened.

So the animals held a council, and first the bear was proposed as messenger, but they were afraid he would eat the cattle. Next came the wolf, but they feared that he might eat the sheep. Then the fox was proposed, but then he might eat the chickens. So at length the hare was chosen to bear the sad tidings, and he promised to perform his office faithfully.

He ran like the wind, and soon reached Aino's home. There he found no one in the house, but on going to the door of the bath-cabin he found some servants there making birch brooms. They had no sooner caught sight of him than they threatened to roast him and eat him, but he replied, "Do not think I have come here to let you roast me. For I come with sad tidings to tell you of the flight of Aino and how she died. The rainbow-coloured stone sank with her to the bottom of the sea, and she perished, singing like a lovely song-bird. There she sleeps in the caverns at the bottom of the sea, and on the shore she has left her silken dress and all her gold and jewels."

When these tidings came to her mother the bitter tears poured from her eyes, and she sang:

"Oh all other mothers, listen:

never try to force your daughters

from the house they long to stay in,

unto husbands whom they love not.

Thus I drove away my daughter,

Aino, fairest in the Northland."

Singing thus she sat and wept, and the tears trickled down until they reached her shoes, and began to flow out over the ground. Here they formed three little streams, which flowed on and grew larger and larger until they became roaring torrents, and in each torrent was a great waterfall. And in the midst of the waterfalls rose three huge rocky pillars, and on the rocks were three green hills, and on each of the hills was a birch-tree, and on each tree sat a cuckoo. And all three sang together.

And the first one sang "Love! Oh Love!" for three whole moons, mourning for the dead maiden.

And the second sang "Suitor! Suitor!" wailing six long moons for the unhappy suitor.

And the third sang sadly "Consolation! Consolation!" never ending all his life long for the comfort of the broken-hearted mother.

How The Stalos Were Tricked

Adapted by Andrew Lang in his Orange Fairy Book from an original in Lapplandische Märchen. The Orange Fairy Book was published by Longman, Green & Co in 1906.

"MOTHER, I HAVE SEEN SUCH A wonderful man," said a little boy one day, as he entered a hut in Lapland, bearing in his arms the bundle of sticks he had been sent out to gather.

"Have you, my son; and what was he like?" asked the mother, as she took off the child's sheepskin coat and shook it on the doorstep.

"Well, I was tired of stooping for the sticks, and was leaning against a tree to rest, when I heard a noise of 'sh-'sh, among the dead leaves. I thought perhaps it was a wolf, so I stood very still. But soon there came past a tall man - oh! twice as tall as father - with a long red beard and a red tunic fastened with a silver girdle, from which hung a silver-handled knife. Behind him followed a great dog, which looked stronger than any wolf, or even a bear. But why are you so pale, mother?"

"It was the Stalo," replied she, her voice trembling, "Stalo the man-eater! You did well to hide, or you might never had come back. But remember that, though he is so tall and strong, he is very stupid, and many a Lapp has escaped from his clutches by playing him some clever trick."

Not long after the mother and son had held this talk, it began to be whispered in the forest that the children of an old man called Patto had vanished one by one, no one knew where. The unhappy father searched the country for miles round without being able to find as much as a shoe or a handkerchief, to show him where they had passed, but at length a little boy came with news that he had seen the Stalo hiding behind a well, near which the children used to play. The boy had waited behind a clump of bushes to see what would happen, and by-and-by he noticed that the Stalo had laid a cunning trap in the path to the well, and that anybody who fell over it would roll into the water and drown there.

And, as he watched, Patto's youngest daughter ran gaily down the path, till her foot caught in the strings that were stretched across the steepest place. She slipped and fell, and in another instant had rolled into the water within reach of the Stalo.

As soon as Patto heard this tale his heart was filled with rage, and he vowed to have his revenge. So he straightway took an old fur coat from the hook where it hung, and putting it on went out into the forest. When he reached the path that led to the well he looked hastily round to be sure that no one was watching him, then laid himself down as if he had been caught in the snare and had rolled into the well, though he took care to keep his head out of the water.

Very soon he heard a "sh-"sh of the leaves, and there was the Stalo pushing his way through the undergrowth to see what chance he had of a dinner. At the first glimpse of Patto's head in the well he laughed loudly, crying, "Ha! ha! This time it is the old ass! I wonder how he will taste?"

And drawing Patto out of the well, he flung him across his shoulders and carried him home. Then he tied a cord round him and hung him over the fire to roast, while he finished a box that he was making before the door of the hut, which he meant to hold Patto"s flesh when it was cooked. In a very short time the box was so nearly done that it only wanted a little more chipping out with an axe; but this part of the work was easier accomplished indoors, and he called to one of his sons who were lounging inside to bring him the tool.

The young man looked everywhere, but he could not find the axe, for the very good reason that Patto had managed to pick it up and hide it in his clothes.

"Stupid fellow! what is the use of you?" grumbled his father angrily; and he bade first one and then another of his sons to fetch him the tool, but they had no better success than their brother.

"I must come myself, I suppose!" said Stalo, putting aside the box. But, meanwhile, Patto had slipped from the hook and concealed himself behind the door, so that, as Stalo stepped in, his prisoner raised the axe, and with one blow the ogre's head was rolling on the ground. His sons were so frightened at the sight that they all ran away.

And in this manner Patto avenged his dead children.

But though Stalo was dead, his three sons were still living, and not very far off either. They had gone to their mother, who was tending some reindeer on the pastures, and told her that by some magic, they knew not what, their father's head had rolled from his body, and they had been so afraid that something dreadful would happen to them that they had come to take refuge with her. The ogress said nothing. Long ago she had found out how stupid her sons were, so she just sent them out to milk the reindeer, while she returned to the other house to bury her husband's body.

Now, three days" journey from the hut on the pastures two brothers Sodno dwelt in a small cottage with their sister Lyma, who tended a large herd of reindeer while they were out hunting. Of late it had been whispered from one to another that the three young Stalos were to be seen on the pastures, but the Sodno brothers did not disturb themselves, the danger seemed too far away.

Unluckily, however, one day, when Lyma was left by herself in the hut, the three Stalos came down and carried her and the reindeer off to their own cottage. The country was very lonely, and perhaps no one would have known in which direction she had gone had not the girl managed to tie a ball of thread to the handle of a door at the back of the cottage and let it trail behind her. Of course the ball was not long enough to go all the way, but it lay on the edge of a snowy track which led straight to the Stalos' house.

When the brothers returned from their hunting they found both the hut and the sheds empty. Loudly they cried, "Lyma! Lyma!" But no voice answered them; and they fell to searching all about, lest perchance their sister might have dropped some clue to guide them. At length their eyes dropped on the thread which lay on the snow, and they set out to follow it.

On and on they went, and when at length the thread stopped the brothers knew that another day's journey would bring them to the Stalos" dwelling. Of course they did not dare to approach it openly, for the Stalos had the strength of giants, and besides, there were three of them; so the two Sodnos climbed into a big bushy tree which overhung a well.

"Perhaps our sister may be sent to draw water here," they said to each other.

But it was not till the moon had risen that the sister came, and as she let down her bucket into the well, the leaves seemed to whisper "Lyma! Lyma!"

The girl started and looked up, but could see nothing, and in a moment the voice came again.

"Be careful - take no notice, fill your buckets, but listen carefully all the while, and we will tell you what to do so that you may escape yourself and set free the reindeer also."

So Lyman bent over the well lower than before, and seemed busier than ever.

"You know," said her brother, "that when a Stalo finds that anything has been dropped into his food he will not eat a morsel, but throws it to his dogs. Now, after the pot has been hanging some time over the fire, and the broth is nearly cooked, just rake up the log of wood so that some of the ashes fly into the pot. The Stalo will soon notice this, and will call you to give all the food to the dogs; but, instead, you must bring it straight to us, as it is three days since we have eaten or drunk. That is all you need do for the present."

Then Lyma took up her buckets and carried them into the house, and did as her brothers had told her. They were so hungry that they ate the food up greedily without speaking, but when there was nothing left in the pot, the eldest one said, "Listen carefully to what I have to tell you. After the eldest Stalo has cooked and eaten a fresh supper, he will go to bed and sleep so soundly that not even a witch could wake him. You can hear him snoring a mile off, and then you must go into his room and pull off the iron mantle that covers him, and put it on the fire till it is almost red hot. When that is done, come to us and we will give you further directions."

"I will obey you in everything, dear brothers," answered Lyman; and so she did.

It had happened that on this very evening the Stalos had driven in some of the reindeer from the pasture, and had tied them up to the wall of the house so that they might be handy to kill for next day's dinner. The two Sodnos had seen what they were doing, and where the beasts were secured; so, at midnight, when all was still, they crept down from their tree and seized the reindeer by the horns which were locked together. The animals were frightened, and began to neigh and kick, as if they were fighting together, and the noise became so great that even the eldest Stalo was awakened by it, and that was a thing which had never occurred before. Raising himself in his bed, he called to his youngest brother to go out and separate the reindeer or they would certainly kill themselves.

The young Stalo did as he was bid, and left the house; but no sooner was he out of the door than he was stabbed to the heart by one of the Sodnos, and fell without a groan. Then they went back to worry the reindeer, and the noise became as great as ever, and a second time the Stalo awoke.

"The boy does not seem to be able to part the beasts," he cried to his second brother, "go and help him, or I shall never get to sleep." So the brother went, and in an instant was struck dead as he left the house by the sword of the eldest Sodno. The Stalo waited in bed a little longer for things to get quiet, but as the clatter of the reindeer's horns was as bad as ever, he rose angrily from his bed muttering to himself:

"It is extraordinary that they cannot unlock themselves; but as no one else seems able to help them I suppose I must go and do it."

Rubbing his eyes, he stood up on the floor and stretched his great arms and gave a yawn which shook the walls. The Sodnos heard it below, and posted themselves, one at the big door and one at the little door at the back, for they did not know what their enemy would come out at.

The Stalo put out his hand to take his iron mantle from the bed, where it always lay, but the mantle was not there. He wondered where it could be, and who could have moved it, and after searching through all the rooms, he found it hanging over the kitchen fire. But the first touch burnt him so badly that he let it alone, and went with nothing, except a stick in his hand, through the back door.

The young Sodno was standing ready for him, and as the Stalo passed the threshold struck him such a blow on the head that he rolled over with a crash and never stirred again. The two Sodnos did not trouble about him, but quickly stripped the younger Stalos of their clothes, in which they dressed themselves. Then they sat still till the dawn should break and they could find out from the Stalos" mother where the treasure was hidden.

With the first rays of the sun the young Sodno went upstairs and entered the old woman's room. She was already up and dressed, and sitting by the window knitting, and the young man crept in softly and crouched down on the floor, laying his head on her lap. For a while he kept silence, then he whispered gently, "Tell me, dear mother, where did my eldest brother conceal his riches?"

"What a strange question! Surely you must know," answered she.

"No, I have forgotten; my memory is so bad."

"He dug a hole under the doorstep and placed it there," said she. And there was another pause.

By-and-by the Sodno asked again, "And where may my second brother's money be?"

"Don't you know that either?" cried the mother in surprise.

"Oh , yes; I did once. But since I fell upon my head I can remember nothing."

"It is behind the oven," answered she. And again was silence.

"Mother, dear mother," said the young man at last, "I am almost afraid to ask you; but I really have grown so stupid of late. Where did I hide my own money?"

But at this question the old woman flew into a passion, and vowed that if she could find a rod she would bring his memory back to him. Luckily, no rod was within her reach, and the Sodno managed, after a little, to coax her back into good humour, and at length she told him that the youngest Stalo had buried his treasure under the very place where she was sitting.

"Dear mother," said Lyman, who had come in unseen, and was kneeling in front of the fire. "Dear mother, do you know who it is you have been talking with?"

The old woman started, but answered quietly, "It is a Sodno, I suppose?"

"You have guessed right," replied Lyma.

The mother of the Stalos looked round for her iron cane, which she always used to kill her victims, but it was not there, for Lyma had put it in the fire.

"Where is my iron cane?" asked the old woman.

"There!" answered Lyma, pointing to the flames.

The old woman sprang forwards and seized it, but her clothes caught fire, and in a few minutes she was burned to ashes.

So the Sodno brothers found the treasure, and they carried it, and their sister and the reindeer, to their own home, and were the richest men in all Lapland.

Wainamoinen's Search For Aino

Adapted by R. Eivind in Finnish Legends for English Children, from the original Song of the Kervala. Finnish Legends for English Children was published in 1893 by T. fisher Unwin, London.

WHEN THE NEWS ABOUT AINO REACHED Wainamoinen he began to weep most bitterly, and the tears fell all that day and night; but the next day he hastened to the water's edge and prayed to the god of dreams to tell him where the water-gods dwelt. And the dream-god answered him lazily, and told him where the island was around which the sea-gods and the mermaids lived.

Then Wainamoinen hastened to his boat-house, and chose a copper boat, and in it placed fishing lines and hooks and nets, and when all was ready he rowed off swiftly towards the forest-covered island which the dream-god had told him of. No sooner had he arrived there than he began to fish, using a line of silver and a hook of gold. But for many days he fished in vain, yet still he persevered. At last one day a wondrous fish was caught, and it played about and struggled a long time until at length it was exhausted, and the hero landed it in the boat.

When Wainamoinen saw it he was astonished at its beauty, but after gazing at it for some time he drew out his knife and was about to cut it up ready for eating. But no sooner had he touched the fish with his knife than it leapt from the bottom of the boat and dived under the water. Then it rose again out of his reach and said to him, "Oh ancient minstrel, I did not come here to be eaten by you, merely to give you food for a day."

"Why did you come then?" asked Wainamoinen.

"I came, Oh minstrel, to rest in your arms and to be your companion and wife for ever," the fish replied, "to keep your home in order and to do whatever you please. For I am not a fish; I am no salmon of the Northern Seas, but You kahainen's youngest sister. I am the one you were fishing for - Aino, whom you love. Once you were wise, but now you are foolish and cruel. You did not know enough to keep me, but would have eaten me for your dinner!"

Then Wainamoinen begged her to return to him, but the fish replied, "Nevermore will Aino's spirit come to you to be so treated," and as it spoke the fish dived out of sight.

Still Wainamoinen did not give up, but took out his nets and began dragging the waters. And he dragged all the waters in the lands of Lapland and of Kalevala, and caught fish of every sort, only Aino, now the water-maiden, never came into his net.

"Fool that I am," he said at length, "surely I was once wise, had at least a bit of wisdom, but now all my power has left me. For I have had Aino in my boat, but did not know until too late that I had even caught her."

And with these words he gave up his search and set off to his home in Kalevala. And on his way he mourned that the joyous song of the sacred cuckoo had ceased, and he sang:

"I shall never learn the secret

how to live and prosper.

If only my ancient mother were still living,

she could give me good advice

that this sorrow might leave me."

Then his mother awoke from her tomb in the depths and spoke to him, "Your mother was but sleeping, and I'll now advise you how this sorrow may pass over. Go at once to the Northland, where dwell wise and lovely maidens, far lovelier than Aino. Take one of them for your wife; she will make you happy and be an honour to your home."

Wainamoinen's Unlucky Journey

Adapted by R. Eivind in Finnish Legends for English Children, from the original Song of the Kervala. Finnish Legends for English Children was published in 1893 by T. fisher Unwin, London.

WAINAMOINEN MADE READY FOR A JOURNEY to the Northland, to the land of cold winters and of little sunshine, where he was to seek a wife. He saddled his swift steed, and mounting, started towards the north. On and on he went upon his magic steed, galloping over the plains of Kalevala. And when he came to the shores of the wide sea, he did not halt, but galloped on over the water without even so much as wetting a hoof of his magic courser.

But wicked You kahainen hated Wainamoinen for what he had done when he defeated him in magic, and so he made ready a bow of steel. He painted it with many bright colours and trimmed it with gold and silver and copper. Then he chose the strongest sinews from the stag, and at length the great bow was ready. On the back was painted a courser, at each end a colt, near the bend a sleeping maiden, near the notch a running hare. And after that he cut some arrows out of oak, put tips of sharpened copper on them, and five feathers on the end. Then he hardened the arrows and steeped them in the blood of snakes and the poison of the adder to give them magic power.

When all was ready You kahainen went out to wait for his enemy. For many days and nights he watched in vain, but still he did not weary, and at last one day at dawn he saw what seemed to be a black cloud on the waters. But by his magic are he knew that it was Wainamoinen on his magic steed. Then he went after his bow, but his mother stopped him and asked him whom he meant to shoot with his bow and poisoned arrows. You kahainen replied, "I have made this mighty bow and these poisoned arrows for the old magician Wainamoinen, that I may destroy my rival."

His mother reproved him, saying, "If you slay Wainamoinen all our joy will vanish, all the singing and music will die with him. It is better that we have his magic music in this world than to have it all go to the underground world Manala, where the spirits of the dead dwell."

You kahainen hesitated for a moment, but then envy and hatred filled his heart, and he replied, "Even though all joy and pleasure vanish from the world, yet will I shoot this rival singer, let the end be what it will."

With these words he hastened out and took his stand in a thicket near the shore. He chose the three strongest arrows from his quiver, and selecting the best among these three, he laid it against the string and aimed at Wainamoinen's heart. And as he still waited for him to come nearer, he sang this incantation:

"Be elastic, bow-string mine,

swiftly fly, Oh oaken arrow,

swift as light, Oh poisoned arrow,

to the heart of Wainamoinen.

If my hand too low shall aim you,

may the gods direct you higher.

If mine eye too high shall aim you,

may the gods direct you lower."

Then he let the arrow fly, but it flew over Wainamoinen's head and pierced and scattered the clouds above. Again he shot a second, but it flew too low and penetrated to the depths of the sea. Then he aimed the third, and it flew from his bow swift as lightning. Straight forward it flew, and struck the magic steed full in the shoulder so that Wainamoinen was plunged headlong into the waves. And then arose a mighty storm-wind, and the old magician was carried far out into the wide-open sea.

But You kahainen believed that he had killed his rival, and so went home, rejoicing and singing as he went. And his mother asked him, "Have you slain great Wainamoinen?" and he replied, "I have slain old Wainamoinen. Into the salt sea he plunged headlong, and the old magician is now at the bottom of the deep."

 But his mother replied, "Woe to earth for what you have done. Joy and singing are gone for ever, for you have slain the great wise singer, you have slain the joy of Kalevala."

Wainamoinen's Rescue

Adapted by R. Eivind in Finnish Legends for English Children, from the original Song of the Kervala. Finnish Legends for English Children was published in 1893 by T. fisher Unwin, London.

BUT WAINAMOINEN WAS NOT DEAD, BUT swam on for eight days and seven nights trying to reach land. And when the evening of the eighth day came and still no land was in sight, he began to grow tired and to despair of ever getting out alive.

But just then he spied an eagle of wonderful size flying towards him from the west. And the eagle flew up to him and asked who he was and how he had come there in the ocean.

And Wainamoinen replied, "I am Wainamoinen, the great singer and magician. I had left my home for the distant Northland, and as I galloped over the ocean and neared the shore, the wicked You kahainen killed my steed with his magic arrows, and I was cast headlong into the waters. And then a mighty wind arose and drove me farther and ever farther out to sea, and now I have been struggling with the winds and waves for eight long weary days, and I fear that I shall perish of cold and hunger before I reach any land."

The eagle replied, "Do not be discouraged, but seat yourself upon my back and I will carry you to land, for I have not forgotten the day when you left the birch-trees standing for the birds to sing in and the eagle to rest on."

So Wainamoinen climbed upon the eagle's broad back and seated himself securely there, and off the eagle flew, straight to the nearest land. There on the shore of the dismal Northland the eagle left him, and flew off to join his mate.

Wainamoinen found himself upon a bare, rocky point of land, without a trace of human life about it, nor any path through the woods by which it was surrounded. And he wept bitterly, for he was far from home, covered with wounds from his battle with the winds and waters, and faint with hunger: three days and three nights he wept without ceasing.

Now the fair and lovely daughter of old Louhi had laid a wager with the Sun, that she would rise before him the next morning. And so she did, and had time to shear six lambs before the Sun had left his couch beneath the ocean. And after this she swept up the floor of the stable with a birch broom, and collecting the sweepings on a copper shovel, she carried them to the meadow near the seashore. There she heard the sound of someone weeping, and hastening back she told her mother of it.

Then Louhi, ancient mistress of the Northland, hurried out from her house and down to the seashore. There she heard the sound of weeping, and quickly pushed off from the shore in a boat and rowed to where the weeping Wainamoinen sat.

When she came to him she said to him, "What folly have you done to be in so sad a state?"

Wainamoinen replied, "It is indeed folly that has brought me into this trouble. I was happy enough at home before I went on this expedition."

Then Louhi asked him to tell her who he was of all the great heroes.

Wainamoinen replied, "Formerly I was honoured as a great singer and magician: I was called the "Singer of Kalevala," the wise Wainamoinen."

Then Louhi said, "Rise, Oh hero, from your lowly couch among the willows, come with me to my home and there tell me the story of your adventures." So she took the starving hero into her boat and rowed him to the shore, and took him to her house. There she gave him food, and the warmth and rest and shelter soon restored to him all his strength. Then Louhi asked him to relate his adventures, and he told her all that had happened to him.

When he had finished Louhi said to him, "Weep no more, Wainamoinen, for you shall be welcome in our homes, you shall live with us and eat our salmon and other fish."

Wainamoinen thanked her for her kindness, but added, "One's own country and table and home are the best and dearest. May the great god, Ukko, the Creator, grant that I may once more reach my dear home and country. It is better to drink clear water from a birch cup in one's own home, than in foreign lands to drink the richest liquors from the golden beakers of strangers."

Then Louhi asked him, "What reward will you give me, if I carry you back to your beloved home, to the plains of Kalevala?"

Wainamoinen asked her what reward she would consider sufficient, whether gold or silver treasures, but Louhi answered, "I ask not for gold or silver, Oh wise Wainamoinen, but can you forge for me the magic Sampo, with its lid of many colours, the magic mill that grinds out flour on one side, and salt from another side, and turns out money from the third? I will give you, too, my daughter, as a reward, to be your wife and to care for your home."

But Wainamoinen answered sadly, "I cannot forge for you the magic Sampo, but take me to my country and I will send you Ilmarinen, who will make it for you, and wed your lovely daughter. Ilmarinen is a wondrous smith; he it was who forged the heavens, and so perfectly did he do it that we cannot see a single mark of the hammer on them."

 Louhi replied, "Only to him who can forge the magic Sampo for me will I give my daughter." Then she harnessed up her sledge and put Wainamoinen in it and made him ready for his journey home. And as he started off she spoke these words to him, "Do not raise your eyes to the heavens, do not look upward while the day lasts, before the evening star has risen, or a terrible misfortune will happen to you."

Then Wainamoinen drove off, and his heart grew light as he left the dismal Northland behind him on his way to Kalevala.

The Birch And The Star

Adapted by Zacharias Topelius in The Birch and the Star, and Other Stories, published by Row, Peterson and Co, 1915.

ABOUT THREE HUNDRED YEARS AGO FINLAND had suffered greatly. There had been war; cities were burned, the harvest destroyed and thousands of people had died; some had perished by the sword, others from hunger, many from dreadful diseases. There was nothing left but tears and want, ashes and ruins.

Then it happened that many families became separated; some were captured and carried away by the enemy, others fled to the forests and desert places or far away to Sweden. A wife knew nothing about her husband, a brother nothing about his sister, and a father and mother did not know whether their children were living or dead. Some fugitives came back and when they found their dear ones, there was such joy that it seemed as if there had been no war, no sorrow. Then the huts were raised from the ashes, the fields again turned yellow with golden harvest. A new life began for the country.

During the time of the war a brother and sister were carried far away to a foreign land. Here they found friendly people who took care of them. Year after year passed and the children grew and suffered no want. But even in their comfort and ease they could not forget their father, mother and native country.

When the news came that there was peace in Finland, and that those who wished might return, the children felt more and more grieved to stay in a foreign land, and they begged permission to return home. The strangers who had taken care of them laughed and said, "Foolish children, you don't realize that your country lies hundreds of miles away from here."

But the children replied, "That does not matter, we can walk home."

The people then said, "Here you have a home, clothes and food and friends who love you; what more do you desire?"

"More than anything else we want to go home," answered the children.

"But there is nothing but poverty and want in your home. There you would have to sleep on miserable moss beds and suffer from cold and hunger. Probably your parents, sisters, brothers and friends are dead long ago, and if you look for them you will find only tracks of wolves in the snow-drifts on the lonely field where your cottage used to stand."

"Yes," said the children, "but we must go home."

"But you have been away from your home for many years, you were only six and seven years old when you were carried away. You have forgotten the road you came on. You can't even remember how your parents look."

"Yes," said the children, "but we must go home."

"Who is going to show you the way?"

"God will help us," answered the boy, "and besides, I remember that a large birch tree stands in front of my father's cottage, and many lovely birds sing there every morning."

"And I remember that a beautiful star shines through the branches of the birch at night," said the little girl.

"Foolish children," said the people in the foreign land, "you must never think about this again; it will only bring you sorrow."

But still the children always thought about going home, not because they were disobedient, but because it was impossible for them to forget their country, impossible to cease longing for father and mother.

One moonlight night the boy could not sleep for the thoughts of home and parents. He asked his sister if she were asleep.

"No, I can't sleep. I am thinking of our home."

"And so am I," said the boy, "come let us pack our clothes and flee. There seems to be a voice in my heart that says, 'Go home, go home,' it is the voice of God I know, so we are doing nothing wrong."

"Yes, let us go," said the sister. And quietly they went away.

It was a lovely night, the moon shone brightly and lit up the paths. "But dear brother, I am afraid we never shall find our home," said the little girl after they had walked a while.

The brother answered, "Let us always go toward the northwest, and we shall surely reach Finland, and when we are there, the birch and the star shall be our sign. If we see the star shining through the leaves of the birch, we shall know that we are at home."

"But don't you think wild beasts may devour us or robbers carry us away?" cried she.

"Remember, sister dear, the hymn which our mother taught us long ago - 'Though you suffer in a foreign land, God will lead you by the hand.'"

"Yes," said the little girl, "God will send his angels to protect us in the foreign land."

And they went bravely on. The boy cut a stout stick from a young oak tree in order to protect his sister and himself, but no evil befell them.

One day they came to a crossroad where they did not know which way to go. Then they saw two little birds that were singing in a tree by the road on the left-hand side. "Come," said the brother, "this road is the right one. I know it from the song of the birds. Perhaps these little birds are sent by God to help us along."

The children went on, and the birds flew from branch to branch, but not faster than the little ones could follow them. The children ate nuts and berries in the woods, drank water from the clear brooks, and slept at night on soft beds of moss. They seemed to be cared for in a most wonderful way. They always had enough to eat, and they always found a place where they could spend the night. They could not tell why, but whenever they saw the little birds, they said, "See, there are God's angels, who are helping us." And so they walked on.

But at last the little girl grew very tired from wandering about so long, and said to her brother, "When shall we begin to look for our birch?"

And he answered, "Not until we hear people speak the language which our father and mother spoke."

Again they walked towards the north and west. Summer was gone, the days in the forests began to grow cold and again the little sister asked about the birch, but her brother begged her to be patient.

The country through which they now wandered gradually began to change. The land which they had left and through which they had walked for weeks and months was a level land, now they had come into a country with mountains, rivers and lakes. The little sister asked, "Tell me brother about how we shall get over the steep mountains?"

Her brother answered, "I shall carry you," and he carried her.

Again the little girl asked, "How shall we cross the rapid rivers and the great lakes?"

The boy answered, "We shall row across," and he rowed across the rivers and lakes; for wherever they came, they found boats, which seemed to be there just for their sakes. Sometimes the brother swam with his little sister across the rivers and they floated easily on the waves. At their side flew the two little birds. One evening when they were very tired, the children came upon the ruins of burned down buildings. Close by stood a large new farmhouse. Outside the kitchen door stood a girl peeling vegetables. "Will you give us something to eat?" asked the boy.

"Yes, come," answered the child, "mother is in the kitchen, she will give you supper, if you are hungry."

Then the brother threw his arms about his sister's neck. "Do you hear, sister? This girl speaks the language that our father and mother spoke. Now we may begin to look for the birch and the star." The children then went into the kitchen where they were received with much friendliness, and were asked where they came from. They answered, "We come from a foreign land and are looking for our home. We have no other mark than this - a large birch tree grows in the yard in front of the house. In the morning birds sing in its branches, and in the evening a large star shines through its leaves."

"Poor children," said the people, full of pity, "thousands of birches grow in this country, thousands of birds sing in the treetops, and thousands of stars shine in the sky. How will you find your birch and your star?"

The boy and girl answered, "God will help us. His angels have led us to our own country. Now we are almost at home."

"Finland is great," said the people, shaking their heads.

"But God is greater!" answered the boy. And they thanked the good people for their kindness and went on their way.

It was fortunate for the children that they did not need to sleep in the woods any longer, but could go from farm to farm. Though there were wide plains between the human dwellings and great poverty everywhere, the children were given food and shelter; all felt sorry for them.

But their birch and star they did not find. From farm to farm they looked; there were so many birches and so many stars, but not the right ones.

"Finland is so large, and we are so small," sighed the little girl, "I don't think we will ever find our home."

The boy said, "Do you believe in God?"

"Yes, you know I do," she answered.

"Remember then," continued the brother, "that greater miracles have been performed. When the three wise men journeyed to Bethlehem, a star went before them to show them the way. God will show us the way too."

"Yes, he will," answered the little girl. She always agreed with her brother. And bravely they trudged on.

One evening at the end of the month of May, they came to a lonely farm. This was in the second year of their wanderings. As they approached the house, they saw a large birch tree which stood in front of it. The light green leaves looked lovely in the bright summer evening and through the leaves shone the bright evening star. "That's our birch!" cried the boy.

"That is our star," whispered the little girl.

Each clasped the neck of the other and praised the good Lord with joyful hearts. "Here is the barn where father's horses stood," began the boy.

"I am sure this is the well where mother raised water for the cattle," answered the girl.

"Here are two small crosses under the birch. I wonder what that means," said the boy.

"I am afraid to go in," said the girl. "What if Father and Mother are not living, or think if they don't know us. You go in first, brother."

In the sitting-room sat an old man and his wife - well, they were really not old, but suffering and sorrow had aged them before their time. The man said to his wife, "Now spring has come again, birds are singing, flowers are peeping up everywhere, but there is no new hope of joy in our hearts. We have lost all our children, two are resting under the birch, and far sadder - two are in the land of the enemy, and we shall never see them on earth. It is hard to be alone when one grows old."

The wife answered, "I have not given up hope. God is mighty, he led the people of Israel out of their imprisonment. If he so wills he has the power to give us back our children."

"Oh , what a blessing that would be," answered the man.

While he was still talking, the door opened. In stepped a boy and a girl who asked for something to eat. "Come nearer children," said the man, "stay with us tonight." And to each other the old people said, "Our children would have been just their ages if we had been allowed to keep them, and they would have been just as beautiful," thought the parents, and they wept.

Then the children could keep still no longer, but embraced their father and mother, crying, "We are your children whom God in a wonderful way has led back from the foreign land."

The parents pressed the children to their hearts and all praised God, who on this lovely spring evening had brought the warmth of joy to them.

And now the children had to tell everything that had happened to them, and though there was much sorrow and many dark days to tell of, now the sorrow was changed to joy. The father felt of the arms of his son and rejoiced to find him so manly and strong. The mother kissed the rosy cheeks of her daughter and said, "I knew something beautiful would happen to-day, because two little strange birds sang so sweetly in the top of the birch this morning."

"We know those birds," said the little girl. "They are angels disguised which have flown before us all the way to lead us home. They sang because they were glad that we had found our home."

"Come, let us go and see the birch," said the boy. "Look, sister, here lie our little brother and sister."

"Yes," said the mother, "but they are now angels with God."

"I know, I know," cried the little girl, "the angels in bird form who have flown before us all the way and who sang of our coming, are our brother and sister. It was they who always seemed to say to us 'Go home to Father and Mother.' It was they who cared for us, so that we did not starve or freeze to death. It was they who sent us boats so that we were not drowned in the rapid rivers. It was also they who said to us, 'That is the right birch, this is the right star.' God sent them to keep us safe."

"See," said the boy, "the star is shining more brightly than ever through the leaves. It is bidding us welcome. Now we have found our home - now our wanderings are ended."

The Rainbow-Maiden

Adapted by R. Eivind in Finnish Legends for English Children, from the original Song of the Kervala. Finnish Legends for English Children was published in 1893 by T. fisher Unwin, London.

THE FAIR RAINBOW-MAIDEN, LOUHI'S DAUGHTER, sat upon a rainbow in the heavens, and was clad in the most splendid dress of gold and silver. She was busy weaving golden webs of wonderful beauty, using a shuttle of gold and a silver weaving-comb.

As Wainamoinen came swiftly along the way which led from the dark and dismal Northland to the plains of Kalevala before he had gone far on his way he heard in the sky above him the humming of the Rainbow-maiden's loom. Without thinking of old Louhi's warning, he looked up and beheld the maiden seated on the gorgeous rainbow weaving beauteous cloths. No sooner had he seen the lovely maiden than he stopped, and calling to her asked her to come to his sledge.

The Rainbow-maiden replied, "Tell me what you wish of me."

"You shall come with me," Wainamoinen replied, "to bake me honey-biscuit, to fill my cup with foaming beer, to sing beside my table, to be a queen within my home in the land of Kalevala."

But the maiden replied, "Yesterday I went at twilight to the flowery meadows. There I heard a thrush singing, and I asked him, 'Tell me, pretty song-bird, how shall I live most happily, as a maiden in my father's home or as a wife by my husband's side?' And the bird sang in reply, 'The summer days are bright and warm, and so is a maiden's freedom; the winter is cold and dark, and so are the lives of married women. They are like dogs chained in a kennel, no favours are given to wives.'"

But Wainamoinen answered the maiden, "The thrush sings only nonsense. Maidens are treated like little children, but wives are like queens. Come to my sledge, Oh maiden, for I am not the least among heroes, nor am I ignorant of magic. Come, and I will make you my wife and queen in Kalevala."

Then the Rainbow-maiden promised to be his wife if he would split a golden hair with a knife that had no edge, and take a bird's egg from the nest with a snare that no one could see. Wainamoinen did both these things, and then begged her to come to his sledge, for he had done what she asked.

But she set another task for him, telling him she would marry him if he could peel a block of sandstone and cut a whip-handle from ice without making a single splinter. And Wainamoinen did both these things, but still the maiden refused to go until he had performed a third task. This was to make from the splinters of her distaff a little ship, and to launch it into the water without touching it.

Then Wainamoinen took the pieces of her distaff and set to work. He took them to a mountain from which he got the iron for his work, and for three days he laboured with hatchet and hammer. But on the evening of the third day a wicked spirit, Lempo, caught his hatchet as he raised it up, and turned it as it fell, so that it hit a rock and broke in fragments, and one of the pieces flew into the magician's knee, and cut it, so that the blood poured out.

Then Wainamoinen began to sing a magic incantation to stop the blood from flowing, but his magic was powerless against the evil Lempo, and he could not stop the blood. Then he gathered certain herbs with wonderful powers, and put them on the wound, but still he could not heal it up, for Lempo's spell was too powerful for his magic.

So he got into his sledge again, and drove off at a gallop to seek for help. Soon he came to a place where the road branched off in three directions. He chose the left-hand one, and galloped on till he reached a house. When he went to the door he found only a boy and a baby inside, and when he had told them what he wanted, the boy said, "There is no one here that can help you , but take the middle road, and perhaps you will find help."

So off he galloped to where the roads branched off, and then along the middle one to another house. There he found an old witch lying on the floor, but she gave him the same answer that the boy had done, and sent him to the right-hand road.

On this road he came to another cottage, where an old man with a long grey beard was sitting by the fire. And when Wainamoinen told him of his trouble, the old man replied, "Greater things have been done by but three of the magic words; water has been turned to land, and land to water." On hearing this answer Wainamoinen rose from his sledge and went into the cottage, and seated himself there. And all this time his knee was bleeding, so that the blood was enough to fill seven huge birchen pots.

Then the old man asked him who he was, and bade him sing to him the origin of the iron that had wounded him so, and Wainamoinen related the following story of how iron was first made:

Long ago after there were air and water, fire was born, and after the fire came iron. Ukko, the creator, rubbed his hands upon his left knee, and there arose three lovely maidens, who were the mothers of iron and steel. These three maidens walked forth on the clouds, and from their bosoms ran the milk of iron, down unto the clouds and then down upon the earth. Ukko's eldest daughter cast black milk over the river-beds, and the second cast white milk over the hills and mountains, and the third red milk over the lakes and oceans; and from the black milk grew the soft black iron-ore; from the white milk the lighter-coloured ore; and from the red milk the brittle red iron-ore.

After the iron had lain in peace for a while, Fire came to visit his brother Iron and tried to eat him up. Then Iron ran from him and took refuge in the swamps and marshes, and that is how we now find iron-ore hidden in the marshes.

Then was born the great smith, Ilmarinen, and the next morning after he was born he built his smithy on a hill near the marshland. There he found the hidden iron-ore, and carried it to his smithy and put it in the furnace to be smelted. And Ilmarinen had not blown more than three strokes of the bellows before the iron began to grow soft as dough. But then Iron cried out to him, "Take me from this furnace, Ilmarinen, save me from this cruel torture!" for the heat of the fire had grown unbearable.

"You are not hurt, but only a little frightened," Ilmarinen replied, "but I will take you out, and you shall be a great warrior and slay many heroes."

But Iron swore by the hammer and anvil, "I will injure trees and mountains, but I'll never kill the heroes. I will be men's servant and their tool, but will not serve for weapons."

So Ilmarinen put the iron on his anvil, and made from it many fine things and tools of every kind. But he could not harden the iron into steel, though he pondered over it for a long time. He made a lye from birch-ashes and water to harden the iron in, but it was all in vain.

Just then a little bee came flying up, and Ilmarinen begged him to bring honey from all the flowers in the meadows, that he might put it in the water and so harden the iron to steel. But a hornet, one of the servants of the evil spirit Lempo, was sitting on the roof and overheard Ilmarinen's words. And the hornet flew off and collected all the evil charms he could find - the hissing of serpents, the venom of adders, the poison of spiders, the stings of every insect - and brought them to Ilmarinen. He thought that the bee had come and brought him honey from the meadows, and so mixed all these poisons with the water in which he was to plunge the iron. And when he thrust the iron into the poisoned water it was turned to hard steel, but the poisons made it forget its oath and grow hard-hearted, and it began to wound men and cause their blood to flow in streams. This was the origin of steel and iron.

When Wainamoinen had finished, the old man rose from the hearth and began an incantation to make the wound close up. First he cursed Iron that it had become so wicked, and then he bade the blood cease to flow by the power of his magic. And as he went on he prayed to great Ukko that if this magic incantation should not prove sufficient, Ukko himself would come and stop the wound.

By the time he had finished his words of magic the blood ceased flowing from the wound. Then the old man sent his son to make a healing salve out of herbs, to take away the soreness from Wainamoinen's knee.

 First the youth made a salve from oak-bark and young shoots, and many sorts of healing grasses. Three days and three nights he steeped them in a copper kettle, but when he had finished the salve would not do. Then he added still other healing herbs, and steeped it for three days more, and at last it was ready. First he tried it on a birch-tree that had been broken down by wicked Lempo. He rubbed the salve on the broken branches and said, "With this salve I anoint you , recover, Oh birch-tree, and grow more beautiful than ever!"

And the tree grew together and became more beautiful and stronger than ever before. Then he tried the salve on broken granite boulders and on fissures in the mountains, and it was so powerful that it closed them all together as if they had never existed. After this he hurried home and gave the magic salve to his father, and told him what he had done with it.

The old man anointed Wainamoinen's knee with it, saying, "Do not rely on your own virtue or power, but in your creator's strength; do not speak with your own wisdom, but with great Ukko's. Whatever in you is good comes from Ukko."

No sooner had the old man put on the salve and said these words, than Wainamoinen was seized with a terrible pain, and lay rolling and writhing on the floor in agony. But the old man bandaged up his knee with a silken bandage, and prayed to Ukko to come to his assistance.

And suddenly the pain left Wainamoinen and his knee became as strong and well as ever. Then he raised his eyes in gratitude to heaven and prayed thus to Ukko, "Praise to you , my Creator, for the aid that you have given me. For you have banished all my pain and trouble. Oh, all you people of Kalevala, both those now living and those to come, boast not of the work that you have done but give to God the praise, for the great Ukko alone can make all things perfect, Ukko is the one master!"

Ilmarinen Forges The Sampo

Adapted by R. Eivind in Finnish Legends for English Children, from the original Song of the Kervala. Finnish Legends for English Children was published in 1893 by T. fisher Unwin, London.

NO SOONER WAS WAINAMOINEN CURED OF his wound than he put his sledge in order and drove off at lightning speed towards Kalevala. For three days he journeyed over hills and valleys, over marshes and meadows, and on the evening of the third day he reached the land of Kalevala once again.

There, on the border line he halted, and began a magic song. And as he sang a fir-tree began to grow from the earth, and kept on growing until its top had grown up above the clouds and reached to the stars. When the tree had finished growing, Wainamoinen sang another magic song, so that the moon was caught fast in the tree's branches and obliged to shine there until Wainamoinen should reverse his spell. And then by another spell he made the stars of the Great Bear fast in the tree-top, and then jumped into his sledge and drove on again to his home, with his cap set awry on his head, mourning because he had promised to send Ilmarinen back to the Northland, to forge the magic Sampo as his ransom.

As he drove on he came to Ilmarinen's smithy, and he stopped and went into him. Ilmarinen welcomed him and asked where he had been so long, and what had happened to him.

Then Wainamoinen told him of his journey to the Northland, and all the dangers he had gone through, and he added, "In a village there I saw a maiden, who is the fairest in all the Northland. All there sing her praises, for her forehead shines like the rainbow and her face is fair as the golden moonlight. She is more beautiful than the sun and all the stars together, but she will not marry any suitor. But do you go, dear Ilmarinen, and see her wondrous beauty; forge the magic Sampo for her mother and then you shall win this lovely maiden to be your wife."

But Ilmarinen replied, "Oh cunning Wainamoinen, I know that you have promised me as a ransom for yourself. But I will never go to that gloomy country, nor do I care for your beautiful maiden; I will not go for all the maids in Pohjola."

Wainamoinen answered, "But I can tell you of still greater wonders, for I have seen a giant fir-tree growing on the border of our own country; its top is higher than the clouds, and in its branches shine the moon and the Great Bear."

"I will not believe your wonderful story," replied Ilmarinen, "until I see the tree with my own eyes and the moon and stars shining in it."

"Come with me," said Wainamoinen, "and I will show you that I speak the truth." So off they set to see the wondrous tree. When they had come to it Wainamoinen asked Ilmarinen to climb the tree and to bring down the moon and stars, and he at once began to climb up towards them.

But, while he was climbing, the fir-tree spoke to him, saying, "Foolish hero, why have you so little knowledge as to try to steal the moon from my branches?" No sooner had the tree said these words to Ilmarinen, than Wainamoinen sang a magic spell, calling up a great storm-wind, and saying to it, "Oh storm-wind, take Ilmarinen and carry him in your airy vessel to the dark and dismal Northland."

And the storm-wind came and heaped up the clouds so that they formed a boat, and seizing Ilmarinen from the tree it placed him in the clouds and rushed off to the north, carrying clouds and all with it. On and on he sailed, rising higher than the moon, tossed about by the wind, until at last he came to the Northland and the storm-wind set him down in Louhi's courtyard.

Old toothless Louhi saw him as he alighted, and asked him, "Who are you that comes through the air, riding on the storm-wind? Have you ever met the great smith Ilmarinen, for I have long been waiting for him to come and forge the magic Sampo for me."

"I do indeed know him well," he replied, "for I myself am Ilmarinen."

At these words Louhi hurried into the house and told her youngest daughter to dress herself in all her most splendid clothes and ornaments, for Ilmarinen was come to make the Sampo for them. So the maiden chose her loveliest silken dresses, and placed a circlet of copper round her brow, a golden girdle round her waist, and pearls about her neck, and in her hair she twisted threads of gold and silver. When she was dressed she looked, with her rosy, red cheeks and bright sparkling eyes, more lovely than any other maiden in all the Northland, and then she hurried to the hall to meet Ilmarinen.

Louhi went to Ilmarinen and led him into the house, where there was a feast spread ready for him. She gave him the best seat at the table, and the choicest viands to eat, and gave him everything he wished for. Then she asked him if he would forge the Sampo for her, and promised him, if he would, her fairest daughter as his wife.

Ilmarinen was charmed with her daughter's beauty, and he promised to do what she asked. But when he went to look for a place to work in, he could find no place, and not even so much as a pair of bellows to blow his fire with. Still he was not discouraged, but for three days he wandered about, looking for a place to build a workshop. On the evening of the third day he saw a huge rock that was suited for his purpose, and there he began to build. The first day he built the chimney and started a fire; the second day he made his bellows and put them in place; the third day he finished his furnace, and had everything ready to begin his work.

Then Ilmarinen made a magic mixture of certain metals and put them in the bottom of the furnace. And he hired some of Louhi's men to work the bellows and keep putting fuel on the fire. Three long summer days the workmen blew the bellows, until at length the base rock began to blossom in flames from the magic heat.

On the evening of the first day Ilmarinen bent over the furnace and took out a magic bow. It gleamed like the moon, had a shaft of copper and tips of silver, and was the most wonderful bow that had ever been made. But it would not rest satisfied unless it killed a warrior every day, and two on feast-days. So Ilmarinen broke it into pieces and threw them back into the furnace, and tried again to forge the Sampo.

On the evening of the second day he looked into the furnace and drew forth a magic vessel. It was all purple, save the ribs that were of gold and the vase of copper, and it was the most beautiful vessel that ever had been made. But wherever it went it always led men into quarrels and fights, so Ilmarinen broke it into pieces and threw it back into the furnace.

On the evening of the third day he took out of the furnace a magic heifer, with horns of gold and the most beautifully-shaped head. But she was ill-tempered and would not stay at home, but rushed through the forest and swamps and wasted all her milk on the ground. So Ilmarinen cut the magic heifer in pieces and threw them back into the furnace.

And on the fourth evening he took out a wonderful plough, the ploughshare of gold and the handles of silver and the beam of copper. But it ploughed up fields of barley and the richest meadows, so Ilmarinen threw it back into the furnace.

Then he drove away all his workmen, and by his magic called up the storm-winds to blow his bellows. They came from the North and South and East and West, and they blew one day and then another and then a third, until the fire leapt out through the windows, the sparks flew from the door, and the smoke rose up and mingled with the clouds. And on the third evening Ilmarinen looked into the furnace and beheld the magic Sampo growing there. Quickly he took it out and placed it on his anvil, and taking a huge hammer the wonderful smith forged the luck-bringing Sampo. From one side it grinds out flour, and from the other salt, and from the third it coins out money. And the lid is all the colours of the rainbow, and as it rocks back and forth it grinds one measure for the day, and one for the market and one for the storehouse.

Then old Louhi joyfully took the luck-bringing Sampo and hid it in the hills of Lapland. She bound it with nine great locks, and by her witchcraft made three roots grow all around it, two deep beneath the mountains and one beneath the seashore.

And when he had finished the Sampo, Ilmarinen came to the lovely daughter of Louhi and asked her if she were ready now to be his wife. But she replied, "If I should go with you, and leave the Northland, all the birds would cease to sing. No, never while I live will I give up my maiden freedom, lest all the birds should leave the forest and the mermaids leave the waters."

So Ilmarinen had made the Sampo all in vain, and he was now far from home and had no way of returning. But Louhi came to him and asked him why he was grieving, and when she learned his trouble, and that he now wished to return to his own home, she provided him with a boat of copper. And when he had set sail she sent the north wind to carry him on his way, and on the evening of the third day he reached his home.

There Wainamoinen met him and asked if he had forged the magic Sampo. "Yes," replied Ilmarinen, "I have forged the Sampo, with its lid of many colours. Louhi has the wondrous Sampo, but I have lost the beauteous maiden."

The Elf Maiden

Adapted by Andrew Lang in his Brown Fairy Book from an original in Lapplandische Märchen. The Brown Fairy Book was published by Longman, Green & Co in 1904.

ONCE UPON A TIME TWO YOUNG men living in a small village fell in love with the same girl. During the winter, it was all night except for an hour or so about noon, when the darkness seemed a little less dark, and then they used to see which of them could tempt her out for a sleigh ride with the Northern Lights flashing above them, or which could persuade her to come to a dance in some neighbouring barn. But when the spring began, and the light grew longer, the hearts of the villagers leapt at the sight of the sun, and a day was fixed for the boats to be brought out, and the great nets to be spread in the bays of some islands that lay a few miles to the north. Everybody went on this expedition, and the two young men and the girl went with them.

They all sailed merrily across the sea chattering like a flock of magpies, or singing their favourite songs. And when they reached the shore, what an unpacking there was! For this was a noted fishing ground, and here they would live, in little wooden huts, till autumn and bad weather came round again.

The maiden and the two young men happened to share the same hut with some friends, and fished daily from the same boat. And as time went on, one of the youths remarked that the girl took less notice of him than she did of his companion. At first he tried to think that he was dreaming, and for a long while he kept his eyes shut very tight to what he did not want to see, but in spite of his efforts, the truth managed to wriggle through, and then the young man gave up trying to deceive himself, and set about finding some way to get the better of his rival.

The plan that he hit upon could not be carried out for some months; but the longer the young man thought of it, the more pleased he was with it, so he made no sign of his feelings, and waited patiently till the moment came. This was the very day that they were all going to leave the islands, and sail back to the mainland for the winter. In the bustle and hurry of departure, the cunning fisherman contrived that their boat should be the last to put off, and when everything was ready, and the sails about to be set, he suddenly called out, "Oh , dear, what shall I do! I have left my best knife behind in the hut. Run, like a good fellow, and get it for me, while I raise the anchor and loosen the tiller."

Not thinking any harm, the youth jumped back on shore and made his way up the steep hank. At the door of the hut he stopped and looked back, then started and gazed in horror. The head of the boat stood out to sea, and he was left alone on the island.

Yes, there was no doubt of it - he was quite alone; and he had nothing to help him except the knife which his comrade had purposely dropped on the ledge of the window. For some minutes he was too stunned by the treachery of his friend to think about anything at all, but after a while he shook himself awake, and determined that he would manage to keep alive somehow, if it were only to revenge himself.

So he put the knife in his pocket and went off to a part of the island, which was not so bare as the rest, and had a small grove of trees. From one of these he cut himself a bow, which he strung with a piece of cord that had been left lying about the huts.

When this was ready the young man ran down to the shore and shot one or two sea-birds, which he plucked and cooked for supper.

In this way the months slipped by, and Christmas came round again. The evening before, the youth went down to the rocks and into the copse, collecting all the driftwood the sea had washed up or the gale had blown down, and he piled it up in a great stack outside the door, so that he might not have to fetch any all the next day. As soon as his task was done, he paused and looked out towards the mainland, thinking of Christmas Eve last year, and the merry dance they had had. The night was still and cold, and by the help of the Northern Lights he could almost see across to the opposite coast, when, suddenly, he noticed a boat, which seemed steering straight for the island. At first he could hardly stand for joy, the chance of speaking to another man was so delightful; but as the boat drew near there was something, he could not tell what, that was different from the boats which he had been used to all his life, and when it touched the shore he saw that the people that filled it were beings of another world than ours. Then he hastily stepped behind the wood stack, and waited for what might happen next.

The strange folk one by one jumped on to the rocks, each bearing a load of something that they wanted. Among the women he remarked two young girls, more beautiful and better dressed than any of the rest, carrying between them two great baskets full of provisions. The young man peeped out cautiously to see what all this crowd could be doing inside the tiny hut, but in a moment he drew back again, as the girls returned, and looked about as if they wanted to find out what sort of a place the island was.

Their sharp eyes soon discovered the form of a man crouching behind the bundles of sticks, and at first they felt a little frightened, and started as if they would run away. But the youth remained so still, that they took courage and laughed gaily to each other. "What a strange creature, let us try what he is made of," said one, and she stooped down and gave him a pinch.

Now the young man had a pin sticking in the sleeve of his jacket, and the moment the girl's hand touched him she pricked it so sharply that the blood came. The girl screamed so loudly that the people all ran out of their huts to see what the matter was. But directly they caught sight of the man they turned and fled in the other direction, and picking up the goods they had brought with them scampered as fast as they could down to the shore. In an instant, boat, people, and goods had vanished completely.

In their hurry they had, however, forgotten two things: a bundle of keys which lay on the table, and the girl whom the pin had pricked, and who now stood pale and helpless beside the wood stack.

"You will have to make me your wife," she said at last, "for you have drawn my blood, and I belong to you."

"Why not? I am quite willing," answered he. "But how do you suppose we can manage to live till summer comes round again?"

"Do not be anxious about that," said the girl, "if you will only marry me all will be well. I am very rich, and all my family are rich also."

Then the young man gave her his promise to make her his wife, and the girl fulfilled her part of the bargain, and food was plentiful on the island all through the long winter months, though he never knew how it got there. And by-and-by it was spring once more, and time for the fisher-folk to sail from the mainland.

"Where are we to go now?" asked the girl, one day, when the sun seemed brighter and the wind softer than usual.

"I do not care where I go," answered the young man, "what do you think?"

The girl replied that she would like to go somewhere right at the other end of the island, and build a house, far away from the huts of the fishing-folk. And he consented, and that very day they set off in search of a sheltered spot on the banks of a stream, so that it would be easy to get water.

In a tiny bay, on the opposite side of the island they found the very thing, which seemed to have been made on purpose for them; and as they were tired with their long walk, they laid themselves down on a bank of moss among some birches and prepared to have a good night's rest, so as to be fresh for work next day. But before she went to sleep the girl turned to her husband, and said, "If in your dreams you fancy that you hear strange noises, be sure you do not stir, or get up to see what it is."

"Oh , it is not likely we shall hear any noises in such a quiet place," answered he, and fell sound asleep.

Suddenly he was awakened by a great clatter about his ears, as if all the workmen in the world were sawing and hammering and building close to him. He was just going to spring up and go to see what it meant, when he luckily remembered his wife's words and lay still. But the time till morning seemed very long, and with the first ray of sun they both rose, and pushed aside the branches of the birch trees. There, in the very place they had chosen, stood a beautiful house - doors and windows, and everything all complete!

"Now you must fix on a spot for your cow-stalls," said the girl, when they had breakfasted off wild cherries, "and take care it is the proper size, neither too large nor too small." And the husband did as he was bid, though he wondered what use a cow-house could be, as they had no cows to put in it. But as he was a little afraid of his wife, who knew so much more than he, he asked no questions.

This night also he was awakened by the same sounds as before, and in the morning they found, near the stream, the most beautiful cow-house that ever was seen, with stalls and milk-pails and stools all complete, indeed, everything that a cow-house could possibly want, except the cows. Then the girl bade him measure out the ground for a storehouse, and this, she said, might be as large as he pleased; and when the storehouse was ready she proposed that they should set off to pay her parents a visit.

The old people welcomed them heartily, and summoned their neighbours, for many miles round, to a great feast in their honour. In fact, for several weeks there was no work done on the farm at all; and at length the young man and his wife grew tired of so much play, and declared that they must return to their own home. But, before they started on the journey, the wife whispered to her husband, "Take care to jump over the threshold as quick as you can, or it will be the worse for you."

The young man listened to her words, and sprang over the threshold like an arrow from a bow; and it was well he did, for, no sooner was he on the other side, than his father-in-law threw a great hammer at him, which would have broken both his legs, if it had only touched them.

When they had gone some distance on the road home, the girl turned to her husband and said, "Till you step inside the house, be sure you do not look back, whatever you may hear or see."

And the husband promised, and for a while all was still; and he thought no more about the matter till he noticed at last that the nearer he drew to the house the louder grew the noise of the trampling of feet behind him. As he laid his hand upon the door he thought he was safe, and turned to look. There, sure enough, was a vast herd of cattle, which had been sent after him by his father-in-law when he found that his daughter had been cleverer than he. Half of the herd were already through the fence and cropping the grass on the banks of the stream, but half still remained outside and faded into nothing, even as he watched them.

However, enough cattle were left to make the young man rich, and he and his wife lived happily together, except that every now and then the girl vanished from his sight, and never told him where she had been. For a long time he kept silence about it; but one day, when he had been complaining of her absence, she said to him, "Dear husband, I am bound to go, even against my will, and there is only one way to stop me. Drive a nail into the threshold, and then I can never pass in or out."

And so he did.

Lemminkainen And Kyllikki

Adapted by R. Eivind in Finnish Legends for English Children, from the original Song of the Kervala. Finnish Legends for English Children was published in 1893 by T. fisher Unwin, London.

LONG, LONG AGO A SON WAS born to Lempo, and he was named Lemminkainen, but some call him Ahti. He grew up amongst the islands and fed upon the salmon until he became a mighty man, handsome to look at and skilled in magic. But he was not as good as he was handsome - he had a wicked heart, and was more famous for his dancing than for great deeds.

Now at the time my story begins, there lived in the Northland a beautiful maiden named Kyllikki. She was so lovely that the Sun had begged her to marry his son and come and live with them. But she refused, and when the Moon came and besought her to marry her son, and the Evening Star sought her for his son, she refused them both. And after that came suitors from all the countries round about, but the lovely Kyllikki would not marry one of them.

When Lemminkainen heard of this, he resolved that he would win her himself. But his aged mother tried to dissuade him, telling him that the maiden was of a higher family than his own, that all the

Northland women would laugh at him, and then if he should try to punish them for their laughter, that the warriors of the Northland would fall on him and kill him. But all this did not make him change his mind, and he started off for the distant Northland.

When he came near to Kyllikki's home, all the women and maidens that saw him began to laugh at him because he looked so poor, and yet dared to try to win the fair Kyllikki's hand. When he heard them laughing, it made him so angry that he drove on without paying any attention to how he was driving, and when he came to the courtyard his sledge hit against the gate-post and broke to pieces, and threw him out into the snow.

He rose up angrier than ever, but all those around only laughed the harder at him, and made all manner of fun of him. Then they offered him a place as a shepherd on the mountains. So Ahti became a shepherd, and spent all the days on the hills, but in the evenings he went to their dances, and when he had shown them what. a skilful dancer he was, he soon became a great favourite with all the women, and they began to praise him instead of laughing at him.

But fair Kyllikki alone would have nothing to do with him - would not even look at him in spite of all his endeavours to win her. At last she was tired out with his attentions, and told him that he had better return home, for she did not like him, and that so long as he stayed there she would not even look at him.

Still he did not go away, but waited until a chance came to carry out his new plan. About a month after this, all the maidens were met together for a dance in a glen among the hills, and among them was Kyllikki. Suddenly Lemminkainen came galloping up in his sledge and seized the fair Kyllikki as she was dancing with the rest, placed her in his sledge, and drove off like the whirlwind, and as he flew by the frightened maidens he cried out to them, "Never tell that I have taken Kyllikki, or I will cast a magic spell over your lovers, so that they will all leave you and go off to the wars and will never come back to dance and make merry with you."

But Kyllikki wept and begged Lemminkainen to give her back her freedom, saying, "Oh , give me back my freedom, cruel Lemminkainen; let me return on foot to my grieving father and mother. If you will not let me go, Oh Ahti, I will curse you and will call upon my seven valiant brothers to pursue and kill you. Once I was happy among my people, but now all my joy has gone since you have come to torment me, Oh cruel-hearted Ahti!"

But all her words could not move Lemminkainen to release her. Then he said to her, "Dearest maiden, fair Kyllikki, cease your weeping and be joyful; I will never harm you nor deceive you. Why should you be sorrowful, for I have a lovely home and friends and riches, and you shall never need to labour. Do not despise me because my family is not mighty, for I have a good spear and a sharp sword, and with these I will gain greatness and power for your sake."

Then Kyllikki asked him, "Oh Ahti, son of Lempo, will you then be to me a faithful husband; will you swear to me never to go to battle nor to strife of any sort?"

"I will swear upon my honour," Lemminkainen replied, "that I will never go to battle, if you will promise in return never to go to dance in the village, however much you may long for it."

So the two swore before the great Ukko, Lemminkainen promising never to go to battle, and Kyllikki that she would never go to the village dances. And then Lemminkainen rejoicing cracked his whip, and they galloped on like the wind over hills and valleys towards the plains of Kalevala.

As they came near to Lemminkainen's home, Kyllikki saw that it looked dreary and poor, and began to weep again, but Lemminkainen comforted her, telling her that now he would build a splendid mansion for her, and so she grew cheerful once more.

They drove up to his mother's cottage, and as they entered his mother asked him how he had fared. Ahti answered, "I have well repaid the scorn of the Northland maidens, for I have brought the fairest of them with me in my sledge. I brought her here well wrapped in bear-skins, to be my loving bride for ever. Beloved mother, make ready for us the best room and prepare a rich feast, that my bride may be content."

His mother answered, "Praised be gracious Ukko, that has given me a daughter. Praise Ukko, my son, that you have won this lovely maiden, the pride of the Northland, who is purer than the snow, more graceful than the swan, and more beautiful than the stars. Let us make our dwelling larger, and decorate the walls most beautifully in honour of your lovely bride, the fairest maid of all creation."

Kyllikki's Broken Vow

Adapted by R. Eivind in Finnish Legends for English Children, from the original Song of the Kervala. Finnish Legends for English Children was published in 1893 by T. fisher Unwin, London.

LEMMINKAINEN AND KYLLIKKI LIVED TOGETHER happily for many years, keeping the promises they had made to each other. But one day Lemminkainen had not come home from fishing by sunset, and then the longing to dance was more than Kyllikki could withstand, and she went into the village and joined the maidens in their dance.

As soon as Lemminkainen came home, his sister Ainikki came to him and told him how Kyllikki had broken her promise and had joined in the dance. Then Lemminkainen grew angry and sad at the same time, and he went to his mother and asked her to steep his clothing in the blood of serpents, for he was going off to battle since Kyllikki could not keep her vow.

Kyllikki tried to persuade him not to leave her, telling him that she had dreamt a dream, in which she saw their home in flames and the fire bursting out through the doors and windows and roof. But Lemminkainen replied, "I have no faith in women's dreams or maidens' vows. Bring me my copper armour, mother, for I long to get to the wars, to go to dismal Pohjola, there to win great stores of gold and silver."

"Stay at home, my dear son," his aged mother said, "and drink the beer in our cellars, sitting peaceably by your own hearth, for we have more than enough gold and silver. Only the other day, as our servants were ploughing the fields they came upon a chest of gold and silver buried in the ground - take this and be content."

When all this had no effect upon Lemminkainen, his mother began to tell him of the magic of the Northland people, and that they would sing him into the fire so that he would be burnt to death. But he replied, "Long ago three Lapland wizards tried to bewitch me, and employed their strongest spells against me, but I stood unmoved. Then I began my own magic songs, and before long I overcame them and sank them to the bottom of the sea, where they are still sleeping and the seaweed is growing through their hair and beards."

Still his mother tried to stop him, and his wife Kyllikki begged his forgiveness in tears. He stood listening to them and brushing out his long black hair, but at last he became impatient, and threw the brush from him and cried out, "I will not stay, but keep that brush, and when you see blood oozing from its bristles, then you may know that some terrible misfortune has overtaken me."

Saying this he left them and put on his armour and harnessed his steed into his sledge. Then he sang a song, calling on all the spirits of the woods and the mountains and the waters and on great Ukko himself to help him against the Northland wizards, and when his song was ended he drove off like the wind.

In the evening of the third day he reached a little village in the Northland. Here he drove into a courtyard and called out, "Is there any one strong enough to attend to my horse and take care of my sledge." There was a child playing on the floor of the house, and it replied that there was no one there to do it. Then Lemminkainen rode on to another house and asked the same question; and a man standing in the doorway replied, "There are plenty here that are mighty enough not only to unharness your steed, but to conquer you and drive you to your home ere the sun has set."

Then Lemminkainen told him that he would return and slay him, and so drove off to the highest house in the village. Here he cast a spell over the watch-dog, so that he should not bark, and drove in. Then he struck on the ground with his whip, and from the ground there arose a vapour that concealed the sledge, and in the vapour was a dwarf that took his steed and unharnessed it and gave it food. But Lemminkainen went on into the house, having first made himself invisible. There he found a great many people singing and making merry, and by the fires the Northland wizards were seated. He made his way on, and then took on his own shape again and entered into the main hall, and cried out to those that were singing to be silent.

As soon as she saw him the mistress of the house ran up to him and asked him who he was, and how he had passed the watch-dog unnoticed. Then Lemminkainen told her who he was, and instantly began to weave his magic spells, while the lightning shot from his fur mantle and flames from his eyes. He sang them all under the power of his magic - some beneath the waters, some into the burning fire, some beneath the heaped-up mountains. Only one poor old man, who was blind and lame, did he leave untouched. And when the old man asked him why it was that he had alone been left, cruel Lemminkainen began to abuse him and to torment him with words, until the old man, Nasshut, grew almost wild with anger, and hobbled away, swearing to have vengeance. Nasshut journeyed on and on, and at last arrived at the river Tuoni, which separates the land of the dead from the land of the living. There he waited until Lemminkainen should come, for he knew, by his wizard's skill, that he would come there soon.

Lemminkainen's Second Wooing

Adapted by R. Eivind in Finnish Legends for English Children, from the original Song of the Kervala. Finnish Legends for English Children was published in 1893 by T. fisher Unwin, London.

AFTER THIS LEMMINKAINEN TRAVELLED ON through dismal Pohjola until he came to the home of aged Louhi. He went in to Louhi and begged her to give him one of her daughters in marriage, but Louhi refused, saying, "You have already taken one wife from Lapland, the fair Kyllikki, and I will give you neither the loveliest nor yet the ugliest of my daughters."

Still Lemminkainen kept urging her, and at last, to get rid of him, she said, "I will never give one of my daughters to a worthless man. You may not ask me again until you bring me the Hisi-reindeer."

Then Lemminkainen set to work to make his arrows and his darts. When these were done he went to Lylikki, the great snow-shoe maker, and bade him make a huge pair of snow-shoes, as he was going to hunt the Hisi-reindeer. At first Lylikki tried to dissuade him, telling him he could never succeed, but perhaps would die in the forest. But Lemminkainen ordered him again to make the snow-shoes, and Lylikki set to work. He made them of wood, only a few inches wide, but longer than Lemminkainen was tall, and with straps in the middle to fasten them on to the feet; and he also made a staff for Lemminkainen to push himself along with, or to keep his balance with when he slid down the hills.

At length they were finished, and Lemminkainen put them on, and his quiver on his back, and took his snow-staff in his hand, and as he set off he cried out, "There is no living thing in all the forest that can escape me now, when I take my mighty strides in Lylikki's snow-shoes."

But the evil spirit Hisi overheard him as he boasted thus, and Hisi set to work to make an enchanted reindeer, that Lemminkainen would never be able to catch. So he took bare willow branches to make the horns, and wood for the head, the feet and legs were made of reeds, and the veins from withered grass, the eyes were made from daisies, the ears from flowers, and the skin of the rough fir-bark, and the muscles from strong, sappy wood. When this magic reindeer was completed it was the swiftest and the finest-looking of all reindeer. And Hisi sent it off to Pohjola, telling it to lure Lemminkainen into the snow-covered mountains and there to wear him out with the cold and the fatigue of the chase. So the reindeer went forth to dismal Pohjola, and there it ran through the courtyards and the outhouses, overturning tubs of water, throwing the kettles from their hooks, and upsetting the dishes that were cooking before the fires. There was a frightful noise there, for all the dogs began to bark, and the children to cry, and the women to laugh, and the men to shout. And then the magic reindeer went on its way.

Now Lemminkainen had set out, as soon as his snow-shoes were ready, and had hunted the whole world over for a trace of the Hisi-reindeer, rushing like the wind over mountains and valleys, until the fire shot from his snow-shoes, and his snow-staff smoked. But after he had wandered over the whole world and still had found no trace of the Hisi-reindeer, he came at last to the corner of Northland where the magic animal had just run through the courts upsetting everything, and the children were still crying and the women laughing when he arrived. Lemminkainen asked what the cause was of their uproar, and they told him how the reindeer had been there.

No sooner had he heard this than off he flew over the snow, and as he went he sang a spell, calling on the powers of Pohjola to enable him to catch the Hisi-beast. After he had sung, he gave three huge strides with his snow-shoes, and at the end of the third he caught up with the Hisi-reindeer, and in another moment had it bound fast. Then he spoke to the reindeer and patted it on the head, and bade it come with him to Louhi. But suddenly the animal made a mighty rush, snapped his bonds in two, and sprang away over the hills and valleys out of sight.

Lemminkainen started off after it, but at the first step his snow-shoes broke right in two and threw him down, breaking his arrows and his snow-staff in his fall. Then he arose and looked sadly at his broken shoes and arrows and stick, and said to himself, "How shall I ever succeed in my hunt, now that my shoes are broken, and the reindeer is once more free?"

Lemminkainen's Death

Adapted by R. Eivind in Finnish Legends for English Children, from the original Song of the Kervala. Finnish Legends for English Children was published in 1893 by T. fisher Unwin, London.

FOR A LONG TIME LEMMINKAINEN SAT considering whether he should give up the chase and return to Kalevala, or still keep on after the Hisi-reindeer. At length he regained hope and courage, and having sung an incantation that made his snow-shoes and arrows and staff whole again, he started off once more.

This time he turned his steps to the home of Tapio, the god of the forest, and as he went he began to sing wondrous songs to Tapio and his wife Mielikki, begging them to help him, and promising them great stores of gold and silver if they would do so.

At last he arrived at Tapio's palace, which had window-frames of gold, and the palace itself was of ivory. And within it Mielikki and her daughters were dressed in golden garments, and wore gold and gems in their hair, and pearls round their necks. And they all promised to help Lemminkainen, and went off to drive the reindeer up to the palace so that he might catch it. Nor had he long to wait before whole troops of reindeer came flocking into the palace courtyard, and Lemminkainen saw among them the Hisi-deer, and caught it.

Then Lemminkainen sang a song of triumph, and having paid to Tapio's wife, Mielikki, the gold and silver he had promised, he hastened off with the reindeer to Louhi's home. But when he gave the Hisi-deer to her, she said, "I will give you my fairest daughter if you catch and bridle for me the fiery Hisi-horse, that breathes smoke and fire from his mouth and nostrils."

So Lemminkainen went off, taking with him a golden bridle to put on the horse. For three days he wandered without catching sight of the Hisi-horse, but on the third day he climbed to the top of a very high mountain, and from there he spied the steed on the plain amongst the fir-trees, breathing smoke and flames from his mouth and nostrils and eyes.

When Lemminkainen saw him he prayed to great Ukko to send a shower of icy hail upon the fiery Hisi-steed, and presently a great shower of hail rained down, and every hailstone was larger than a man's head. After the hail was over, Lemminkainen came up to the fiery horse and coaxed him to let the golden bridle be slipped over his head. Then off they went like the wind, the horse obeying Lemminkainen perfectly, and in a very short time they arrived at Louhi's house. When he had given the Hisi-horse to Louhi, Lemminkainen asked again for the hand of her fairest daughter. But Louhi told him she would not give him her daughter until he had killed the swan that swam on Tuoni's river, which flows between the land of the living and the dead.

Then Lemminkainen started off fearlessly to seek the graceful swan of Tuoni, and journeyed on and on until at length he came to the coal-black river. There the old shepherd of Pohjola, Nasshut, was waiting for him, and, though blind, he heard Lemminkainen's footsteps, and sent a serpent from the death-river to meet him. The serpent stung Lemminkainen just over the heart, so that he fell down dead almost instantly, only having time to call upon his ancient mother to help him.

And Nasshut cast his body into the dismal river Tuoni, where it was washed down through the rapids to the Deathland, Tuonela. There the son of the ruler of the Deathland took the body, and cutting it into five portions, cast them back into the stream, saying, "Swim there now, Oh Lemminkainen! Float for ever in this river, so that you may hunt the wild swan at your leisure."

And thus the handsome Lemminkainen died, and was cast into the river of Tuoni, that flows along the Deathland.

Lemminkainen's Restoration

Adapted by R. Eivind in Finnish Legends for English Children, from the original Song of the Kervala. Finnish Legends for English Children was published in 1893 by T. fisher Unwin, London.

LEMMINKAINEN'S MOTHER BEGAN TO GROW uneasy at his long absence, and to fear that some trouble had befallen him. At last one day, as his wife, the fair Kyllikki, was in her room, she noticed that drops of blood had begun to flow from the bristles of Lemminkainen's hair-brush. Then she began to weep and mourn, and ran and told his mother, who came and saw the blood oozing from the brush, and cried out, "Woe is me, for my son, my hero, is in some terrible distress; some awful misfortune has happened to him."

Saying this she hurried off, and went straight to Louhi's house. There she asked what had become of her son, but Louhi only replied that she did not know, that he had driven off long ago in a sledge she had given him, and perhaps the wolves or bears had eaten him.

"You are only telling falsehoods," replied Lemminkainen's mother, "for no bears or wolves can devour him; he would put them to sleep with his magic singing. Now, tell me truly, Oh Louhi, where have you sent my son, or I will destroy all your storehouses and even your magic Sampo."

And then Louhi said that she had given him a copper boat, and he had floated off on the river; perhaps he had perished in the rapids below. But Lemminkainen's mother answered, "You are still speaking falsely. Tell me the truth this time, or I will send plague and death upon you."

Then Louhi answered the third time, "I will tell you the truth. I sent him to fetch me the Hisi-reindeer, and then after the fire-breathing horse, and last of all, after the swan that swims the death-stream, Tuoni, that he might gain the hand of my fairest daughter. He may have perished there, for he has not come back since to ask for my daughter's hand."

No sooner had Louhi said this than the anxious mother hurried off to hunt for her son. Over hills and valleys, through marsh and forest, and over the wide waters she went, but looked for him in vain. Then she asked the Trees if they had seen him but they answered, "We have more than enough to think of with our own griefs. We are cut down with cruel axes and burned to death, and no one pities us."

So she wandered on and on, and finally she asked the Paths if they had seen her son pass by. But the Paths replied, "Our own lives are too wretched to think of other people's sorrows. We are trodden under foot by beasts and men, and the heavy carts cut us in pieces."

Next she asked the Moon, but the Moon replied, "I have trouble enough of my own. I have to wander all alone in both summer and winter nights, and have no rest."

Next she questioned the Sun, and he was kinder than the rest, and told her how her son had died in the gloomy river Tuoni.

Then she hastened to Ilmarinen, the wondrous smith, and bade him make a huge rake for her out of copper, with teeth a hundred fathoms long and the handle five hundred fathoms. Ilmarinen quickly forged a magic rake, and she hurried off with it to the gloomy river Tuoni, praying as she went, "Oh Sun, whom Ukko has created, shine for me now with magic power into the kingdom of death, into dark Manala, and lull all the evil spirits there to sleep."

The Sun came and sat upon a birch-tree near the river of Tuoni, and shone upon the Deathland, Tuonela, until all the spirits fell asleep. Then he rose, and hovering over them, warmed them into a yet deeper slumber, and then hurried back to his place in the sky.

Meanwhile Lemminkainen's mother had raked a long time in the coal-black river, but could find nothing. Then she waded in deeper and deeper, until she could reach into the deepest caverns with her rake. First, she found his jacket, and then the rest of his clothing; and finally, the third time she swept her rake along, it brought up Lemminkainen's body, but the hands and arms and head were still missing. Still she went on with her search, and at length all the pieces were gathered together.

When she had laid them beside each other, in their proper positions, she began to pray to the goddess of the veins, Suonetar, and the maiden of the ether, to come and join the different parts together, and to sew up the wounds and make him whole. And then she prayed to the mighty Ukko to help them, and to heal every part that was wounded or bruised, to touch them with his magic touch, and restore Lemminkainen to life.

And Ukko did so, and Lemminkainen lived once more, but he was still blind and deaf and dumb. But his mother considered deeply how she might restore these senses to him, and at length she called the little bee to her, and bade it go out and. collect honey from the healing plants in the meadows. So the bee flew away and returned very soon laden with honey from all the healing plants, and she anointed her son with this, but it only gave him his sight, and still left him deaf and dumb.

Again the mother sent off the bee, telling it to go across the seven oceans, and to alight on an enchanted isle in the eighth. There it would find magic honey to bring back. The bee did as it was told and found the magic honey-balm in tiny earthen vessels, and flew back with seven vessels in its arms and seven on each shoulder, all filled with the magic honey-balm. Lemminkainen's mother anointed him with this, and he could hear, but still remained speechless.

Then the mother bade the bee fly up to the seventh heaven and to bring down from there the honey of Ukko's wisdom, which was so abundant there. When the bee declared that it could not fly so high, she told it the way and sent it off. So the bee flew up and up, and at the end of the first day it rested on the moon. At the end of the second day it reached the shoulders of the Great Bear, and on the third day it flew over the Great Bear's head and reached the seventh heaven of Ukko. There it found three golden kettles, and in the first was a balm that gave ease to the heart, and. the balm in the second gave happiness, but the balm of the third kettle gave life. So the bee took some of the life-giving balm and hastened back to earth.

Then Lemminkainen's mother anointed him with this magic balm, speaking a magic spell as she rubbed him with it, and immediately he awoke, and his first words were, "Truly I have been sleeping long, but yet my sleep was a sweet one, for I knew neither joy nor sorrow."

When his mother asked how he had gone there and who it was that had harmed him, he told her all - how Louhi had sent him for the swan, and how old Nasshut, the blind Northland shepherd, had sent the serpent against him and killed him, for he did not know the charm to cure the sting of serpents. Then his mother upbraided him for his ignorance, and told him how the serpent was born from the marrow of the duck and the brain of swallows, mixed with Suojatar's saliva, and she told him too what the spell was to use against them. Thus his mother brought him back to life and health, and he was wiser and handsomer than ever, but still he was downhearted.

His mother asked him the reason of this, and he replied that he was still thinking of Louhi's daughter and longing for her as his bride, but that first he must shoot the wild. swan. But his mother answered, "Do not think of the wild swan, nor yet of Louhi's daughters. Return with me to Kalevala to your home, and thank and praise your Maker, Ukko, that he has saved you, for I alone could never have saved you from dismal Manala."

So Lemminkainen hastened home with his mother, - back again to his pleasant home in Kalevala.

The Fox And The Lapp

Adapted by Andrew Lang in his Brown Fairy Book from an original in Lapplandische Märchen. The Brown Fairy Book was published by Longman, Green & Co in 1904.

ONCE UPON A TIME A FOX lay peeping out of his hole, watching the road that ran by at a little distance, and hoping to see something that might amuse him, for he was feeling very dull and rather cross. For a long while he watched in vain; everything seemed asleep, and not even a bird stirred overhead. The fox grew crosser than ever, and he was just turning away in disgust from his place when he heard the sound of feet coming over the snow. He crouched eagerly down at the edge of the road and said to himself, "I wonder what would happen if I were to pretend to be dead! This is a man driving a reindeer sledge, I know the tinkling of the harness. And at any rate I shall have an adventure, and that is always something!"

So he stretched himself out by the side of the road, carefully choosing a spot where the driver could not help seeing him, yet where the reindeer would not tread on him; and all fell out just as he had expected. The sledge-driver pulled up sharply, as his eyes lighted on the beautiful animal lying stiffly beside him, and jumping out he threw the fox into the bottom of the sledge, where the goods he was carrying were bound tightly together by ropes. The fox did not move a muscle though his bones were sore from the fall, and the driver got back to his seat again and drove on merrily.

But before they had gone very far, the fox, who was near the edge, contrived to slip over, and when the Laplander saw him stretched out on the snow he pulled up his reindeer and put the fox into one of the other sledges that was fastened behind, for it was market-day at the nearest town, and the man had much to sell.

They drove on a little further, when some noise in the forest made the man turn his head, just in time to see the fox fall with a heavy thump on to the frozen snow. "That beast is bewitched!" he said to himself, and then he threw the fox into the last sledge of all, which had a cargo of fishes. This was exactly what the cunning creature wanted, and he wriggled gently to the front and bit the cord which tied the sledge to the one before it so that it remained standing in the middle of the road.

Now there were so many sledges that the Lapp did not notice for a long while that one was missing; indeed, he would have entered the town without knowing if snow had not suddenly begun to fall. Then he got down to secure more firmly the cloths that kept his goods dry, and going to the end of the long row, discovered that the sledge containing the fish and the fox was missing. He quickly unharnessed one of his reindeer and rode back along the way he had come, to find the sledge standing safe in the middle of the road; but as the fox had bitten off the cord close to the noose there was no means of moving it away.

The fox meanwhile was enjoying himself mightily. As soon as he had loosened the sledge, he had taken his favourite fish from among the piles neatly arranged for sale, and had trotted off to the forest with it in his mouth. By-and-by he met a bear, who stopped and said, "Where did you find that fish, Mr. Fox?"

"Oh, not far off," answered he, "I just stuck my tail in the stream close by the place where the elves dwell, and the fish hung on to it of itself."

"Dear me," snarled the bear, who was hungry and not in a good temper, "if the fish hung on to your tail, I suppose he will hang on to mine."

"Yes, certainly, grandfather," replied the fox, "if you have patience to suffer what I suffered."

"Of course I can," replied the bear, "what nonsense you talk! Show me the way."

So the fox led him to the bank of a stream, which, being in a warm place, had only lightly frozen in places, and was at this moment glittering in the spring sunshine.

"The elves bathe here," he said, "and if you put in your tail the fish will catch hold of it. But it is no use being in a hurry, or you will spoil everything."

Then he trotted off, but only went out of sight of the bear, who stood still on the bank with his tail deep in the water. Soon the sun set and it grew very cold and the ice formed rapidly, and the bear's tail was fixed as tight as if a vice had held it; and when the fox saw that everything had happened just as he had planned it, he called out loudly:

"Be quick, good people, and come with your bows and spears. A bear has been fishing in your brook!"

And in a moment the whole place was full of little creatures each one with a tiny bow and a spear hardly big enough for a baby; but both arrows and spears could sting, as the bear knew very well, and in his fright he gave such a tug to his tail that it broke short off, and he rolled away into the forest as fast as his legs could carry him. At this sight the fox held his sides for laughing, and then scampered away in another direction. By-and-by he came to a fir tree, and crept into a hole under the root. After that he did something very strange.

Taking one of his hind feet between his two front paws, he said softly, "What would you do, my foot, if someone was to betray me?"

"I would run so quickly that he should not catch you."

"What would you do, mine ear, if someone was to betray me?"

"I would listen so hard that I should hear all his plans."

"What would you do, my nose, if someone was to betray me?"

"I would smell so sharply that I should know from afar that he was coming."

"What would you do, my tail, if someone was to betray me?"

"I would steer you so straight a course that you would soon be beyond his reach. Let us be off; I feel as if danger was near."

But the fox was comfortable where he was, and did not hurry himself to take his tail's advice. And before very long he found he was too late, for the bear had come round by another path, and guessing where his enemy was beginning to scratch at the roots of the tree. The fox made himself as small as he could, but a scrap of his tail peeped out, and the bear seized it and held it tight. Then the fox dug his claws into the ground, but he was not strong enough to pull against the bear, and slowly he was dragged forth and his body flung over the bear's neck. In this manner they set out down the road, the fox's tail being always in the bear's mouth.

After they had gone some way, they passed a tree-stump, on which a bright coloured woodpecker was tapping.

"Ah! those were better times when I used to paint all the birds such gay colours," sighed the fox.

"What are you saying, old fellow?" asked the bear.

"I? Oh, I was saying nothing," answered the fox drearily. "Just carry me to your cave and eat me up as quick as you can."

The bear was silent, and thought of his supper; and the two continued their journey till they reached another tree with a woodpecker tapping on it.

"Ah! those were better times when I used to paint all the birds such gay colours," said the fox again to himself.

"Couldn't you paint me too?" asked the bear suddenly.

But the fox shook his head; for he was always acting, even if no one was there to see him do it.

"You bear pain so badly," he replied, in a thoughtful voice, "and you are impatient besides, and could never put up with all that is necessary. Why, you would first have to dig a pit, and then twist ropes of willow, and drive in posts and fill the hole with pitch, and, last of all, set it on fire. Oh, no; you would never be able to do all that."

"It does not matter a straw how hard the work is," answered the bear eagerly, "I will do it every bit." And as he spoke he began tearing up the earth so fast that soon a deep pit was ready, deep enough to hold him.

"That is all right," said the fox at last, "I see I was mistaken in you. Now sit here, and I will bind you." So the bear sat down on the edge of the pit, and the fox sprang on his back, which he crossed with the willow ropes, and then set fire to the pitch. It burnt up in an instant, and caught the bands of willow and the bear's rough hair; but he did not stir, for he thought that the fox was rubbing the bright colours into his skin, and that he would soon be as beautiful as a whole meadow of flowers. But when the fire grew hotter still he moved uneasily from one foot to the other, saying, imploringly, "It is getting rather warm, old man." But all the answer he got was, "I thought you would never be able to suffer pain like those little birds."

The bear did not like being told that he was not as brave as a bird, so he set his teeth and resolved to endure anything sooner than speak again; but by this time the last willow band had burned through, and with a push the fox sent his victim tumbling into the grass, and ran off to hide himself in the forest. After a while he stole cautiously and found, as he expected, nothing left but a few charred bones. These he picked up and put in a bag, which he slung over his back.

By-and-by he met a Lapp driving his team of reindeer along the road, and as he drew near, the fox rattled the bones gaily.

"That sounds like silver or gold," thought the man to himself. And he said politely to the fox:

"Good-day, friend! What have you got in your bag that makes such a strange sound?"

"All the wealth my father left me," answered the fox. "Do you feel inclined to bargain?"

"Well, I don't mind," replied the Lapp, who was a prudent man, and did not wish the fox to think him too eager, "but show me first what money you have got."

"Ah, but I can't do that," answered the fox, "my bag is sealed up. But if you will give me those three reindeer, you shall take it as it is, with all its contents."

The Lapp did not quite like it, but the fox spoke with such an air that his doubts melted away. He nodded, and stretched out his hand; the fox put the bag into it, and unharnessed the reindeer he had chosen.

"Oh, I forgot!" he exclaimed, turning round, as he was about to drive them in the opposite direction, "you must be sure not to open the bag until you have gone at least five miles, right on the other side of those hills out there. If you do, you will find that all the gold and silver has changed into a parcel of charred bones." Then he whipped up his reindeer, and was soon out of sight.

For some time the Lapp was satisfied with hearing the bones rattle, and thinking to himself what a good bargain he had made, and of all the things he would buy with the money. But, after a bit, this amusement ceased to content him, and besides, what was the use of planning when you did not know for certain how rich you were? Perhaps there might be a great deal of silver and only a little gold in the bag; or a great deal of gold, and only a little silver. Who could tell? He would not, of course, take the money out to count it, for that might bring him bad luck. But there could be no harm in just one peep! So he slowly broke the seal, and untied the strings, and behold, a heap of burnt bones lay before him! In a minute he knew he had been tricked, and flinging the bag to the ground in a rage, he ran after the fox as fast as his snow-shoes would carry him.

Now the fox had guessed exactly what would happen, and was on the lookout. Directly he saw the little speck coming towards him, he wished that the man's snow-shoes might break, and that very instant the Lapp's shoes snapped in two. The Lapp did now know that this was the fox's work, but he had to stop and fetch one of his other reindeer, which he mounted, and set off again in pursuit of his enemy. The fox soon heard him coming, and this time he wished that the reindeer might fall and break its leg. And so it did; and the man felt it was a hopeless chase, and that he was no match for the fox.

So the fox drove on in peace till he reached the cave where all his stores were kept, and then he began to wonder whom he could get to help him kill his reindeer, for though he could steal reindeer he was too small to kill them. "After all, it will be quite easy," thought he, and he bade a squirrel, who was watching him on a tree close by, take a message to all the robber beasts of the forest, and in less than half an hour a great crashing of branches was heard, and bears, wolves, snakes, mice, frogs, and other creatures came pressing up to the cave.

When they heard why they had been summoned, they declared themselves ready each one to do his part. The bear took his crossbow from his neck and shot the reindeer in the chin; and, from that day to this, every reindeer has a mark in that same spot, which is always known as the bear's arrow. The wolf shot him in the thigh, and the sign of his arrow still remains; and so with the mouse and the viper and all the rest, even the frog; and at the last the reindeer all died. And the fox did nothing, but looked on.

"I really must go down to the brook and wash myself," said he (though he was perfectly clean), and he went under the bank and hid himself behind a stone. From there he set up the most frightful shrieks, so that the animals fled away in all directions. Only the mouse and the ermine remained where they were, for they thought that they were much too small to be noticed.

The fox continued his shrieks till he felt sure that the animals must have got to a safe distance; then he crawled out of his hiding-place and went to the bodies of the reindeer, which he now had all to himself. He gathered a bundle of sticks for a fire, and was just preparing to cook a steak, when his enemy, the Lapp, came up, panting with haste and excitement.

"What are you doing there?" cried he, "why did you palm off those bones on me? And why, when you had got the reindeer, did you kill them?"

"Dear brother," answered the fox with a sob, "do not blame me for this misfortune. It is my comrades who have slain them in spite of my prayers."

The man made no reply, for the white fur of the ermine, who was crouching with the mouse behind some stones, had just caught his eye. He hastily seized the iron hook which hung over the fire and flung it at the little creature; but the ermine was too quick for him, and the hook only touched the top of its tail, and that has remained black to this day. As for the mouse, the Lapp threw a half-burnt stick after him, and though it was not enough to hurt him, his beautiful white skin was smeared all over with it, and all the washing in the world would not make him clean again. And the man would have been wiser if he had let the ermine and the mouse alone, for when he turned round again he found he was alone.

Directly the fox noticed that his enemy's attention had wandered from himself he watched his chance, and stole softly away till he had reached a clump of thick bushes, when he ran as fast as he could, till he reached a river, where a man was mending his boat.

"Oh, I wish, I wish, I had a boat to mend too!" he cried, sitting up on his hind-legs and looking into the man's face.

"Stop your silly chatter!" answered the man crossly, "or I will give you a bath in the river."

"Oh, I wish, I do wish, I had a boat to mend," cried the fox again, as if he had not heard. And the man grew angry and seized him by the tail, and threw him far out in the stream close to the edge of an island; which was just what the fox wanted. He easily scrambled up, and sitting on the top, he called, "Hasten, hasten, Oh fishes, and carry me to the other side!" And the fishes left the stones where they had been sleeping, and the pools where they had been feeding, and hurried to see who could get to the island first.

"I have won," shouted the pike. "Jump on my back, dear fox, and you will find yourself in a trice on the opposite shore."

"No, thank you," answered the fox, "your back is much too weak for me. I should break it."

"Try mine," said the eel, who had wriggled to the front.

"No, thank you," replied the fox again, "I should slip over your head and be drowned."

"You won't slip on MY back," said the perch, coming forward.

"No; but you are really TOO rough," returned the fox.

"Well, you can have no fault to find with ME," put in the trout.

"Good gracious! are YOU here?" exclaimed the fox. "But I'm afraid to trust myself to you either."

At this moment a fine salmon swam slowly up.

"Ah, yes, you are the person I want," said the fox, "but come near, so that I may get on your back, without wetting my feet."

So the salmon swam close under the island, and when he was touching it the fox seized him in his claws and drew him out of the water, and put him on a spit, while he kindled a fire to cook him by. When everything was ready, and the water in the pot was getting hot, he popped him in, and waited till he thought the salmon was nearly boiled. But as he stooped down the water gave a sudden fizzle, and splashed into the fox's eyes, blinding him. He started backwards with a cry of pain, and sat still for some minutes, rocking himself to and fro. When he was a little better he rose and walked down a road till he met a grouse, who stopped and asked what the matter was.

"Have you a pair of eyes anywhere about you?" asked the fox politely.

"No, I am afraid I haven't," answered the grouse, and passed on.

A little while after the fox heard the buzzing of an early bee, whom a gleam of sun had tempted out. "Do you happen to have an extra pair of eyes anywhere?" asked the fox.

"I am sorry to say I have only those I am using," replied the bee. And the fox went on till he nearly fell over an asp who was gliding across the road.

"I should be SO glad if you would tell me where I could get a pair of eyes," said the fox. "I suppose you don't happen to have any you could lend me?"

"Well, if you only want them for a short time, perhaps I could manage," answered the asp, "but I can't do without them for long."

"Oh, it is only for a very short time that I need them," said the fox, "I have a pair of my own just behind that hill, and when I find them I will bring yours back to you. Perhaps you will keep these till them." So he took the eyes out of his own head and popped them into the head of the asp, and put the asp's eyes in their place. As he was running off he cried over his shoulder, "As long as the world lasts the asps" eyes will go down in the heads of foxes from generation to generation."

And so it has been; and if you look at the eyes of an asp you will see that they are all burnt; and though thousands and thousands of years have gone by since the fox was going about playing tricks upon everybody he met, the asp still bears the traces of the day when the sly creature cooked the salmon.

Wainamoinen's Boat-Building

Adapted by R. Eivind in Finnish Legends for English Children, from the original Song of the Kervala. Finnish Legends for English Children was published in 1893 by T. fisher Unwin, London.

WAINAMOINEN STARTED TO BUILD A BOAT from the Rainbow-maiden's distaff, but he had soon used up all his timber, and the boat was far from finished. So he asked Sampsa (the planter of the first trees that grew on earth) to go and search out the needful timber in order to finish the boat.

Sampsa started off with a golden axe upon his shoulder and a copper hatchet in his belt. He wandered through the mountain forests, and at length came upon a great aspen, and was just going to cut it down, when the aspen asked him what he wanted. "I wish to take your timber for a vessel," Sampsa replied, "that the wise magician Wainamoinen is building."

Then the aspen answered, "All the boats that have been made of my wood have been. but failures; they float but a little way, and then sink to the ocean's bottom, for my trunk is full of hollow places, where the worms have eaten my wood."

So Sampsa left the aspen and searched still further, until he came to a pine-tree that was even taller than the aspen was. Sampsa struck a blow with his axe, and at the same time asked the pine-tree if it would furnish good timber for Wainamoinen's boat. But the pine-tree answered, "All the ships that have been made from me are useless. I am full of imperfections, for the ravens live among my branches and bring ill-luck."

And Sampsa was obliged to leave the pine-tree and go on until he came to a tremendous oak-tree, whose trunk was thicker than the height of even the tallest men. And he asked the oak-tree if it would furnish wood for Wainamoinen's boat. "I will gladly furnish the wood," replied the oak-tree, "for I am tall and sound and strong. The warm sun shines upon me for three months in the summer, and the sacred cuckoo dwells in my branches and brings good fortune." So Sampsa quickly felled the oak, and brought the timber, skilfully hewn, to Wainamoinen.

The wise magician Wainamoinen then began to put his boat together by the aid of magic spells. The first magic song that. he sang joined the framework together, and the second song fastened the planking into the ribs, and the third put the rowlocks in place and made the oars. But alas! when all this was done, there were still three magic words needed to complete the stem and stern and bulwarks.

Wainamoinen saw that all his labour was in vain unless he found the three magic words, for unless the stern and stem were fastened and the bulwarks built, the boat could never put to sea. He pondered long over where he might find the lost words, and after a while he concluded that they might be found in the brains of swallows and the heads of swans and the plumage of the sea-duck. But though he killed great numbers of these birds, he could not find the three lost words. Then he thought that he might find them on the tongues of reindeers or of the squirrels; but though he killed great numbers of them, and found many words on their tongues, the three lost words were not there.

Then he said to himself, "I will seek the lost words in the kingdom of Manala; there are countless words to be found there in the Deathland." So off he went, travelling for three weeks over hill and dale, through marshes and thickets, until at length he came to the river of Tuoni. There he called out in a voice like thunder, "Bring a boat, Oh, daughter of Tuoni, and ferry me over this black and fatal river."

Tuoni's daughter, a wee little dwarf, but very wise and ancient, bade him first say why he wished to come into the Deathland while he was still alive. And first Wainamoinen answered that Tuoni himself, the death-god, had sent him. But the maid replied, "Had Tuoni brought you, he would now be with you, and you would be wearing his cap and gloves."

So Wainamoinen answered again, "I was slain by an iron weapon." But the maid would not believe him, because he had no bleeding wound. Then he said the third time, that he had been washed there by the river. But still the maid would not believe him, for his clothing was not wet. And the fourth time he said that fire had burnt him.

But the maid replied, "If the fire had brought you to Manala, your hair and eyebrows and beard would be all singed and burnt. But now I ask you for the last time what it is that has brought you, living, here. Tell me the truth this time."

Then Wainamoinen told her that he had been building a boat by magic, but that he yet lacked one spell, and had come there to seek it. When he had said this, Tuoni's daughter came across and rowed him to the opposite side, having first tried to dissuade him from coming. But Wainamoinen was not afraid; and when he had landed he walked straight up to the abode of Tuoni.

There Tuonetar, Tuoni's wife, gave him a golden goblet filled with beer, saying, "Drink Tuoni's beer, Oh wise and ancient Wainamoinen!" But he carefully inspected the liquor before he tasted it, and saw that it was black and full of the spawn of frogs and poisonous serpent-broods; and he said to Tuonetar, "I have not come here to drink Tuoni's poisons, for they that do so will surely be destroyed."

Tuonetar then asked him why he had come, and he told her of his boat-building, and how he still needed the three magic words, and that he hoped to find them there. "Tuoni will never reveal them," Tuonetar said, "nor shall you ever leave these gates alive;" and as she spoke she waved the slumber-wand over Wainamoinen's head, and he sank into a deep sleep. And to make sure of his not escaping, Tuoni's son, a hideous wizard with only three fingers, wove nets of iron and of copper, and set them all through the river, to catch Wainamoinen if by any chance he should get so far.

But Wainamoinen soon freed himself from Tuonetar's slumber-spell, and knowing in how great danger he was, he instantly transformed himself into a serpent, and wriggled his way to the river, and through the nets that had been set to catch him, until at length he came out safe into the land of the living again; and the next morning, when Tuoni's wizard son went to look at his nets, he found all kinds of evil fish and serpents, but not the wise old magician.

But Wainamoinen prayed to Ukko, "I thank you, Oh Ukko, that you have protected me; but never suffer any other of your heroes, not even the wisest, to go against the laws of nature to the awful Tuonela. For there are but few who return from there."

And then Wainamoinen called together the people on the plains of Kalevala, and spoke to the young men and maidens, saying, "Listen, all you young people. Never disobey your parents; never harm the innocent, nor wrong the weak, nor utter falsehood, else you will pay the penance for it in the gloomy prison of Manala; for there is the dwelling-place of the wicked, and a place for the guilty. Beneath the burning rocks there are fiery couches, with pillows of hissing serpents, and coverlets of green writhing vipers. And the wicked there drink the blood of adders, but have nothing to eat at all. If you would be happy, shun this abode of the wicked ones in Tuonela."

Wainamoinen Finds The Lost Words

Adapted by R. Eivind in Finnish Legends for English Children, from the original Song of the Kervala. Finnish Legends for English Children was published in 1893 by T. fisher Unwin, London.

WAINAMOINEN HAD FAILED TO FIND THE three magic words in the Deathland, and now he sat and pondered where he should go next to seek them. While he was thinking over this, a shepherd came to him and said, "You can find a thousand words of wisdom on the tongue of the dead hero Wipunen. I know the road that leads to his grave: first, you must journey a long distance over the points of needles, and then a long way upon the edges of sharp swords, and then a third road on the edges of hatchets."

Then Wainamoinen considered how he should be able to walk over the needles and swords and hatchets, and at last hit on a plan. He went to the smith Ilmarinen and bade him make shoes of iron, and gloves of copper, and a magic staff of the strongest metal. Wainamoinen then said, "Lay steel upon the inside and forge within the might of magic. I am going on a journey to procure the magic sayings, to find the lost-words of the Master from the mouth of the magician, from the tongue of wise Wipunen."

Ilmarinen replied, "Wise Wipunen died long ago and disappeared these many ages. He no longer lays his snares of copper, he no longer sets traps of iron. You cannot learn from him wisdom and you will not find in him the lost-words."

Wainamoinen, old and hopeful, paid no heed nor was he discouraged. In his metal shoes and armour, he hastened forward on his journey, running the first day fleetly onward across the sharpened points of needles. On the second day he strode wearily on the edges of the broadswords, and then on the third day he swung himself forward on the edges of the hatchets.

Then wise Wipunen, wisdom-singer, ancient bard, and great magician, lay stretched out before Wainamoinen, with his magic songs and sayings and words beside him. On Wipunen's shoulder grew the aspen, on each temple grew the birch-tree, on his mighty chin the alder, from his beard grew willow-bushes, from his mouth the dark green fir-tree, and the oak-tree grew from his forehead.

Wainamoinen, drew closer, brandishing his sword and laying bare his hatchet from his magic leathern scabbard. He swung his axe and felled the aspen from Wipunen's shoulder. Then he felled the birch-tree from his temples, the alder from his chin and the branching willows from his beard. Finally he pulled the dark-green fir-tree from Wipunen's mouth and felled the oak-tree from his forehead.

Finally Wainamoinen thrust his staff of iron through the mouth of wise Wipunen, prying open his jaws, and spoke the words of a spell:

"Rise, Oh master of magicians,

From the sleep of Tuonela,

From your everlasting slumber!"

Wise Wipunen, the ancient singer, quickly woke from his sleeping, feeling the deep pangs of torture from the cruel staff of iron. He bit with mighty force against the metal, biting in two the softer iron, but he could not bite the hard steel asunder. Wipunen opened wide his mouth in anguish.

Wainamoinen. in his iron-shoes and armour, stepped forward and carelessly stumbled headlong into the spacious mouth and fauces of the magic bard. Wipunen, full of song-charms, opened wide his mouth and swallowed Wainamoinen and his magic, together with his shoes, and staff, and iron armour.

Then wise Wipunen said, "Many things before I've eaten. I've dined on goat, and sheep, and reindeer, bear, and ox, and wolf, and wild-boar, but never in my recollection have I tasted sweeter morsels!"

Wainamoinen replied, "Now I see the evil symbols, now I see misfortune hanging o'er me in these darksome Hisi-hurdles and in these catacombs of Kalma."

Wainamoinen thought long and hard about how he might live and prosper and conquer this condition. In his belt he wore a poniard with a handle hewn from birch-wood. Taking that wood Wainamoinen built a boat through magic science, and in this boat he rowed swiftly through the entrails of the Wipunen. He rowed on through every gland and vessel of the wisest of magicians.

Old Wipunen, the master-singer, barely felt the hero's presence and gave no heed to Wainamoinen. Taking this chance, Wainamoinen straightway set himself to forging, hammering metals and made a smithy from his armour. From his sleeves he made the bellows. From his fur coat he made the air-valve and from his stockings he made the muzzle. He used his knees instead of an anvil, made a hammer of his fore-arm, and like the storm-wind he roared the bellows. Wainamoinen forged form three long days in the body of Wipunen, deep in the sorcerer's abdomen.

Finally old Wipunen, full of magic, spoke these words in wonder, guessing, "Who are you of ancient heroes? Who of all the host of heroes? Many heroes I have eaten, and of men a countless number, but I have not eaten such as you. Smoke arises from my nostrils. From my mouth the fire is streaming. In my throat are iron-clinkers."

Then Wipunen swore, "Go, monster, away to wander. Flee this place, you plague of Northland, before I go to seek your mother and tell the ancient dame about your mischief. I will burden her with your evil conduct and she will bear a great weight, a mother's pain and anguish when her child runs wild and lawless. Why did you come here, monster? Why do your torture me so? Are you Hisi sent from heaven, some calamity from Ukko? Are you, perchance, some new creation ordered here to do me evil? If you are some evil genius, some calamity from Ukko, sent to me by my Creator, then am I resigned to suffer. God does not forsake the worthy, not ruin those that trust him. Never are the good forsaken. If you were created by men, if some hero sent you here, then I shall find your race of evil and destroy your wicked tribe-folk. Leave my body, cease your forging, let me rest in peace and slumber. Or if you will not leave me, I will call on all the great magicians of the past, the spirits of the mountains and woods and seas and rivers, on Ilmatar, daughter of the ether, to assist me. Or if these be not sufficient, I will call on mighty Ukko to drive you forth. If you are from the winds, then return to the copper mountains where they live; if from the sea, return to it; if from the forests, then return to them, or I will drive you to the bottom of the coal-black river of Tuoni, from where you shall never move again."

"I am well contented here," said Wainamoinen, "in these roomy caverns. I can eat your heart and flesh and for drink I will take your blood. And I will set my forge still deeper in your vitals, and will swing my hammer still harder on your heart and lungs and liver. I shall never leave you until I learn all your wisdom, and the three lost words, that all your magic knowledge may not perish with you from the earth."

Then Wipunen began to sing all his knowledge and his magic spells for Wainamoinen. He sang the origin of witchcraft, the source of good and evil and how by the will of Ukko the water was first divided from the ether. And next he sang of how the moon and sun were made, and from where the colours of the rainbow came, and how the stars were sprinkled in the sky. Three whole days and nights he sang, until the stars and the moon stood still to listen, and the very waves of the sea and the tides ceased to rise and fall, and the rivers stopped in their courses.

At length Wainamoinen had learned all the wisdom of the great magician, and the three lost words, and he made ready to leave Wipunen's body, bidding him open wide his mouth that he might get out and leave him for ever.

"I have eaten many things, Oh Wainamoinen," said Wipunen, "bears and reindeer, wolves and oxen, but never such a thing as you. Now you have found the wisdom that you seekest, go in peace and never come back to me."

Then he opened his mouth wide, and Wainamoinen glided forth and hastened swiftly as the deer to Kalevala. First he went into the smithy, and Ilmarinen asked him if he had learned the lost words that would enable him to finish his vessel. "I have learned a thousand magic words," answered Wainamoinen, "and among them are the lost words that I sought."

Thereupon he hastened off to where his vessel lay, and with the three lost words he joined the stem and stern and raised the bulwarks. Thus he had built the vessel with magic alone, and by magic he launched it too, not touching it with foot or knee or hand, using only magic to push it. Thus was the task completed which should gain for him the Rainbow-maiden in her beauty.

The Gifts Of The Magician

Adapted by Andrew Lang in his Crimson Fairy Book from an original in Finnische Märchen. The Crimson Fairy Book was published by Longman, Green & Co in 1903.

ONCE UPON A TIME THERE WAS an old man who lived in a little hut in the middle of a forest. His wife was dead, and he had only one son, whom he loved dearly. Near their hut was a group of birch trees, in which some black-game had made their nests, and the youth had often begged his father's permission to shoot the birds, but the old man always strictly forbade him to do anything of the kind.

One day, however, when the father had gone to a little distance to collect some sticks for the fire, the boy fetched his bow, and shot at a bird that was just flying towards its nest. But he had not taken proper aim, and the bird was only wounded, and fluttered along the ground. The boy ran to catch it, but though he ran very fast, and the bird seemed to flutter along very slowly, he never could quite come up with it; it was always just a little in advance. But so absorbed was he in the chase that he did not notice for some time that he was now deep in the forest, in a place where he had never been before.

Then he felt it would be foolish to go any further, and he turned to find his way home.

He thought it would be easy enough to follow the path along which he had come, but somehow it was always branching off in unexpected directions. He looked about for a house where he might stop and ask his way, but there was not a sign of one anywhere, and he was afraid to stand still, for it was cold, and there were many stories of wolves being seen in that part of the forest. Night fell, and he was beginning to start at every sound, when suddenly a magician came running towards him, with a pack of wolves snapping at his heels. Then all the boy's courage returned to him. He took his bow, and aiming an arrow at the largest wolf, shot him through the heart, and a few more arrows soon put the rest to flight. The magician was full of gratitude to his deliverer, and promised him a reward for his help if the youth would go back with him to his house.

"Indeed there is nothing that would be more welcome to me than a night's lodging," answered the boy, "I have been wandering all day in the forest, and did not know how to get home again.

"Come with me, you must be hungry as well as tired," said the magician, and led the way to his house, where the guest flung himself on a bed, and went fast asleep. But his host returned to the forest to get some food, for the larder was empty.

While he was absent the housekeeper went to the boy's room and tried to wake him. She stamped on the floor, and shook him and called to him, telling him that he was in great danger, and must take flight at once. But nothing would rouse him, and if he did ever open his eyes he shut them again directly.

Soon after, the magician came back from the forest, and told the housekeeper to bring them something to eat. The meal was quickly ready, and the magician called to the boy to come down and eat it, but he could not be wakened, and they had to sit down to supper without him. By-and-by the magician went out into the wood again for some more hunting, and on his return he tried afresh to waken the youth. But finding it quite impossible, he went back for the third time to the forest.

While he was absent the boy woke up and dressed himself. Then he came downstairs and began to talk to the housekeeper. The girl had heard how he had saved her master's life, so she said nothing more about his running away, but instead told him that if the magician offered him the choice of a reward, he was to ask for the horse which stood in the third stall of the stable.

By-and-by the old man came back and they all sat down to dinner. When they had finished the magician said, "Now, my son, tell me what you will have as the reward of your courage?"

"Give me the horse that stands in the third stall of your stable," answered the youth. "For I have a long way to go before I get home, and my feet will not carry me so far."

"Ah! my son," replied the magician, "it is the best horse in my stable that you want! Will not anything else please you as well?"

But the youth declared that it was the horse, and the horse only, that he desired, and in the end the old man gave way. And besides the horse, the magician gave him a zither, a fiddle, and a flute, saying, "If you are in danger, touch the zither; and if no one comes to your aid, then play on the fiddle; but if that brings no help, blow on the flute."

The youth thanked the magician, and fastening his treasures about him mounted the horse and rode off. He had already gone some miles when, to his great surprise, the horse spoke, and said, "It is no use your returning home just now, your father will only beat you. Let us visit a few towns first, and something lucky will be sure to happen to us."

This advice pleased the boy, for he felt himself almost a man by this time, and thought it was high time he saw the world. When they entered the capital of the country everyone stopped to admire the beauty of the horse. Even the king heard of it, and came to see the splendid creature with his own eyes. Indeed, he wanted directly to buy it, and told the youth he would give any price he liked. The young man hesitated for a moment, but before he could speak, the horse contrived to whisper to him:

"Do not sell me, but ask the king to take me to his stable, and feed me there; then his other horses will become just as beautiful as I."

The king was delighted when he was told what the horse had said, and took the animal at once to the stables, and placed it in his own particular stall. Sure enough, the horse had scarcely eaten a mouthful of corn out of the manger, when the rest of the horses seemed to have undergone a transformation. Some of them were old favourites which the king had ridden in many wars, and they bore the signs of age and of service. But now they arched their heads, and pawed the ground with their slender legs as they had been wont to do in days long gone by. The king's heart beat with delight, but the old groom who had had the care of them stood crossly by, and eyed the owner of this wonderful creature with hate and envy. Not a day passed without his bringing some story against the youth to his master, but the king understood all about the matter and paid no attention. At last the groom declared that the young man had boasted that he could find the king's war horse which had strayed into the forest several years ago, and had not been heard of since. Now the king had never ceased to mourn for his horse, so this time he listened to the tale which the groom had invented, and sent for the youth. "Find me my horse in three days," said he, "or it will be the worse for you."

The youth was thunderstruck at this command, but he only bowed, and went off at once to the stable.

"Do not worry yourself," answered his own horse. "Ask the king to give you a hundred oxen, and to let them be killed and cut into small pieces. Then we will start on our journey, and ride till we reach a certain river. There a horse will come up to you, but take no notice of him. Soon another will appear, and this also you must leave alone, but when the third horse shows itself, throw my bridle over it."

Everything happened just as the horse had said, and the third horse was safely bridled. Then the other horse spoke again, "The magician's raven will try to eat us as we ride away, but throw it some of the oxen's flesh, and then I will gallop like the wind, and carry you safe out of the dragon's clutches."

So the young man did as he was told, and brought the horse back to the king.

The old stableman was very jealous, when he heard of it, and wondered what he could do to injure the youth in the eyes of his royal master. At last he hit upon a plan, and told the king that the young man had boasted that he could bring home the king's wife, who had vanished many months before, without leaving a trace behind her. Then the king bade the young man come into his presence, and desired him to fetch the queen home again, as he had boasted he could do. And if he failed, his head would pay the penalty.

The poor youth's heart stood still as he listened. Find the queen? But how was he to do that, when nobody in the palace had been able to do so! Slowly he walked to the stable, and laying his head on his horse's shoulder, he said, "The king has ordered me to bring his wife home again, and how can I do that when she disappeared so long ago, and no one can tell me anything about her?"

"Cheer up!" answered the horse, "we will manage to find her. You have only got to ride me back to the same river that we went to yesterday, and I will plunge into it and take my proper shape again. For I am the king's wife, who was turned into a horse by the magician from whom you saved me."

Joyfully the young man sprang into the saddle and rode away to the banks of the river. Then he threw himself off, and waited while the horse plunged in. The moment it dipped its head into the water its black skin vanished, and the most beautiful woman in the world was floating on the water. She came smiling towards the youth, and held out her hand, and he took it and led her back to the palace. Great was the king's surprise and happiness when he beheld his lost wife stand before him, and in gratitude to her rescuer he loaded him with gifts.

You would have thought that after this the poor youth would have been left in peace; but no, his enemy the stableman hated him as much as ever, and laid a new plot for his undoing. This time he presented himself before the king and told him that the youth was so puffed up with what he had done that he had declared he would seize the king's throne for himself.

At this news the king waxed so furious that he ordered a gallows to be erected at once, and the young man to be hanged without a trial. He was not even allowed to speak in his own defence, but on the very steps of the gallows he sent a message to the king and begged, as a last favour, that he might play a tune on his zither. Leave was given him, and taking the instrument from under his cloak he touched the strings. Scarcely had the first notes sounded than the hangman and his helper began to dance, and the louder grew the music the higher they capered, till at last they cried for mercy. But the youth paid no heed, and the tunes rang out more merrily than before, and by the time the sun set they both sank on the ground exhausted, and declared that the hanging must be put off till to-morrow.

The story of the zither soon spread through the town, and on the following morning the king and his whole court and a large crowd of people were gathered at the foot of the gallows to see the youth hanged. Once more he asked a favour - permission to play on his fiddle, and this the king was graciously pleased to grant. But with the first notes, the leg of every man in the crowd was lifted high, and they danced to the sound of the music the whole day till darkness fell, and there was no light to hang the musician by.

The third day came, and the youth asked leave to play on his flute. "No, no," said the king, "you made me dance all day yesterday, and if I do it again it will certainly be my death. You shall play no more tunes. Quick! the rope round his neck."

At these words the young man looked so sorrowful that the courtiers said to the king, "He is very young to die. Let him play a tune if it will make him happy." So, very unwillingly, the king gave him leave; but first he had himself bound to a big fir tree, for fear that he should be made to dance.

When he was made fast, the young man began to blow softly on his flute, and bound though he was, the king's body moved to the sound, up and down the fir tree till his clothes were in tatters, and the skin nearly rubbed off his back. But the youth had no pity, and went on blowing, till suddenly the old magician appeared and asked, "What danger are you in, my son, that you have sent for me?"

"They want to hang me," answered the young man, "the gallows are all ready and the hangman is only waiting for me to stop playing."

"Oh, I will put that right," said the magician; and taking the gallows, he tore it up and flung it into the air, and no one knows where it came down. "Who has ordered you to be hanged?" asked he.

The young man pointed to the king, who was still bound to the fir; and without wasting words the magician took hold of the tree also, and with a mighty heave both fir and man went spinning through the air, and vanished in the clouds after the gallows.

Then the youth was declared to be free, and the people elected him for their king; and the stable helper drowned himself from envy, for, after all, if it had not been for him the young man would have remained poor all the days of his life.

The Rival Suitors

Adapted by R. Eivind in Finnish Legends for English Children, from the original Song of the Kervala. Finnish Legends for English Children was published in 1893 by T. fisher Unwin, London.

NOW THE RAINBOW-MAIDEN WAS REALLY THE same as old Louhi's fairest daughter, whom Wainamoinen had wooed, and for whom Ilmarinen had made the magic Sampo, and Wainamoinen had learned this. So when the magic boat was finished, he made ready for a journey to the Northland, to try once more to win the fair Pohjola maiden for his bride.

He ornamented the magic vessel with gold and silver, and painted it scarlet, and on the masts he set sails of linen, red, white, and blue. Then he stepped on board, and called on Ukko to protect and help him, and on the winds to aid him on his way, and off the magic boat flew towards Pohjola, never needing an oar to help it.

Annikki, Ilmarinen's sister, was down by the seashore just at dawn that morning, and as she gazed out over the sea, she saw a blue speck in the distance. At first she thought it was a flock of birds, and then as it drew nearer it looked like a great tree floating on the water, but at last she saw that it was a vessel with but one man in it, and when it came still nearer she recognised Wainamoinen.

She called out to him and asked him where he was going. He replied that he was come a-fishing, but Annikki said, "Your boat is not rigged like a fisher-boat, nor have you lines or nets with you. Tell me the truth, Oh Wainamoinen!" And he answered the second time, that he had come to kill wild geese and ducks. But Annikki told him that she knew that was untrue, for he had no hunting dogs in the vessel with him, nor any weapons. Then he told her that he was sailing to the wars. Annikki replied, "My father often used to sail to war, but in a ship with many rowers, and with many armed heroes on board, but your vessel is surely not fitted for battle. Now tell me the truth, Oh wise Wainamoinen, or else I will send a storm-wind after you and break your ship in pieces."

Then he told her the truth, that he was going to woo the Rainbow-maiden, Louhi's daughter, and then Annikki knew that he spoke the truth. She hurried off to her brother's smithy and said to him, "Dearest brother, if you will forge for me a silver loom and gold and silver finger-rings and earrings, golden girdles and golden ornaments for my hair, I will tell you something that is very important for you to know."

So Ilmarinen promised, and his sister said, "Oh Ilmarinen, if you hopest ever to wed the fair maid of Pohjola, you must hasten and make your sledge ready, for Wainamoinen is now sailing there in a magic boat to win her before you." Then Ilmarinen bade his sister prepare a magic soap and make a bath ready for him while he was forging the gold and silver ornaments that she had bargained for.

When Ilmarinen had finished his work he found the bath and the magic soap all ready for him, and he began to wash off the grime and dirt and soot of the smithy. When he was through, and came out of the bath, he had grown wonderfully bright and handsome, for the magic soap had made his cheeks rosy and his eyes bright as moonlight. Then he put on his finest garments, soft linen, and silken stockings, a blue vest and scarlet trousers, and a fur coat of sealskin, held by buttons made of jewels, and a belt with golden buckles. After he was dressed he ordered his magic sledge to be harnessed, and on the front placed six cuckoos and seven blue-birds that they might sing and charm the Northland maiden.

When all was ready Ilmarinen prayed to great Ukko to send snow that it might cover all the country and let his sledge glide easily to Pohjola. And the snow came, and Ilmarinen wrapped himself up warmly in bear-skins, and drove off like the wind, first invoking Ukko's blessing on his journey. On he went, over hill and dale, with the cuckoos and blue-birds singing on the sledge, and then he drove along the seashore to the north in a cloud of snow and sand and mist and sea-foam, looking out for Wainamoinen's vessel. On the evening of the third day he caught up with Wainamoinen, and called out to him, "Oh ancient Wainamoinen, let us woo the maiden peacefully, and let her choose which one of us she will." To this Wainamoinen agreed; and having promised not to use deceit of any sort against one another, they hurried on their way, Wainamoinen calling up the south wind to help him, and Ilmarinen's steed shaking the hills of Northland as he galloped on.

Soon they drew near to Louhi's dwelling, and the watchdogs began to bark more loudly than they had ever done before. Louhi's husband told his daughter to go and see what the trouble was, but she replied that she was busy grinding barley, and could not go. Then he told his wife to go, but she was too busy cooking dinner. So the father grew angry, and said, "Women are always busy either baking or sleeping; go, my son, and learn what all the trouble is." But the son refused because he was busy splitting wood.

So at last Louhi's husband was obliged to go himself, for the dogs kept barking louder and louder. There, as soon as he had reached the gate, he saw a scarlet-coloured ship sailing into the bay, and a sledge driving up along the shore at full speed. Then he hastened back into the house, and told them all that he had seen. And Louhi took a branch and gave it to her daughter, saying, "Place this on the fire, my daughter, and if in burning it drips blood, then these strangers bring war and bloodshed; but if clear water, then they come in peace."

So the maiden put the branch on the fire, and as they watched it they saw honey trickling out, and from this Louhi knew that the two men were coming as suitors. Then they hastened out into the courtyard, and saw the vessel in the harbour, painted scarlet, and an ancient, white-bearded magician at the helm; and on the land they saw a brightly-coloured sledge, with cuckoos and bluebirds singing on the front, and driven by a young and handsome hero.

Louhi immediately recognised them both, and said to her daughter, "Will you have one of these suitors, dearest daughter? He that comes in the ship is good old Wainamoinen, bringing countless treasures for you from Kalevala. The other in the sledge, with the singing birds, is the blacksmith Ilmarinen, who brings no presents save himself. When they come into the house bring a pitcher of honey-drink, and give it to the one that you will follow. Give it to old Wainamoinen, for he brings you countless treasures."

But the daughter replied, "I will never marry a man for riches, but for his real worth. Mothers did not use to sell their daughters thus in the olden times to suitors whom they did not love. I shall choose Ilmarinen for his true worth and wisdom."

Old Louhi grew angry at this, and tried to change her daughter's mind, but all she could say did not move her; and just then Wainamoinen came to the house, and addressed the maiden thus, "Come with me, Oh lovely maiden, be my bride and honoured wife, and share my joys and sorrows with me."

The maiden answered, "Have you built the magic vessel, using neither hand nor foot to touch it?"

"I have built it, and brought it here," answered Wainamoinen. "It is finely made by magic, and will live in the worst of storms; nothing can ever sink it."

But then the maiden said to him, "I will not wed a husband born in the sea. Storms would bring us trouble, and the winds rack our hearts. I cannot go with you, cannot marry you, Oh Wainamoinen."

Ilmarinen's Wooing

Adapted by R. Eivind in Finnish Legends for English Children, from the original Song of the Kervala. Finnish Legends for English Children was published in 1893 by T. fisher Unwin, London.

JUST AS WAINAMOINEN HAD RECEIVED HIS answer, Ilmarinen came hurrying into the house and into the guest-room. There servants brought him honey-drink in silver pitchers, but he said, "I will never taste the drink of Northland till I see the Rainbow-maiden. With her I will gladly drink, for I have come here to seek her hand."

Then Louhi said to him, "The maiden is not ready to receive you, and you may not woo her before you have ploughed the field of hissing serpents. Once the evil spirit Lempo ploughed it, but it has never been done since."

Ilmarinen wandered off sadly, but while he was pondering over what he should do, he saw the lovely maid herself. He went up to her and said, "Long ago I forged the Sampo for you, and then you promised to become my wife. But now your mother demands that I first plough the field of serpents before I win you." But the maiden comforted him, and told him how to plough the field with a plough of gold and silver and copper.

So Ilmarinen went off and built a smithy, and placed in the furnace gold and silver and copper and iron. And from these he forged a plough, with ploughshare of gold and beam of silver and copper handles; and for himself he made boots and gloves and armour of iron; and as he worked he sang magic spells to give his work power to overcome the serpents. Then he harnessed to the plough the fire-breathing Hisi-horse, and went into the field. There were serpents of every sort, creeping and crawling over one another, and hissing horribly, but Ilmarinen cast a spell over them, and ploughed the field, so that all the snakes were buried in the furrows. And then he went to Louhi, and claimed her daughter's hand.

But Louhi refused to let him have her daughter until he should catch the great bear of Manala, and bring him to her. So he went off to the maid again, and told her what old Louhi had demanded of him. The lovely maiden instructed him how to prepare a muzzle for the bear, forging it of steel on a rock beneath the water, at a spot where three currents met together, and the straps were to be of steel and copper mixed. And Ilmarinen made a muzzle as she had directed, and set off for Manala, the dismal Deathland. As he went he prayed to the goddess of the mists to send a fog where the great bear of Manala was, so that he might not see Ilmarinen as he approached. And the goddess sent the fog, and Ilmarinen was able to creep up to the bear and throw the magic muzzle over his head, and then to lead him to Louhi without any trouble.

When he had brought the bear to her, he asked her again for her lovely daughter's hand. But Louhi said to him, "You must perform one more task still, and then, when that is done, you shall have my dear daughter. Catch for me the monster-pike that lives in the river of Tuoni, but you may not use hook, nor line, nor nets, nor boat. Hundreds have been sent to catch it, but all have died in Tuoni's dark waters."

And now Ilmarinen was deeply discouraged, and went off to tell the maiden of this third task, which he thought it was impossible to do. But she told him to forge an eagle in his magic furnace, and that the eagle would catch the monster-pike for him. So Ilmarinen went to work and forged an eagle in his smithy: talons of iron, beak of steel and copper. And when the eagle was entirely made from iron and copper, he mounted on its back and bade it fly away to the river of Tuoni, there to catch the monster-pike.

When they had reached the bank, Ilmarinen dismounted and began to search for the pike, while the eagle hovered over the water. While Ilmarinen was searching, a huge monster rose from the depths and tried to seize him, but the eagle swooped down, and with one bite of his mighty beak, wrenched off the monster's head. Still Ilmarinen continued his search, until at last the monster-pike itself rose up to seize him. But as it came to the surface, the giant-eagle swooped down upon it, and buried its talons in the pike's flesh.

Then the fish, maddened with the pain, rushed down to the deepest caverns, dragging the eagle with it until the bird had to loosen its hold and soar aloft again. A second time the eagle swooped down and struck deep into the pike's shoulders; but the pike dived to the bottom again and escaped. At last the eagle made a third descent, and this time grasped the pike firmly with his beak of steel, and planted his talons firmly on the rocks, and this time he succeeded in dragging the pike from out the river.

Then the eagle flew off with the pike to the top of a tall pine-tree, and there ate the body of his victim, leaving the head for Ilmarinen. But the eagle himself soared up into the air, up beyond the clouds and at length disappeared behind the sun.

Ilmarinen returned to Louhi with the pike's head and again claimed her daughter in marriage. Louhi answered him, "You have performed this last task but badly, since you only brought me the worthless head. But still, since you have completed the other tasks also, I will give you my fair daughter. You have won the Maid of Beauty, to be the help and joy of all your future life."

But while Ilmarinen was rejoicing in his good fortune, the aged Wainamoinen wandered sorrowfully homewards, bewailing his sad lot, thus to be compelled to live without a wife to cheer his home. "Woe is me," he sang, "that I did not woo and marry in my youth, for the old men cannot hope to conquer the young ones when they go a-wooing.

The Brewing Of Beer

Adapted by R. Eivind in Finnish Legends for English Children, from the original Song of the Kervala. Finnish Legends for English Children was published in 1893 by T. fisher Unwin, London.

GREAT PREPARATIONS WERE NOW MADE IN Louhi's home for her daughter's wedding with Ilmarinen. In distant Karjala, a part of Kalevala, was a great ox, the largest in the world. It took a weasel seven days to travel round his neck and shoulders; the swallow had to fly a whole day without resting, to get from one horn-tip to the other; the squirrel travelled thirty days, starting from the tail, before he reached the shoulders. This great ox was led by a thousand heroes to Pohjola, to Louhi's house, but when he had come there, no one could be found to kill him.

Then there came an aged hero from Karjala, and went up to the ox to kill him with his war-club. But the ox turned and gave him one fierce glance, and the old warrior dropped his club and ran away and hid in the forest. Then they sent forth far and near to find someone to kill the ox, but no one came. At last there arose from the sea a tiny dwarf, who, when he stepped on land, grew suddenly into a giant, with hands of iron, a copper-coloured face, a hat of flint upon his head, and sandstone shoes upon his feet. As soon as this sea-spirit saw the ox, he rushed at it and killed it with one blow of his golden sword. Thus was the meat provided for the feast.

The banquet-hall was so large that when a dog barked at one door no one could hear him at the opposite side, and when a cock crowed on the roof no one on the ground could hear him. Louhi went in there, to see that all was being put in readiness, but while she was there she said aloud as if to herself, "Where will I get the liquor for my guests, for I know nothing of the secret of beer-brewing?"

An old man was sitting beside the fire, and he answered her, "Beer comes from barley, hops, and water. The seed of the hops were scattered loosely over the earth, and from them arose the graceful hop-vine, climbing over everything. The barley was planted in the land of Kalevala, and it grew and flourished there.

"Then the hops, clinging to the trees, began to hum, and the barley and the water in the wells to sing, saying, "Let us join our forces together, that we may live united, for that is far better than to be separated as we now are.' So the ancient maiden Osmotar took six golden grains of barley, seven hops, and seven cups of water, and set them in a caldron on the fire. There she let them steep and boil during the warm summer days, and at length poured off the liquor into tubs made of birch-wood. Now she pondered long how she should make the liquor ferment and cause it to foam and sparkle.

"Then Osmotar called one of the Kalevala maidens and bade her step into the birchen tub. The maiden did so, and on looking around she saw a splinter of wood lying on the bottom. She picked it up, thinking it was worthless, but nevertheless she took it to Osmotar. Osmotar rubbed her hands upon her knees and turned the bit of wood into a white squirrel. As soon as she had made the squirrel, she sent it off to Tapio's kingdom, to the great forest, and commanded it to bring her cones from the magic fir-trees and young shoots from the magic pines. And the squirrel hurried off and travelled through the forest until it came to Tapio's home. There it found three magic pine-trees growing, and three fir-trees beside them, and having taken the young shoots and the cones and stowed them in its pouch, it came back again to Osmotar. But when she put the cones and pine-shoots into the beer, it still refused to ferment.

"So Osmotar made the Kalevala maiden get into the birchen tub once more, and this time the maiden found a chip upon the bottom. When she took it to Osmotar, the latter rubbed her hands upon her knees again, and turned the chip into a magic golden-breasted marten. Then she sent the marten off to the dens of the mountain bears, to gather the foam from their angry lips as they fought with one another. The marten flew away, and soon returned with the foam that it had gathered from the mouths of the raging bears. But when Osmotar added it to the liquor there was no effect, and the beer remained as still as ever.

"For a third time, then, the maid of Kalevala stepped into the tub, and this time found a pod on the bottom. Osmotar took the pod and rubbed it between her hands and knees, and there flew out of it a honeybee. She sent the bee off to the Islands of the Sea, telling it to go to a meadow there, where a maiden lay asleep, and growing by the maiden's side there were honey-grasses and fragrant flowers. From these the bee was to collect the honey and bring it back. The bee flew off straight over the ocean, and on the evening of the third day reached the Isles of the Sea, where it found the maiden fast asleep amongst the flowers, clad in a silver robe, with a girdle of copper. By her grew the loveliest and sweetest of flowers and grasses, and the bee loaded itself down with their honey and returned to Osmotar with it. This time, when the honey was placed in the beer it began to ferment and rise and bubble and foam until it filled all the tubs and ran over on the sands.

"When the beer was ready, all the heroes of Kalevala came to drink it, and Lemminkainen drank so much that he became intoxicated. But Osmotar, now that she had made the beer, did not know how to keep it, for it was still running out of the tubs and over everything. While she was sitting and grieving over this, the robin sang to her from an aspen, and told her to put it into strong oaken barrels bound with copper hoops, and thus the last difficulty was overcome.

"Thus was beer first brewed from hops and barley," continued the old man, "and the beer of Kalevala is famed to strengthen the feeble, to cheer the sad, to make the old young, and the timid brave. It makes the heart joyful and puts wise sayings on the tongue, but the fool it makes still more foolish."

Thus the old man ended his account of the origin of beer, and Louhi, who had listened to him carefully, took all the tubs she had and put hops and barley in them, and water on top, and then lit huge fires to heat stones, that she might drop them in the mixture and make it boil. She made such a great quantity of beer that the springs were emptied and the forests grew small, and such a vast column of smoke went up as filled half of Pohjola and was seen even in distant Karjala and Lemminkainen's home. And all the people there thought it arose from some mighty battle between great heroes. But Lemminkainen pondered over it, and at last he found out that it was the fires for Louhi's beer-making for the wedding feast, and he grew bitterly angry, for Louhi had refused him her daughter's hand, and now had given her to Ilmarinen.

But now the beer was ready and was stored away in casks hooped with copper, and thousands of delicate dishes were made ready for the feast. But when all was nearly ready the beer began to grow impatient in its casks, and cried out for the guests to come that songs might be sung in its honour. So Louhi sent first for a pike and a salmon to sing its praises, but they could not do it. Next she sent for a boy, but the boy was too ignorant to sing the praises of the beer, and all this time the beer was calling out more and more loudly from its prison. Then Louhi determined to invite the guests at once, lest the beer should break forth from the casks.

So she called one of her servants and said to her, "Go, my trusted servant, and call together all the Pohjola people to the banquet. Go out into the highways too, and bring in all the poor and blind and cripples, the old and the young, that they may be merry at my daughter's wedding. And ask all the people of Karjala and the ancient Wainamoinen, but be sure you do not invite wild Lemminkainen." At this the servant asked why she was not to ask Lemminkainen, and Louhi answered, "Lemminkainen must not come, for he loves war and strife, and would bring disturbance and sorrow to our feast, and scoff at our maidens."

And the servant, having learned from Louhi how she should recognise Lemminkainen, set off and invited rich and poor, old and young, the deaf, the blind, and the cripples in all Pohjola and Karjala, but did not ask Lemminkainen.

Ilmarinen's Wedding Feast

Adapted by R. Eivind in Finnish Legends for English Children, from the original Song of the Kervala. Finnish Legends for English Children was published in 1893 by T. fisher Unwin, London.

AT LENGTH THE GUESTS BEGAN TO arrive, and Ilmarinen came escorted by hundreds of his friends, driving a coal-black steed, and with the same birds singing on his sledge as when he came to woo the Rainbow-maiden, Louhi's fairest daughter. When he alighted from his sledge, Louhi sent her best servants to take the steed and give him the very best of food in a manger of pure gold. But as Ilmarinen advanced to enter the house, they found that he was too tall to pass through the doorway without stooping, which would have been very unlucky: so Louhi had to have the top beam taken away before he could enter.

Inside the dwelling was so changed that no one would have recognised it. Louhi had cast a magic spell over it, and all the beams and door and window-sills were made from bones that gleamed like ivory; the windows were adorned with trout-scales, and the fires were set in flowers; and the seats and tables and floors were of gold and silver and copper, with marble hearth-stones and silken carpets on the floors. Louhi bade Ilmarinen welcome when he came into the guest-hall, and calling up her servant-maidens, she gazed at her daughter's suitor. The maidens bore wax tapers, and by their light the bridegroom looked handsomer than ever, and his eyes sparkled like the waves of the sea.

Then Louhi bade the maidens lead Ilmarinen to the seat of honour at the table in the great hall, and then all the other guests took their places, and the feast began. First of all the daintiest dishes of every sort were served by Louhi to the bridegroom - honey-biscuits, river-salmon, butter, bacon, and every delicacy one can think of - and after he was served, the servants took the dishes around to the others. After this the foaming beer was brought in silver pitchers, and all were served in the same order.

All the heroes and magicians assembled there began to grow merry, and Wainamoinen said that someone should sing the praises of the beer. But no one else could be found to do it, and all pressed Wainamoinen to sing, so at last he arose and began. He sang of the beer first, and then from his great stock of wisdom he sang them one song after the other of the days of old, until every guest grew happy from his magic power of song. But when Wainamoinen had finished his singing, he added, "Yet I am but a poor singer. For if great Ukko should sing his perfect songs of wisdom, he would sing the oceans into honey and the sands to berries, and the pebbles into barley, the rivers into beer, the fruit to gold, and the mountains into bread. Grant your blessing, great Ukko, upon this feast of ours. Send joy and health and comfort to all those here, that we may ever look back with pleasure to Ilmarinen's marriage with the fair Maiden of the Rainbow."

Thus Wainamoinen, the great singer, ended his singing, and the time had come for the bride and bridegroom to leave for their distant home in Kalevala. But first must Osmotar, the wise maiden, instruct the bride as to her future life. Osmotar told her that she must henceforth be thoughtful and not foolish, that she must love her husband's kinsfolks as her own. Osmotar told her, too, never to be idle, and then instructed her in all the many household duties of the wives of Kalevala, but at the same time impressed it upon her how wicked she would be if with all this she were to forget her own parents. After this Osmotar turned to the bridegroom and bade him ever love his bride and honour her, nor ever treat her ill.

Thus she advised them both, and they made ready to leave. But the Maiden of the Rainbow wept, because she was leaving all the joys and pleasures of her youth, and those she loved, to go to a distant land, where all would be new and strange, and perhaps, too, hard for her. Yet at length all the farewells had been said, the last goodbye was spoken, and the two got into their sledge and the next instant the swift black steed flew off like an arrow, rushing on toward the land of Kalevala, leaving far behind them the gloomy Northland, which was yet so dear to the Rainbow-maiden, and which she was never to see again.

Three days they journeyed onward over hill and valley without stopping, and the third evening brought them in sight of Ilmarinen's smithy, and they could see the smoke rising from the chimneys of their home. There they found that they had been expected for a long time, and there was great rejoicing when their sledge drove up, with the birds singing merrily on its front, and all bright and happy.

Lakko, Ilmarinen's mother, received them at the door and welcomed the fair Rainbow-maiden most heartily, and when the bridal pair had taken off their furs, she served them with the very best of food and drink - choicest bits of reindeer, wheaten biscuit, honey-cakes, and fish of all sorts, and the best of beer. And while they ate, the others, who had been old Louhi's guests, began to arrive, and soon there was a great feast going on, almost as great a one as there had been before at Louhi's.

While they were all feasting, Wainamoinen arose and began to sing again. This time he sang the praises of the bridegroom's father and mother, and the bride and groom, and ended up with praising the guests that were assembled there. Then he and many of the guests took their leave and journeyed off together to their homes. Three days they drove on together, and Wainamoinen kept on singing all the time, until suddenly his song was cut short, for his sledge ran into a birch-tree and was broken into pieces. But Wainamoinen considered the case and then said, "Is there any one here who will go to Tuonela, to the Deathland, for the auger of Tuoni, that I may mend my sledge with it?" But no one would venture on so perilous a journey, so at length Wainamoinen went himself and obtained Tuoni's magic auger, and with its aid, on his return, he put together his magic sledge again.

Then he harnessed up his steed once more and galloped off to his home. Thus ended Ilmarinen's wedding and the feasts that followed it.

The Mermaid And The Boy

Adapted by Andrew Lang in his Brown Fairy Book from an original by Josef Calasanz Poestion in Lapplandische Märchen. The Brown Fairy Book was published by Longman, Green & Co in 1904.

LONG, LONG AGO, THERE LIVED A king who ruled over a country by the sea. When he had been married about a year, some of his subjects, inhabiting a distant group of islands, revolted against his laws, and it became needful for him to leave his wife and go in person to settle their disputes. The queen feared that some ill would come of it, and implored him to stay at home, but he told her that nobody could do his work for him, and the next morning the sails were spread, and the king started on his voyage.

The vessel had not gone very far when she ran upon a rock, and stuck so fast in a cleft that the strength of the whole crew could not get her off again. To make matters worse, the wind was rising too, and it was quite plain that in a few hours the ship would be dashed to pieces and everybody would be drowned, when suddenly the form of a mermaid was seen dancing on the waves which threatened every moment to overwhelm them.

"There is only one way to free yourselves," she said to the king, bobbing up and down in the water as she spoke, "and that is to give me your solemn word that you will deliver to me the first child that is born to you."

The king hesitated at this proposal. He hoped that someday he might have children in his home, and the thought that he must yield up the heir to his crown was very bitter to him; but just then a huge wave broke with great force on the ship's side, and his men fell on their knees and entreated him to save them.

So he promised, and this time a wave lifted the vessel clean off the rocks, and she was in the open sea once more.

The affairs of the islands took longer to settle than the king had expected, and some months passed away before he returned to his palace. In his absence a son had been born to him, and so great was his joy that he quite forgot the mermaid and the price he had paid for the safety of his ship. But as the years went on, and the baby grew into a fine big boy, the remembrance of it came back, and one day he told the queen the whole story. From that moment the happiness of both their lives was ruined. Every night they went to bed wondering if they should find his room empty in the morning, and every day they kept him by their sides, expecting him to be snatched away before their very eyes.

At last the king felt that this state of things could not continue, and he said to his wife, "After all, the most foolish thing in the world one can do is to keep the boy here in exactly the place in which the mermaid will seek him. Let us give him food and send him on his travels, and perhaps, if the mermaid ever blocs come to seek him, she may be content with some other child." And the queen agreed that his plan seemed the wisest.

So the boy was called, and his father told him the story of the voyage, as he had told his mother before him. The prince listened eagerly, and was delighted to think that he was to go away all by himself to see the world, and was not in the least frightened; for though he was now sixteen, he had scarcely been allowed to walk alone beyond the palace gardens. He began busily to make his preparations, and took off his smart velvet coat, putting on instead one of green cloth, while he refused a beautiful bag which the queen offered him to hold his food, and slung a leather knapsack over his shoulders instead, just as he had seen other travellers do. Then he bade farewell to his parents and went his way.

All through the day he walked, watching with interest the strange birds and animals that darted across his path in the forest or peeped at him from behind a bush. But as evening drew on he became tired, and looked about as he walked for some place where he could sleep. At length he reached a soft mossy bank under a tree, and was just about to stretch himself out on it, when a fearful roar made him start and tremble all over. In another moment something passed swiftly through the air and a lion stood before him.

"What are you doing here?" asked the lion, his eyes glaring fiercely at the boy.

"I am flying from the mermaid," the prince answered, in a quaking voice.

"Give me some food then," said the lion, "it is past my supper time, and I am very hungry."

The boy was so thankful that the lion did not want to eat him, that he gladly picked up his knapsack which lay on the ground, and held out some bread and a flask of wine.

"I feel better now," said the lion when he had done, "so now I shall go to sleep on this nice soft moss, and if you like you can lie down beside me." So the boy and the lion slept soundly side by side, till the sun rose.

"I must be off now," remarked the lion, shaking the boy as he spoke, "but cut off the tip of my ear, and keep it carefully, and if you are in any danger just wish yourself a lion and you will become one on the spot. One good turn deserves another, you know."

The prince thanked him for his kindness, and did as he was bid, and the two then bade each other farewell.

"I wonder how it feels to be a lion," thought the boy, after he had gone a little way; and he took out the tip of the ear from the breast of his jacket and wished with all his might. In an instant his head had swollen to several times its usual size, and his neck seemed very hot and heavy; and, somehow, his hands became paws, and his skin grew hairy and yellow. But what pleased him most was his long tail with a tuft at the end, which he lashed and switched proudly. "I like being a lion very much," he said to himself, and trotted gaily along the road.

After a while, however, he got tired of walking in this unaccustomed way - it made his back ache and his front paws felt sore. So he wished himself a boy again, and in the twinkling of an eye his tail disappeared and his head shrank, and the long thick mane became short and curly. Then he looked out for a sleeping place, and found some dry ferns, which he gathered and heaped up.

But before he had time to close his eyes there was a great noise in the trees nearby, as if a big heavy body was crashing through them.

The boy rose and turned his head, and saw a huge black bear coming towards him.

"What are you doing here?" cried the bear.

"I am running away from the mermaid," answered the boy; but the bear took no interest in the mermaid, and only said, "I am hungry; give me something to eat."

The knapsack was lying on the ground among the fern, but the prince picked it up, and, unfastening the strap, took out his second flask of wine and another loaf of bread. "We will have supper together," he remarked politely; but the bear, who had never been taught manners, made no reply, and ate as fast as he could. When he had quite finished, he got up and stretched himself.

"You have got a comfortable-looking bed there," he observed. "I really think that, bad sleeper as I am, I might have a good night on it. I can manage to squeeze you in," he added, "you don't take up a great deal of room." The boy was rather indignant at the bear's cool way of talking; but as he was too tired to gather more fern, they lay down side by side, and never stirred till sunrise next morning.

"I must go now," said the bear, pulling the sleepy prince on to his feet, "but first you shall cut off the tip of my ear, and when you are in any danger just wish yourself a bear and you will become one. One good turn deserves another, you know." And the boy did as he was bid, and he and the bear bade each other farewell.

"I wonder how it feels to be a bear," thought he to himself when he had walked a little way; and he took out the tip from the breast of his coat and wished hard that he might become a bear. The next moment his body stretched out and thick black fur covered him all over. As before, his hands were changed into paws, but when he tried to switch his tail he found to his disgust that it would not go any distance. "Why it is hardly worth calling a tail!" said he. For the rest of the day he remained a bear and continued his journey, but as evening came on the bear-skin, which had been so useful when plunging through brambles in the forest, felt rather heavy, and he wished himself a boy again. He was too much exhausted to take the trouble of cutting any fern or seeking for moss, but just threw himself down under a tree, when exactly above his head he heard a great buzzing as a bumble-bee alighted on a honeysuckle branch. "What are you doing here?" asked the bee in a cross voice, "at your age you ought to be safe at home."

"I am running away from the mermaid," replied the boy; but the bee, like the lion and the bear, was one of those people who never listen to the answers to their questions, and only said, "I am hungry. Give me something to eat."

The boy took his last loaf and flask out of his knapsack and laid them on the ground, and they had supper together. "Well, now I am going to sleep," observed the bee when the last crumb was gone, "but as you are not very big I can make room for you beside me," and he curled up his wings, and tucked in his legs, and he and the prince both slept soundly till morning. Then the bee got up and carefully brushed every scrap of dust off his velvet coat and buzzed loudly in the boy's ear to waken him.

"Take a single hair from one of my wings," said he, "and if you are in danger just wish yourself a bee and you will become one. One good turn deserves another, so farewell, and thank you for your supper." And the bee departed after the boy had pulled out the hair and wrapped it carefully in a leaf.

"It must feel quite different to be a bee from what it does to be a lion or bear," thought the boy to himself when he had walked for an hour or two. "I dare say I should get on a great deal faster," so he pulled out his hair and wished himself a bee.

In a moment the strangest thing happened to him. All his limbs seemed to draw together, and his body to become very short and round; his head grew quite tiny, and instead of his white skin he was covered with the richest, softest velvet. Better than all, he had two lovely gauze wings which carried him the whole day without getting tired.

Late in the afternoon the boy fancied he saw a vast heap of stones a long way off, and he flew straight towards it. But when he reached the gates he saw that it was really a great town, so he wished himself back in his own shape and entered the city.

He found the palace doors wide open and went boldly into a sort of hall which was full of people, and where men and maids were gossiping together. He joined their talk and soon learned from them that the king had only one daughter who had such a hatred to men that she would never suffer one to enter her presence. Her father was in despair, and had had pictures painted of the handsomest princes of all the courts in the world, in the hope that she might fall in love with one of them; but it was no use; the princess would not even allow the pictures to be brought into her room.

"It is late," remarked one of the women at last, "I must go to my mistress." And, turning to one of the lackeys, she bade him find a bed for the youth.

"It is not necessary," answered the prince, "this bench is good enough for me. I am used to nothing better." And when the hall was empty he lay down for a few minutes. But as soon as everything was quiet in the palace he took out the hair and wished himself a bee, and in this shape he flew upstairs, past the guards, and through the keyhole into the princess's chamber. Then he turned himself into a man again.

At this dreadful sight the princess, who was broad awake, began to scream loudly. "A man! a man!" cried she; but when the guards rushed in there was only a bumble-bee buzzing about the room. They looked under the bed, and behind the curtains, and into the cupboards, then came to the conclusion that the princess had had a bad dream, and bowed themselves out. The door had scarcely closed on them than the bee disappeared, and a handsome youth stood in his place.

"I knew a man was hidden somewhere," cried the princess, and screamed more loudly than before. Her shrieks brought back the guards, but though they looked in all kinds of impossible places no man was to be seen, and so they told the princess.

"He was here a moment ago - I saw him with my own eyes," and the guards dared not contradict her, though they shook their heads and whispered to each other that the princess had gone mad on this subject, and saw a man in every table and chair. And they made up their minds that - let her scream as loudly as she might - they would take no notice.

Now the princess saw clearly what they were thinking, and that in future her guards would give her no help, and would perhaps, besides, tell some stories about her to the king, who would shut her up in a lonely tower and prevent her walking in the gardens among her birds and flowers. So when, for the third time, she beheld the prince standing before her, she did not scream but sat up in bed gazing at him in silent terror.

"Do not be afraid," he said, "I shall not hurt you"; and he began to praise her gardens, of which he had heard the servants speak, and the birds and flowers which she loved, till the princess's anger softened, and she answered him with gentle words. Indeed, they soon became so friendly that she vowed she would marry no one else, and confided to him that in three days her father would be off to the wars, leaving his sword in her room. If any man could find it and bring it to him he would receive her hand as a reward. At this point a cock crew, and the youth jumped up hastily saying, "Of course I shall ride with the king to the war, and if I do not return, take your violin every evening to the seashore and play on it, so that the very sea-kobolds who live at the bottom of the ocean may hear it and come to you."

Just as the princess had foretold, in three days the king set out for the war with a large following, and among them was the young prince, who had presented himself at court as a young noble in search of adventures. They had left the city many miles behind them, when the king suddenly discovered that he had forgotten his sword, and though all his attendants instantly offered theirs, he declared that he could fight with none but his own.

"The first man who brings it to me from my daughter's room," cried he, "shall not only have her to wife, but after my death shall reign in my stead."

At this the Red Knight, the young prince, and several more turned their horses to ride as fast as the wind back to the palace. But suddenly a better plan entered the prince's head, and, letting the others pass him, he took his precious parcel from his breast and wished himself a lion. Then on he bounded, uttering such dreadful roars that the horses were frightened and grew unmanageable, and he easily outstripped them, and soon reached the gates of the palace. Here he hastily changed himself into a bee, and flew straight into the princess's room, where he became a man again.

She showed him where the sword hung concealed behind a curtain, and he took it down, saying as he did so, "Be sure not to forget what you have promised to do."

The princess made no reply, but smiled sweetly, and slipping a golden ring from her finger she broke it in two and held half out silently to the prince, while the other half she put in her own pocket. He kissed it, and ran down the stairs bearing the sword with him. Some way off he met the Red Knight and the rest, and the Red Knight at first tried to take the sword from him by force. But as the youth proved too strong for him, he gave it up, and resolved to wait for a better opportunity.

This soon came, for the day was hot and the prince was thirsty. Perceiving a little stream that ran into the sea, he turned aside, and, unbuckling the sword, flung himself on the ground for a long drink. Unluckily, the mermaid happened at that moment to be floating on the water not very far off, and knew he was the boy who had been given her before he was born. So she floated gently in to where he was lying, she seized him by the arm, and the waves closed over them both. Hardly had they disappeared, when the Red Knight stole cautiously up, and could hardly believe his eyes when he saw the king's sword on the bank. He wondered what had become of the youth, who an hour before had guarded his treasure so fiercely; but, after all, that was no affair of his! So, fastening the sword to his belt, he carried it to the king.

The war was soon over, and the king returned to his people, who welcomed him with shouts of joy. But when the princess from her window saw that her betrothed was not among the attendants riding behind her father, her heart sank, for she knew that some evil must have befallen him, and she feared the Red Knight. She had long ago learned how clever and how wicked he was, and something whispered to her that it was he who would gain the credit of having carried back the sword, and would claim her as his bride, though he had never even entered her chamber. And she could do nothing; for although the king loved her, he never let her stand in the way of his plans.

The poor princess was only too right, and everything came to pass exactly as she had foreseen it. The king told her that the Red Knight had won her fairly, and that the wedding would take place next day, and there would be a great feast after it.

In those days feasts were much longer and more splendid than they are now; and it was growing dark when the princess, tired out with all she had gone through, stole up to her own room for a little quiet. But the moon was shining so brightly over the sea that it seemed to draw her towards it, and taking her violin under her arm, she crept down to the shore.

"Listen! listen! said the mermaid to the prince, who was lying stretched on a bed of seaweeds at the bottom of the sea. "Listen! that is your old love playing, for mermaids know everything that happens upon earth."

"I hear nothing," answered the youth, who did not look happy. "Take me up higher, where the sounds can reach me."

So the mermaid took him on her shoulders and bore him up midway to the surface. "Can you hear now?" she asked.

"No," answered the prince, "I hear nothing but the water rushing; I must go higher still."

Then the mermaid carried him to the very top. "You must surely be able to hear now?" said she.

"Nothing but the water," repeated the youth. So she took him right to the land.

"At any rate you can hear now?" she said again.

"The water is still rushing in my ears," answered he, "but wait a little, that will soon pass off." And as he spoke he put his hand into his breast, and seizing the hair wished himself a bee, and flew straight into the pocket of the princess. The mermaid looked in vain for him, and coated all night upon the sea; but he never came back, and never more did he gladden her eyes. But the princess felt that something strange was about her, though she knew not what, and returned quickly to the palace, where the young man at once resumed his own shape. Oh, what joy filled her heart at the sight of him! But there was no time to be lost, and she led him right into the hall, where the king and his nobles were still sitting at the feast. "Here is a man who boasts that he can do wonderful tricks," said she, "better even than the Red Knight's! That cannot be true, of course, but it might be well to give this impostor a lesson. He pretends, for instance, that he can turn himself into a lion; but that I do not believe. I know that you have studied the art of magic," she went on, turning to the Red Knight, "so suppose you just show him how it is done, and bring shame upon him."

Now the Red Knight had never opened a book of magic in his life; but he was accustomed to think that he could do everything better than other people without any teaching at all. So he turned and twisted himself about, and bellowed and made faces; but he did not become a lion for all that.

"Well, perhaps it is very difficult to change into a lion. Make yourself a bear," said the princess. But the Red Knight found it no easier to become a bear than a lion.

"Try a bee," suggested she. "I have always read that anyone who can do magic at all can do that." And the old knight buzzed and hummed, but he remained a man and not a bee.

"Now it is your turn," said the princess to the youth. "Let us see if you can change yourself into a lion." And in a moment such a fierce creature stood before them, that all the guests rushed out of the hall, treading each other underfoot in their fright. The lion sprang at the Red Knight, and would have torn him in pieces had not the princess held him back, and bidden him to change himself into a man again. And in a second a man took the place of the lion.

"Now become a bear," said she; and a bear advanced panting and stretching out his arms to the Red Knight, who shrank behind the princess.

By this time some of the guests had regained their courage, and returned as far as the door, thinking that if it was safe for the princess perhaps it was safe for them. The king, who was braver than they, and felt it needful to set them a good example besides, had never left his seat, and when at a new command of the princess the bear once more turned into a man, he was silent from astonishment, and a suspicion of the truth began to dawn on him. "Was it he who fetched the sword?" asked the king.

"Yes, it was," answered the princess; and she told him the whole story, and how she had broken her gold ring and given him half of it. And the prince took out his half of the ring, and the princess took out hers, and they fitted exactly. Next day the Red Knight was hanged, as he richly deserved, and there was a new marriage feast for the prince and princess.

The Origin Of The Serpent

Adapted by R. Eivind in Finnish Legends for English Children, from the original Song of the Kervala. Finnish Legends for English Children was published in 1893 by T. fisher Unwin, London.

AS LEMMINKAINEN WAS PLOUGHING HIS FIELDS one day, he heard the noise of sledges as if a vast number of people were on their way past. At once he guessed the reason, for they were the guests going to Ilmarinen's wedding, while he alone had not been invited. Then his face turned pale with anger, and he left his ploughing and hastened off to his house. When he arrived there, he asked his mother to give him a hearty meal, and after that he went to the bath-house and after the bath put on his finest garments, as if going to a feast.

His mother asked him where he was going and he told her that he was bound for the great feast that Louhi had prepared. But his mother tried to keep him from going, telling him that they did not want him there, or else they would have invited him, but he answered, "This sword with its sharp edges constantly reminds me that I am needed in distant Pohjola." His mother spoke again, saying, "Do not go, my dear son, for Death will meet you thrice upon the way." Lemminkainen replied that he did not fear Death, but would overcome him, but at the same time asked his mother what the first danger would be.

"When you have travelled for one day," she replied, "you will come to a stream of fire, with a fiery cataract, and in the fire-fall a rock, and on the rock a fiery hill, and on its top an eagle made of flames, who devours all that approach him."

Lemminkainen answered that he would easily pass this danger, and asked to know the second. His mother told him, "When you have travelled two days, you will come to a fiery pit filled with red-hot stones, and no one has ever been able to pass over it."

But Lemminkainen thought but little of this second danger, and asked his mother to tell him what the third one was. She replied, "When you have gone one day farther, and have come to Pohjola, the wolf and the black bear will attack you, and many hundred men have perished in their jaws." But he told her how easily he would overcome them and then have conquered all the dangers of the journey. Then his mother added, "There are three things still to conquer. When you reach Louhi's dwelling, you will find walls built of iron rising up to the sky, and surrounded by railings of spears on which are serpents and all manner of venomous creatures twisting and creeping about; and right before the gateway lies the largest of them all, longer than the rafters of a house. And beyond all this, you will find great hosts of armed warriors, who have grown angry over their beer and they will certainly kill you. And if you should come into the courtyard, you will find it full of sharp stakes, to hold the heads of those that go there unbidden. Do not forget how you once fared in Pohjola, that had I not saved you, then you would now be at the bottom of Tuoni's river."

Yet after she had warned him of all this, Lemminkainen would not be persuaded to remain at home, but put on his magic armour of copper and took his father's sword, and his own strongest bow. Then he had his steed hitched to a sledge and went out into the courtyard to drive off. There his mother bade him farewell and gave him some last words of advice, telling him that if he should come to the feast, to drink but half of his goblet of beer, for there were serpents in the other half, and to behave modestly and not to try to take the best of everything for himself.

When she had ended, Lemminkainen jumped upon his sledge, cracked his whip, and drove off like the wind. He had not gone far before a flock of wild birds flew across his road and dropped a few feathers on the ground. Lemminkainen stopped and picking them up put them carefully in his leather pouch, "for," he thought, "no one knows what may happen." As soon as he had picked up the feathers he was off again, but he had not gone far when his steed stopped in terror, for there, right in front of them, was a broad river of fire, and a fire-fall with a rock in the middle, and on the rock a fiery hill, and on the hill a flaming eagle.

The Eagle asked him where he was going, and Lemminkainen replied that he was hurrying to Louhi's feast and begged the Eagle to let him pass. "Truly you shall pass," the Eagle answered, "but only through the flames and down my throat." But Lemminkainen was not dismayed. He took out the feathers from his pouch and rubbed them between his fingers, and presently there arose a whole flock of birds and flew straight down the eagle's mouth so that its hunger was satisfied, then Lemminkainen was able to pass over the river by the help of his magic, and to drive on his way.

He drove for another day and then hips. horse suddenly stopped again in terror, for there was a huge pit full of fire right in front, which stretched as far as one could see to east and west. Yet Lemminkainen was not discouraged, but prayed to great Ukko, that he would send a great storm from all the four points of the compass, and fill the pit with snow. And the snow came and as it fell into the seething pit of fire it melted and formed a lake; and Lemminkainen quickly cast a spell upon this lake so that a solid bridge of ice was formed over it, and he drove over in perfect safety.

Thus the second danger was passed and he drove on more swiftly than ever. After another day's journey, when he had come near to Louhi's abode, his horse stopped again, trembling with fear. This time there were a fierce wolf and a great black bear in the road. But Lemminkainen put his hand into his leather pouch and pulled out a tuft of wool. This he rubbed between his hands and breathed on it, and it changed into a whole flock of sheep, on which the bear and the wolf jumped and left Lemminkainen to pursue his journey in peace.

In a very short time he had reached Louhi's house. But there he found the great wall of iron and the fence of spears and the horrible snakes and lizards that his mother had told him of. Yet he pulled out his magic broad sword and cut an opening through the wall and the fence of spears and the mass of serpents, and passed through to the gateway. There he found a huge serpent with a hundred eyes, each as large as bowls, and a thousand tongues long as javelins, and teeth like hatchets. Lemminkainen sang one spell, but it was not powerful enough, and the huge monster started to rush at him and seize him in its awful mouth. But Lemminkainen just in time began to sing a stronger spell.

For evil things cannot bear to have their wicked origin told, and if therefore one sings the source of any evil, one makes it harmless at once, so Lemminkainen sang, "If you will not give room for me to pass, I will sing of your evil origin, will tell how your horrid head was made. Suoyatar, your evil mother, once spat upon the waves of the sea. The spittle was rocked by the waves and warmed by the sun, until after a long time it was washed ashore. There the daughters of Ukko, the Creator, saw it, and said, 'What would happen if great Ukko were to breathe the breath of life into this writhing, senseless mass?' But Ukko overheard them and said, 'Naught but evil comes from evil, therefore I will not give it life.'

"Now, wicked Lempo heard what Ukko had said, and he himself breathed into it the breath of life, and shaped it to the form of a serpent, adding to the spittle all manner of evil things, every poisonous plant and thing from the Deathland. This was your origin, Oh Serpent, vilest thing of all creation; therefore clear the pathway that I may enter the halls of the hostess Louhi."

Thus sang Lemminkainen, and the serpent uncoiled itself and crawled away, while Ahti himself went on through the gateway.

The Unwelcome Guest

Adapted by R. Eivind in Finnish Legends for English Children, from the original Song of the Kervala. Finnish Legends for English Children was published in 1893 by T. fisher Unwin, London.

THUS LEMMINKAINEN CAME UNBIDDEN TO Louhi's abode, but he had arrived too late for the feast. He entered the house with such a mighty tread that the floors bent under him and the walls and ceilings creaked as he advanced. Louhi's husband was seated in the guest-room, and Lemminkainen said to him, "The same greeting to you that you give to me! Are there food and beer here for a stranger and barley for a hungry steed?"

Louhi's husband answered, "I have never yet refused a place in my stables for a stranger's horse, and if you will act honestly there is a place for you between the iron kettles."

Lemminkainen said, "When my father Lempo comes to a house as a guest, he is well received and given the place of honour. Why should I, his son, be put between the pots and kettles to be covered with soot?" With these words he walked up to the table, and taking his seat he waited to be served.

Then Louhi said to him, "Oh Lemminkainen, you were not invited here, and I feel that you bring sorrow with you. All our dinner was eaten and our beer drunk yesterday, and we have nothing left for you."

This made Lemminkainen very angry, and he replied, "Oh toothless mistress of Pohjola, you have managed your feast very badly, for you have had delicacies of every sort for the others, who gave but trifling presents, while for me, who have sent the most of all, you have nothing at all after my long journey."

Then Louhi called up one of her meanest servants and bade her serve the guest. And there came a little short woman, who made ready a soup out of fish-bones and fish-heads and crusts of bread and turnip-stalks, and brought him the worst of the servants" beer to quench his thirst with. Lemminkainen looked into the pitchers of beer, and saw snakes and worms and lizards floating about in them. This made him furiously angry, yet he resolved to drink the beer at any rate, and then to punish them for their evil treatment of him. So he drew a fish-hook out of his magic wallet, and with it he caught all the evil creatures in the beer and killed them with his sword, and drank the beer.

When he had done this, he turned to the host and upbraided him for his bad treatment, and finally said that as the Pohjola folk could not treat guests decently, perhaps he could purchase good beer at least. At this Louhi's husband grew angry and conjured up a little lake in the floor at Lemminkainen's feet, and bade him quench his thirst at that. But Lemminkainen conjured up a bull with gold and silver horns, that drank up all the water. Then Louhi's husband conjured up a wolf to devour the bull, but Ahti called up a rabbit to draw off the wolf's attention. Next the host conjured up a dog to eat the rabbit, but Ahti drew away the dog by means of a squirrel that he called up by his magic. At that the host made a golden marten to catch the squirrel, and Lemminkainen a scarlet-coloured fox which ate the golden marten. Next the host conjured a hen to distract the scarlet fox, and Lemminkainen made a hawk to tear the hen to pieces.

Then old Louhi's husband cried, "We shall never be happy here until you are driven out, Oh evil Ahti," and with these words he drew his sword and challenged Lemminkainen to combat. So Ahti drew his sword also, and when the two were measured, they found that Ahti's was the shorter by half an inch.

Then Lemminkainen said to his host, "Although you have the longer sword, yet you shall begin the fight."

After this they placed themselves in position, and the host of Pohjola began. But so powerful was Lemminkainen's magic that he only hit the walls and floor and rafters, but could not touch Ahti himself. Then Lemminkainen said sneeringly, "What harm have the walls and rafters done, that you should cut them to pieces. But come, let us go out into the courtyard, that the hall may not be covered with blood."

So they went out into the yard, and there they spread out an ox-hide, and took up their places on it to continue the fight. Lemminkainen again allowed the host to begin, and the latter struck three mighty blows, but still could not harm Ahti. Then the battle began in real earnest, and the sparks flew from their swords until it seemed as if there were a sheet of flame flowing from Lemminkainen's sword and down upon the head and shoulders of his opponent. And when he saw this, Lemminkainen said, "Oh you son of Pohjola, see how your neck is shining like the ocean at dawn."

The other turned without thinking, to see what it was, and quick as lightning Lemminkainen whirled his sword round his head, and with one blow cut off the host's head as easily as one cuts the top from a turnip, and the head rolled along on the ground. In the yard were hundreds of sharp stakes, and on all but one there was a human head. So Lemminkainen quickly took the host's head and stuck it on the empty stake, and then went into the house and ordered Louhi to bring him water to wash his hands, as he had just slain her husband.

But Louhi hastened out and called in hundreds of armed warriors to avenge her husband's death. And in a very short time Lemminkainen saw that he must either flee or else be killed if he remained.

The Isle Of Refuge

Adapted by R. Eivind in Finnish Legends for English Children, from the original Song of the Kervala. Finnish Legends for English Children was published in 1893 by T. fisher Unwin, London.

LEMMINKAINEN HASTENED FROM LOUHI'S HOUSE and looked around for his sledge and steed to escape from the Pohjola men. But both had disappeared, and in their place he found only a clump of willows. As he stood there, wondering what he should do next, the noise of armed men running together grew louder and louder, and he knew that they would soon reach him. So Lemminkainen changed himself into an eagle, and rose up into the clouds. As he flew towards the south he met a grey hawk flying northward, and called to it, "Oh Gray Hawk, fly to Pohjola and tell the warriors of the Northland that they will never catch the Eagle, Lemminkainen, ere he reaches his home in distant Kalevala."

Then he flew on home and taking on again his own form, he went to his mother's house. When she saw the troubled look in his face, she guessed that some great danger threatened him, and began to ask him if it were this, or that, or the other that troubled him, but to all her questions he answered "no." At length she bade him tell her, then, what his trouble was, and he replied, "All the men of

Northland are sharpening their swords and spears to kill your unlucky son Ahti, for I have slain the host of Pohjola, Louhi's husband, in a quarrel, and the men of Northland will soon come here to avenge it."

His mother then reminded him how she had warned him of the journey and its troubles, and asked him where he was going to take refuge. Lemminkainen replied that he did not know, and asked his mother to help him, and she answered, "If I should turn you into a tree, you might be cut down for firewood. Or if into a berry, the maidens might pluck you. Or if to a fish, you would never have a happy life. But if you will swear to me not to go to war again for sixty years, then I will tell you of a distant isle, far off across the ocean, where you may rest in safety."

So Lemminkainen gave his promise, on his honour, not to fight for sixty years, and then his mother told him how to find the isle of refuge. He must sail across nine seas and in the middle of the tenth he would come to the island, where his father had once taken refuge long before. There he must stay until the third year was come, and then he might return to his home.

Lemminkainen took enough provisions in his boat for a long journey, and then bidding farewell to his mother and his home he sailed away. When he had raised the linen sails, he called up a fair wind to drive him onward, and for three months he sailed on without a moment's rest, until at length he reached the magic Isle of Refuge.

First, he asked the people of the island if there was room there for his boat, and on receiving their consent he drew it up out of the water. Next he asked them if he might take refuge and conceal himself there, and they granted this too; but when he asked for a little ground to cultivate, and a place in the forest to cut down the trees, they told him that the whole island had long ago been divided up amongst them, and that he must live in one of their houses if he wished to stay on the island.

But Lemminkainen was not satisfied with this, and told them that he only wished to be allowed to go into the forest and sing some few magic songs there, and this they willingly allowed him to do. So he went into the forest and began to sing the most wondrous spells, making oak-trees to grow up around him, and on each branch an acorn, and on each acorn sat a cuckoo. Then the cuckoos began to sing, and gold fell from every beak, and silver from their wings, and copper from their feathers, until the isle was abundantly supplied with precious metals. Then Lemminkainen sang again, and turned the sand to gems and the pebbles into pearls, and he covered the whole island with flowers, and made little lakes with gold and silver ducks swimming in them, until everyone was delighted, and the maidens most of all.

Then Ahti said, "If I were in a fine castle I would conjure up the most wonderful feasts and sing the grandest songs you have ever heard." No sooner had he said this than they led him to their finest castle, and there he conjured up a splendid feast, with knives and forks and all the dishes made of gold and silver. From this time on Ahti was treated as an honoured guest, and spent his time most delightfully. In every village on the island were seven castles, and in each castle were seven daughters, and all of these made Lemminkainen welcome as he went from one to another according to his fancy. Thus he spent the whole of his years of exile; but there was one maid, old and ugly, and living in a remote village, whom he neglected.

At length the time of his return was come, and he made up his mind to leave. But just as he had decided to go, the maid whom he had neglected came to him and bade him beware, for she was going to take revenge for his slighting her; but Lemminkainen scarcely heard her, for he was so busy thinking about his journey home. But the maiden went around to all the men of the island, and told them evil stories about Lemminkainen, and then she went and burned his boat.

The next morning Lemminkainen started off to bid his friends the maidens farewell, but he had not gone far before he saw the men getting their weapons ready to come and attack him, and he saw that he must fly immediately if he wished to escape alive. So he hastened down to his boat, but when he reached it there were only the ashes left. At first he did not know what to do, but he spied seven broken pieces of planks and a few fragments from a broken distaff, and taking these he began to sing some mystic spells over them. No sooner had he finished his incantations than a magic boat stood ready before him, and he got into it and sailed away. But before he was far from the shore all the maidens came down to the beach and began to weep and beg him to come back and dwell with them for ever. But Lemminkainen answered them that he felt a great longing to see his home once more and his mother, yet that he was truly sorrowful to leave them, but it must be so. And so he sailed on until the isle was out of sight.

The boat sailed on and on for two days and nights, but on the third day came a mighty storm-wind, and tossed the vessel about until it broke all in pieces, and left Lemminkainen struggling in the waters. He swam for long days and nights, struggling with the waves, until at length he reached a rocky point projecting out into the ocean. There he landed and soon found his way to a castle that was built upon the rocks. He told the mistress of the castle how he had been in the water for days and days, and was almost perishing from hunger, and she, being a kind-hearted woman, gave him a splendid feast of bread and butter, veal and bacon, and fish and honey-cakes, and when he had eaten that and rested, she gave him a new boat, loaded with provisions, in which to finish his journey.

So off he sailed again, and after many weary days of sailing he at length reached his beloved island-home. But when he landed and went up to where the house had stood, there was not a sign of anything left. The whole place was all overgrown with trees and bushes.

Then Lemminkainen sat down and began to weep; but it was not for the loss of his home and all his riches that he wept but for his beloved mother. As he sat there he caught sight of an eagle flying in the air above, and Ahti asked him if he knew what had happened to his mother. But the eagle could only tell him that his people had all perished long go. Next he asked the raven, and the raven told him that his people had been killed by his enemies from Pohjola.

On hearing this Lemminkainen began again to mourn her loss, and to look about for some dear relic that he might keep in remembrance of her. But as he looked he suddenly came on a faint pathway leading away from the house, and on it he saw the prints of light feet. He began to follow it eagerly, over hill and valley until he reached the gloomy forest. There it led him to a hidden glade, right in the middle of the island, and there he found a humble cabin, and his grey-haired mother weeping in it.

Ahti cried aloud for joy at the sight of her, and then he told her how he had mourned her as dead. She asked him in return how he had spent those years on the Isle of Refuge, and he told her all; how charming the life there was, and how he had enjoyed himself there, but that at the end all the men of the isle had come to hate him, because the maidens admired him so much, and how through their jealousy and the hatred of the one maid whom he had neglected, he had nearly lost his life. And when he had ended his story they both gave thanks to great Ukko that they had found each other again.

The Frost-Fiend

Adapted by R. Eivind in Finnish Legends for English Children, from the original Song of the Kervala. Finnish Legends for English Children was published in 1893 by T. fisher Unwin, London.

WHEN THE NEXT DAY BEGAN TO dawn, Lemminkainen went to the beach, that was hidden behind a projecting point, where his vessels lay. He found them still there, but as he approached he heard the rigging wailing in the wind, and saying, "Must we lie here for ever and rot, since Ahti has sworn not to go to war for sixty long years?"

Then Lemminkainen cried out to his vessels, "Mourn no more, my good warships, for soon you shall be filled with warriors and hastening to the battle." When he had uttered these words he hurried back to his mother and bade her sorrow no longer over the insult that the Pohjola warriors had offered to her, for he was going now to make war on them in order to punish them for it.

His mother, when she heard his intention, besought him earnestly not to go to war and break his oath to her, for some great misfortune would surely come upon him. But he paid no heed to her, and went to seek his friend Kura to accompany him on his expedition. When he came to the isle on which Kura lived, he went up to the house and said, "Oh my dear friend Kura, do you not remember the time when we fought together long ago against the men of dismal Northland? Come with me now and be my companion in another war against them."

Now Kura's father was sitting by the window, whittling out a javelin, and his mother was near the door skimming milk, and his brother and sisters were also working nearby. And all of them cried out that Kura could not go to war, for he was but lately married, and they bade Lemminkainen leave him.

But Kura himself jumped up from where he was lying before the fire, and began to put on his armour in great haste. On his helmet were wolves of bronze, and a horse on each javelin. Then Kura took his mighty spear, and going forth into the court he hurled it towards the north; and it flew on and on, whistling through the air, until at length it fell upon the earth of the distant Northland. And after this Kura touched his javelin against Lemminkainen's spear and promised to be his faithful comrade in the expedition. So the two great warriors made all needful preparation and set forth to sail to dismal Pohjola.

But Louhi knew by magic are that they were coming, and she called the Black-frost to her, and gave him these commands, "Hasten forth, Oh Black-frost, and freeze all the wide sea. Freeze Lemminkainen's vessel fast in the ice, and freeze the magician himself in his vessel, so that he may never more awaken from his icy sleep until I myself may choose to free him."

So the Black-frost hastened off to do her bidding. And first he stripped the leaves off the trees and took all the colour from the flowers on his way to the seashore. When he reached the shore, the first night he froze all the rivers that empty into the sea and the waters along the shore, but he did not touch the open sea that night. But on the second night he froze all the sea, and the ice kept growing thicker and thicker all around Lemminkainen's vessel, until at last the Black-frost even began to freeze Lemminkainen's hands and feet and ears.

But when Lemminkainen felt this he began to sing an incantation against the Black-frost, saying, "Black-frost, evil child of the Northland and only son of Winter, you may freeze the trees and waters and the very stones, but let me be in peace. Freeze the iron mountains till they burst in sunder; freeze Wuoksi and Imatra, but do not try to harm me, for I will sing your origin and make you powerless. For you were born on the borders of the ever-dismal Northland, and were fed by crawling snakes. The Northwind rocked you to sleep in the marshes, and thus you grew, a thing of evil, and at last the name of Frost was given you. And as you became larger, you did learn to rend the trees in winter and to cover all the lakes with ice. But if you will not leave me now, I will cast you into Lempo's fiery hearth, and will lay you on the anvil, that Ilmarinen may pound you to pieces with his mighty hammer."

Now the Frost-fiend knew how great a magician Lemminkainen was, and therefore he agreed that he would leave the two warriors unharmed, but keep their ship frozen up as it was. And so Ahti and Kura had to leave their vessel and journey over the ice to land. At length they reached the country called Starvation-land, and there they found a house, but there was no food in it. So they went on still farther, over hill and valley, and as they went, Lemminkainen gathered soft moss from the tree-trunks and made stockings of it to keep their feet warm.

On and on they went, seeking for some pathway to guide them, but all was one snow-covered wilderness. Then Kura said, "Alas, Oh Ahti; we came here to take vengeance on the men of Pohjola, but I fear that we shall leave our own bones here, and our flesh be food for eagles and ravens. We shall never learn the pathway that can guide us to our homes. My poor mother will never know what has become of me - whether I have perished in the heat of battle, or on some lonely hill, or in some dismal forest. She can only mourn me as one dead, and sit and weep bitter tears."

Then Lemminkainen said, "My aged mother, think of our former happy days, when all went well and all was joy and happiness. But now sorrow and misfortune are come upon me, yet shall we not despair; for we are young and strong, and will give way neither to hunger nor to evil sorcerers, but will use the prayer my father used to pray, saying, "Guard us, Oh you great Creator; shield us in your arms, and give us of your wisdom. Be our guardian and our Father, that your children may not wander from the path which you have given them.""

Then when Lemminkainen had finished speaking, he took his cares and made fleet coursers of them, and the reins he made of days of evil, and from his pains he made the saddles. Then he and Kura galloped off each to his own home, and thus Lemminkainen was once more returned to his aged mother's arms. Now let us leave him there, and Kura with his bride and kinsfolk, and speak hereafter of other heroes.

The Sea King's Gift

Adapted by Andrew Lang in his Lilac Fairy Book from an original by Zacharias Topelius in The Birch and the Star, and Other Stories. The Lilac Fairy Book was published by Longman, Green & Co in 1910.

THERE WAS ONCE A FISHERMAN WHO was called Salmon, and his Christian name was Matte. He lived by the shore of the big sea; where else could he live? He had a wife called Maie; could you find a better name for her? In winter they dwelt in a little cottage by the shore, but in spring they flitted to a red rock out in the sea and stayed there the whole summer until it was autumn. The cottage on the rock was even smaller than the other; it had a wooden bolt instead of an iron lock to the door, a stone hearth, a flagstaff, and a weather-cock on the roof.

The rock was called Ahtola, and was not larger than the market-place of a town. Between the crevices there grew a little rowan tree and four alder bushes. Heaven only knows how they ever came there; perhaps they were brought by the winter storms. Besides that, there flourished some tufts of velvety grass, some scattered reeds, two plants of the yellow herb called tansy, four of a red flower, and a pretty white one; but the treasures of the rock consisted of three roots of garlic, which Maie had put in a cleft. Rock walls sheltered them on the north side, and the sun shone on them on the south. This does not seem much, but it sufficed Maie for a herb plot.

All good things go in threes, so Matte and his wife fished for salmon in spring, for herring in summer, and for cod in winter. When on Saturdays the weather was fine and the wind favourable, they sailed to the nearest town, sold their fish, and went to church on Sunday. But it often happened that for weeks at a time they were quite alone on the rock Ahtola, and had nothing to look at except their little yellow-brown dog, which bore the grand name of Prince, their grass tufts, their bushes and blooms, the sea bays and fish, a stormy sky and the blue, white-crested waves. For the rock lay far away from the land, and there were no green islets or human habitations for miles round, only here and there appeared a rock of the same red stone as Ahtola, besprinkled day and night with the ocean spray.

Matte and Maie were industrious, hard-working folk, happy and contented in their poor hut, and they thought themselves rich when they were able to salt as many casks of fish as they required for winter and yet have some left over with which to buy tobacco for the old man, and a pound or two of coffee for his wife, with plenty of burned corn and chicory in it to give it a flavour. Besides that, they had bread, butter, fish, a beer cask, and a buttermilk jar; what more did they require? All would have gone well had not Maie been possessed with a secret longing which never let her rest; and this was, how she could manage to become the owner of a cow.

"What would you do with a cow?" asked Matte. "She could not swim so far, and our boat is not large enough to bring her over here; and even if we had her, we have nothing to feed her on."

"We have four alder bushes and sixteen tufts of grass," replied Maie.

"Yes, of course," laughed Matte, "and we have also three plants of garlic. Garlic would be fine feeding for her."

"Every cow likes salt herring," replied his wife. "Even Prince is fond of fish."

"That may be," said her husband. "Methinks she would soon be a dear cow if we had to feed her on salt herring. All very well for Prince, who fights with the gulls over the last morsel. Put the cow out of your head, mother, we are very well off as we are."

Maie sighed. She knew well that her husband was right, but she could not give up the idea of a cow. The buttermilk no longer tasted as good as usual in the coffee; she thought of sweet cream and fresh butter, and of how there was nothing in the world to be compared with them.

One day as Matte and his wife were cleaning herring on the shore they heard Prince barking, and soon there appeared a gaily painted boat with three young men in it, steering towards the rock. They were students, on a boating excursion, and wanted to get something to eat.

"Bring us a junket, good mother," cried they to Maie.

"Ah! if only I had such a thing!" sighed Maie.

"A can of fresh milk, then," said the students, "but it must not be skim."

"Yes, if only I had it!" sighed the old woman, still more deeply.

"What! haven't you got a cow?"

Maie was silent. This question so struck her to the heart that she could not reply.

"We have no cow," Matte answered, "but we have good smoked herring, and can cook them in a couple of hours."

"All right, then, that will do," said the students, as they flung themselves down on the rock, while fifty silvery-white herring were turning on the spit in front of the fire.

"What's the name of this little stone in the middle of the ocean?" asked one of them.

"Ahtola," answered the old man.

"Well, you should want for nothing when you live in the Sea King's dominion."

Matte did not understand. He had never read Kalevala and knew nothing of the sea gods of old, but the students proceeded to explain to him.

"Ahti," said they, "is a mighty king who lives in his dominion of Ahtola, and has a rock at the bottom of the sea, and possesses besides a treasury of good things. He rules over all fish and animals of the deep; he has the finest cows and the swiftest horses that ever-chewed grass at the bottom of the ocean. He who stands well with Ahti is soon a rich man, but one must beware in dealing with him, for he is very changeful and touchy. Even a little stone thrown into the water might offend him, and then as he takes back his gift, he stirs up the sea into a storm and drags the sailors down into the depths. Ahti owns also the fairest maidens, who bear the train of his queen Wellamos, and at the sound of music they comb their long, flowing locks, which glisten in the water."

"Oh!" cried Matte, "have your worships really seen all that?"

"We have as good as seen it," said the students. "It is all printed in a book, and everything printed is true."

"I'm not so sure of that," said Matte, as he shook his head.

But the herring were now ready, and the students ate enough for six, and gave Prince some cold meat which they happened to have in the boat. Prince sat on his hind legs with delight and mewed like a pussy cat. When all was finished, the students handed Matte a shining silver coin, and allowed him to fill his pipe with a special kind of tobacco. They then thanked him for his kind hospitality and went on their journey, much regretted by Prince, who sat with a woeful expression and whined on the shore as long as he could see a flip of the boat's white sail in the distance.

Maie had never uttered a word, but thought the more. She had good ears, and had laid to heart the story about Ahti. "How delightful," thought she to herself, "to possess a fairy cow! How delicious every morning and evening to draw milk from it, and yet have no trouble about the feeding, and to keep a shelf near the window for dishes of milk and junkets! But this will never be my luck."

"What are you thinking of?" asked Matte.

"Nothing," said his wife; but all the time she was pondering over some magic rhymes she had heard in her childhood from an old lame man, which were supposed to bring luck in fishing.

"What if I were to try?" thought she.

Now this was Saturday, and on Saturday evenings Matte never set the herring-net, for he did not fish on Sunday. Towards evening, however, his wife said, "Let us set the herring-net just this once."

"No," said her husband, "it is a Saturday night."

"Last night was so stormy, and we caught so little," urged his wife, "to-night the sea is like a mirror, and with the wind in this direction the herring are drawing towards land."

"But there are streaks in the north-western sky, and Prince was eating grass this evening," said the old man.

"Surely he has not eaten my garlic," exclaimed the old woman.

"No; but there will be rough weather by to-morrow at sunset," replied Matte.

"Listen to me," said his wife, "we will set only one net close to the shore, and then we shall be able to finish up our half-filled cask, which will spoil if it stands open so long."

The old man allowed himself to be talked over, and so they rowed out with the net. When they reached the deepest part of the water, she began to hum the words of the magic rhyme, altering the words to suit the longing of her heart:

Oh, Ahti, with the long, long beard,

Who dwellest in the deep blue sea,

Finest treasures have I heard,

And glittering fish belong to you.

The richest pearls beyond compare

Are stored up in your realm below,

And Ocean's cows so sleek and fair

Feed on the grass in your green meadow.

King of the waters, far and near,

I ask not of your golden store,

I wish not jewels of pearl to wear,

Nor silver either, ask I for,

But one is odd and even is two,

So give me a cow, sea-king so bold,

And in return I'll give to you

A slice of the moon, and the sun's gold.

"What's that you're humming?" asked the old man.

"Oh, only the words of an old rhyme that keeps running in my head," answered the old woman; and she raised her voice and went on:

Oh, Ahti, with the long, long beard,

Who dwellest in the deep blue sea,

A thousand cows are in your herd,

I pray you give one onto me.

"That's a stupid sort of song," said Matte. "What else should one beg of the sea-king but fish? But such songs are not for Sunday."

His wife pretended not to hear him, and sang and sang the same tune all the time they were on the water. Matte heard nothing more as he sat and rowed the heavy boat, while thinking of his cracked pipe and the fine tobacco. Then they returned to the island, and soon after went to bed.

But neither Matte nor Maie could sleep a wink; the one thought of how he had profaned Sunday, and the other of Ahti's cow.

About midnight the fisherman sat up, and said to his wife, "Dost you hear anything?"

"No," said she.

"I think the twirling of the weathercock on the roof bodes ill," said he, "we shall have a storm."

"Oh, it is nothing but your fancy," said his wife.

Matte lay down, but soon rose again.

"The weathercock is squeaking now," said he.

"Just fancy! Go to sleep," said his wife; and the old man tried to.

For the third time he jumped out of bed.

"Ho! how the weather-cock is roaring at the pitch of its voice, as if it had a fire inside it! We are going to have a tempest, and must bring in the net."

Both rose. The summer night was as dark as if it had been October, the weather-cock creaked, and the storm was raging in every direction. As they went out the sea lay around them as white as now, and the spray was dashing right over the fisher-hut. In all his life Matte had never remembered such a night. To launch the boat and put to sea to rescue the net was a thing not to be thought of. The fisherman and his wife stood aghast on the doorstep, holding on fast by the doorpost, while the foam splashed over their faces.

"Did I not tell you that there is no luck in Sunday fishing?" said Matte sulkily; and his wife was so frightened that she never even once thought of Ahti's cows.

As there was nothing to be done, they went in. Their eyes were heavy for lack of slumber, and they slept as soundly as if there had not been such a thing as an angry sea roaring furiously around their lonely dwelling. When they awoke, the sun was high in the heavens, the tempest had cased, and only the swell of the sea rose in silvery heavings against the red rock.

"What can that be?" said the old woman, as she peeped out of the door.

"It looks like a big seal," said Matte.

"As sure as I live, it's a cow!" exclaimed Maie. And certainly it was a cow, a fine red cow, fat and flourishing, and looking as if it had been fed all its days on spinach. It wandered peacefully up and down the shore, and never so much as even looked at the poor little tufts of grass, as if it despised such fare.

Matte could not believe his eyes. But a cow she seemed, and a cow she was found to be; and when the old woman began to milk her, every pitcher and pan, even to the baler, was soon filled with the most delicious milk.

The old man troubled his head in vain as to how she came there, and sallied forth to seek for his lost net. He had not proceeded far when he found it cast up on the shore, and so full of fish that not a mesh was visible.

"It is all very fine to possess a cow," said Matte, as he cleaned the fish, "but what are we going to feed her on?"

"We shall find some means," said his wife; and the cow found the means herself. She went out and cropped the seaweed which grew in great abundance near the shore, and always kept in good condition. Every one Prince alone excepted, thought she was a clever beast; but Prince barked at her, for he had now got a rival.

From that day the red rock overflowed with milk and junkets, and every net was filled with fish. Matte and Maie grew fat on this fine living, and daily became richer. She churned quantities of butter, and he hired two men to help him in his fishing. The sea lay before him like a big fish tank, out of which he hauled as many as he required; and the cow continued to fend for herself. In autumn, when Matte and Maie went ashore, the cow went to sea, and in spring, when they returned to the rock, there she stood awaiting them.

"We shall require a better house," said Maie the following summer, "the old one is too small for ourselves and the men."

"Yes," said Matte. So he built a large cottage, with a real lock to the door, and a store-house for fish as well; and he and his men caught such quantities of fish that they sent tons of salmon, herring, and cod to Russian and Sweden.

"I am quite overworked with so many folk," said Maie, "a girl to help me would not come amiss."

"Get one, then," said her husband; and so they hired a girl.

Then Maie said, "We have too little milk for all these folk. Now that I have a servant, with the same amount of trouble she could look after three cows."

"All right, then," said her husband, somewhat provoked, "you can sing a song to the fairies."

This annoyed Maie, but nevertheless she rowed out to sea on Sunday night and sang as before:

Oh, Ahti, with the long, long beard,

Who dwellest in the deep blue sea,

A thousand cows are in your herd,

I pray you give three unto me.

The following morning, instead of one, three cows stood on the island, and they all ate seaweed and fended for themselves like the first one.

"Are you satisfied now?" said Matte to his wife.

"I should be quite satisfied," said his wife, "if only I had two servants to help, and if I had some finer clothes. Don't you know that I am addressed as Madam?"

"Well, well," said her husband. So Maie got several servants and clothes fit for a great lady.

"Everything would now be perfect if only we had a little better dwelling for summer. You might build us a two-storey house, and fetch soil to make a garden. Then you might make a little arbour up there to let us have a sea-view; and we might have a fiddler to fiddle to us of an evening, and a little steamer to take us to church in stormy weather."

"Anything more?" asked Matte; but he did everything that his wife wished. The rock Ahtola became so grand and Maie so grand that all the sea-urchins and herring were lost in wonderment. Even

Prince was fed on beefsteaks and cream scones till at last he was as round as a butter jar.

"Are you satisfied now?" asked Matte.

"I should be quite satisfied," said Maie, "if only I had thirty cows. At least that number is required for such a household."

"Go to the fairies," said Matte.

His wife set out in the new steamer and sang to the sea-king. Next morning thirty cows stood on the shore, all finding food for themselves.

"Do you realise, good man, that we are far too cramped on this wretched rock, and where am I to find room for so many cows?"

"There is nothing to be done but to pump out the sea."

"Rubbish!" said his wife. "Who can pump out the sea?"

"Try with your new steamer, there is a pump in it."

Maie knew well that her husband was only making fun of her, but still her mind was set upon the same subject. "I never could pump the sea out," thought she, "but perhaps I might fill it up, if I were to make a big dam. I might heap up sand and stones, and make our island as big again."

Maie loaded her boat with stones and went out to sea. The fiddler was with her, and fiddled so finely that Ahti and Wellamos and all the sea's daughters rose to the surface of the water to listen to the music.

"What is that shining so brightly in the waves?" asked Maie.

"That is sea foam glinting in the sunshine," answered the fiddler.

"Throw out the stones," said Maie.

The people in the boat began to throw out the stones, splash, splash, right and left, into the foam. One stone hit the nose of Wellamos chief lady-in-waiting, another scratched the sea queen herself on the cheek, a third plumped close to Ahti's head and tore off half of the sea-king's beard; then there was a commotion in the sea, the waves bubbled and bubbled like boiling water in a pot.

"From where comes this gust of wind?" said Maie; and as she spoke the sea opened and swallowed up the steamer. Maie sank to the bottom like a stone, but, stretching out her arms and legs, she rose to the surface, where she found the fiddler's fiddle, and used it as a float. At the same moment she saw close beside her the terrible head of Ahti, and he had only half a beard!"

"Why did you throw stones at me?" roared the sea-king.

"Oh, your majesty, it was a mistake! Put some bear's grease on your beard and that will soon make it grow again."

"Dame, did I not give you all you asked for - nay, even more?"

"Truly, truly, your majesty. Many thanks for the cows."

"Well, where is the gold from the sun and the silver from the moon that you promised me?"

"Ah, your majesty, they have been scattered day and night upon the sea, except when the sky was overcast," slyly answered Maie.

"I'll teach you!" roared the sea-king; and with that he gave the fiddle such a "puff" that it sent the old woman up like a sky-rocket on to her island. There Prince lay, as famished as ever, gnawing the carcase of a crow. There sat Matte in his ragged grey jacket, quite alone, on the steps of the old hut, mending a net.

"Heavens, mother," said he, "where are you coming from at such a whirlwind pace, and what makes you in such a dripping condition?"

Maie looked around her amazed, and said, "Where is our two-storey house?"

"What house?" asked her husband.

"Our big house, and the flower garden, and the men and the maids, and the thirty beautiful cows, and the steamer, and everything else?"

"You are talking nonsense, mother," said he. "The students have quite turned your head, for you sang silly songs last evening while we were rowing, and then you could not sleep till early morning. We had stormy weather during the night, and when it was past I did not wish to waken you, so rowed out alone to rescue the net."

"But I've seen Ahti," replied Maie.

"You've been lying in bed, dreaming foolish fancies, mother, and then in your sleep you walked into the water."

"But there is the fiddle," said Maie.

"A fine fiddle! It is only an old stick. No, no, old woman, another time we will be more careful. Good luck never attends fishing on a Sunday."

Kullervo's Birth

Adapted by R. Eivind in Finnish Legends for English Children, from the original Song of the Kervala. Finnish Legends for English Children was published in 1893 by T. fisher Unwin, London.

MANY AGES AGO THERE WAS A mother who had three sons, and one of them grew up to be a prosperous merchant, but the other two were carried off - one to distant Pohjola and one to Karjala. And the one in Pohjola was named Untamo, but the one in Karjala was called Kalerwoinen.

One day Untamo set his nets near Kalerwoinen's home to catch salmon, but in the evening Kalerwoinen came by and took all the fish out of the nets and carried them off home. When Untamo found it out he went to his brother, and soon they fell to blows; but neither could conquer the other, though they gave one another sound beatings. After this had happened, Kalerwoinen sowed some barley near Untamo's barns; and Untamo's sheep broke into the field and ate the barley, and then Kalerwoinen's dog killed the sheep. This made Untamo so angry that he collected a great army and marched against his brother to put him and all his tribe to death. And when they reached Kalerwoinen's home they burned all the houses and killed everyone except Kalerwoinen's daughter Untamala.

Now not long after this a child was born to Untamala, and she named him Kullervo. Then they laid the fatherless infant in the cradle and began to rock him, but he began at once to make the cradle rock without assistance, and he rocked for three whole days, so hard that his hair stood quite on end. On the third day he began to kick until he had burst his swaddling clothes, and then he crept out of the cradle and broke that also in pieces. When Kullervo was only three months old he began to speak, and the first words which he uttered were these, "When I have grown big and strong I will avenge the murder of my grandfather Kalerwoinen and his people."

At this Untamo was greatly alarmed, and took counsel with his people as to what should be done with the child. At length they hit upon a plan. They took the child and bound him firmly in a willow basket and then put him in the lake among the bulrushes. After three days had passed they went to see if he were dead, but he had broken loose from the basket and was sitting on the waves, fishing with a copper rod and a golden line; so they took him back again to the house. Next Untamo ordered a great heap of dried brushwood to be collected together, and a pile was made higher than the tree-tops; on the top of this they set the boy and then set fire to the pile. It burned three whole days, and then Untamo sent men to see if the child was dead; but they found him sitting in the middle of the fire raking the coals together with a copper rod, and not a hair of his head was even singed.

Then they took him home and considered again how they should kill him, and this time they took him and crucified him on an oak-tree. And on the third day they came and found that he had painted an armed warrior on every leaf, made fast though he was to the tree, and so they took him down and brought him home again. This time they saw that they could not harm him, so Untamo told him that he would take him as a servant, and that if he did well he should be paid well.

When Kullervo had grown a little, he was set to take care of a baby, and was given very careful instructions as to how to rock it and attend to all its wants; but the cruel Kullervo treated it harshly, and in the evening killed it and burned the cradle in the fire. So Untamo was afraid to give him any further employment about the house, but bade him go out and cut down the forest on the mountain side. Then Kullervo went to the smith and bade him make a huge axe of copper, and when it was ready he spent one day in sharpening it and another in making the handle, and then hastened off to the forest. There he chose the biggest tree on all the mountain side and felled it at one blow. Six more huge trees were cut down just as easily, but then Kullervo grew disgusted with the work, and pronounced a curse over the whole mountain, and stopped working.

So when Untamo came in the evening to see how he was getting on, and found only seven trees felled, he saw that he must set Kullervo to some other task. The next day, therefore, he took him into a field and bade him build a fence round it. As soon as Untamo was gone, Kullervo set to work, using whole trees and raising the fence higher than the clouds; and when he had finished there was no gate to enter by, and the fence was so high that no one could climb over it. When Untamo came and saw what he had done, and that no one could now get into the field, he told Kullervo that he was unfitted for such work, and must go and thresh the rye and barley.

Then Kullervo made a flail and set to work. And he threshed so hard that al the grain was beaten to powder and the straw was broken up into useless pieces. But when Untamo saw this, he grew very angry, and cried out that Kullervo was a wretched workman who spoiled whatever he touched, and the next day he took him off and sold him to the blacksmith Ilmarinen in distant Karjala. And the price Ilmarinen paid was three old worn-out kettles, seven worthless sickles, and three old scythes and hoes and axes, surely quite enough for such a fellow as Kullervo.

Kullervo And Ilmarinen's Wife

Adapted by R. Eivind in Finnish Legends for English Children, from the original Song of the Kervala. Finnish Legends for English Children was published in 1893 by T. fisher Unwin, London.

AS SOON AS THE PURCHASE WAS completed, Kullervo asked Ilmarinen and his wife to give him some work for the next day. So they decided to make him a shepherd. But the wife, once the Rainbow-maiden, did not like the new servant, so she baked him a cheat-loaf - a very thick loaf, half of barley, half of oatmeal, and with a great flint-stone in the centre, and around the flint-stone was melted butter. Then she gave it to Kullervo and told him not to eat it until he was out on the pasture-ground.

The next morning Ilmarinen's wife showed Kullervo the cattle, and bade him take them to the open glades among the forests, where they would find food in abundance. Then she addressed a prayer to Ukko that he would guard the flock in case the shepherd should neglect them. And she sought the aid too of all the goddesses of the forest and the daughters of summer and the spirits of the fountains and the brooks, to care for her cattle and watch over them. And she also sang a spell to keep away the bear from coming and devouring them. And when all these prayers and spells were ended she sent Kullervo off with the herds.

Kullervo drove them off to their pastures in the woods, carrying his lunch in a basket on his arm. And as he walked he sang of his hard lot as a slave, and how he was given only the scraps and crusts to eat, while his master and mistress fed on honey-cakes and wheaten biscuit. At length the time came for him to eat his luncheon, and he sat down and drew the cheat-loaf from the basket. But instead of eating it at once he turned it carefully over and over in his hands, and thought, "Many loaves are fine to look at on the outside, but are nothing but chaff inside," and he drew out his knife to try the loaf.

This knife was the one thing that his mother had kept of all her father's possessions, and Kullervo looked upon it as something sacred. Now as he plunged it into the cheat-loaf it hit right upon the hard flint in the centre and broke in several pieces. Then Kullervo sat down and began to weep over his loss, and to ponder how he should revenge it. But a raven was sitting in a tree nearby and overhead him talking to himself, and the raven said, "Why are you so distressed, Kullervo? Drive the herd away, one half to the wolves" and the other half to the bears" dens, so that they may all be devoured. And then when it is time to return home call together the wolves and bears and make them look like cattle, by your magic are, and drive them home for your mistress to milk. Thus you will repay this insult."

At these words Kullervo jumped up and did as the raven had said. And when the sun was setting in the west, Kullervo hastened homeward, driving bears and wolves before him, but by a magic spell he made them look like cattle. And as he went, he said to them, "Seize my hateful mistress when she comes to milk the cattle, and tear and rend her in pieces." And he took a cow-horn and made a bugle of it and blew till the hills rang, to announce his return.

When he reached the cow-yard, Ilmarinen's wife greeted him joyfully, for it was late and she had feared that something had happened. And she told her oldest maid-servant to go and milk the cows as she herself was busy. But Kullervo said, "You should go yourself, for the cows are in better condition to-night than they have ever been before." And so she went, and when she saw them she cried out in wonder, "Truly my cattle are beautiful to-night, for their hair glistens like the fur of lynxes, and is soft as ermine skin."

With these words she seated herself to begin milking, but all at once the wolves and bears appeared in their true shapes and began to tear her to pieces. Then she cried out to Kullervo, when she saw what he had done, but he answered, "If I have done evil you have done still greater evil, for you have baked a stone inside my bread, and I have broken on it my knife, the only relic of my mother's people."

Then Ilmarinen's wife began to beg him to aid her, and promised him the best of everything to eat, and that he should never have to work again. But Kullervo would not listen to her prayers, but rejoiced at her agony, and then the wolves and bears made one more onset, and she fell and died. Such was the end of the beauteous Rainbow-maiden, for whom so many had wooed, and who had become the pride and joy of Kalevala.

Kullervo's Life And Death

Adapted by R. Eivind in Finnish Legends for English Children, from the original Song of the Kervala. Finnish Legends for English Children was published in 1893 by T. fisher Unwin, London.

THEN KULLERVO HASTENED OFF, BEFORE Ilmarinen should come home and find out what had happened. And after he was at a safe distance he began to play upon the bugle he had made, until Ilmarinen ran out of his smithy to see who it could be, and there before him in the courtyard Ilmarinen saw the body of his wife and learned what had happened: and he sat down and wept bitterly, for all the joy of his life was now gone from him.

But Kullervo hastened on, and as he went he mourned his hard lot. When he had gone a little way he met an old witch on the road, and she asked him where he was going. "I shall journey to the dismal Northland," answered Kullervo, "there to slay the wicked Untamo, who has killed all my kinsfolk." Then the witch said, "You are wrong, for your father and your sisters escaped from Untamo's wrath, and now your mother has joined them and they are living happily together on the distant borders of Kalevala." And when Kullervo begged her to tell him the way to them she did so, and he hastened off to find them.

At length he reached his parents" abode, but at first they did not recognise him. But when he spoke to his mother she knew him at once, and embraced him and kissed him, and made him welcome in his new home. And then they related to one another all that had happened in the years they had been apart, and his mother ended by saying, "Praised be Ukko that you have come back to us; but there is yet one absent one - your eldest sister strayed away many years ago, hunting berries on the hills, and we have never seen or heard of her since."

So Kullervo settled down to live with his parents, and began to work with the others. The first day they all went out to fish for salmon, and Kullervo was put at the oars to row their boat. Then he asked whether he should row with all his strength, or only a little part of it, and they told him that he could not pull too hard. So he put forth all his giant's strength, and in a minute the boat was all broken to pieces.

His father said, "I see that you are too clumsy to row; perhaps you will do better to drive the salmon into the nets." And Kullervo asked again whether he should use all his strength, and he received the same answer as before. So he set to work beating the water to scare the fish into the net; but he beat so hard that he mixed all the mud on the bottom with the water, and pounded the salmon all to pulp and destroyed all the nets.

Then his father saw that he was not fit for such work, so he sent him off to pay the yearly taxes. Kullervo did so, and after he had paid them he started off in his sledge to drive home again. He had not driven far when he met a lovely maiden, whom he asked to get into his sledge and come with him to his home and marry him. But she made fun of him, and he drove off in anger. When he had driven still farther he met another maiden, still more lovely than the first, and this one he at length persuaded to get into his sledge and come home with him and marry him. But when they had driven along for two days towards his home, the maiden asked him about his kinsfolk, and he told her that he was Kalervo's son.

No sooner had the maiden heard this than she gave a great cry of anguish and cried out, "Alas, then, you are my brother! For I am Kalervo"s daughter, who wandered off one day to pick berries and never returned," and with these words she jumped from the sledge and hastened weeping to a river nearby. There she plunged beneath the icy waters and was never seen again alive, but her lifeless body floated down to the black river of Tuoni.

But Kullervo unharnessed his steed from the sledge and galloped off home and there related to his mother all that had occurred, and how he had unknowingly been the cause of his sister's death, and when he had finished his story, he added, "Woe is me that I did not die long ago. But now I must hasten off to gloomy Pohjola, there to slay the wicked Untamo, and myself be also slain." Having said this he also made ready his armour and ground his broadsword until it was as sharp as a razor. But before he went, he asked his father and brother and sister and mother if they would grieve when they heard of his death. And all but his mother told him that they would never sorrow over the death of such an evil fellow. But his mother alone said that, in spite of all the evil he had done, her mother's love was still strong and that she would weep over him for years to come.

Thereupon Kullervo went forth on his journey to the icy Northland, but before he had gone far a messenger came and told him that his father was dead and asked Kullervo to come back and help bury him, but he would not come. And a little later he was told of the death of his brother and then of his sister, and last of all of his mother. Still he refused to come to bury any of them, only, when the news of his mother's death reached him, he mourned that he had not been with her in her last moments, and bade the servants bury her with every possible honour and respect.

Now as he neared the home of Untamo's tribe, he prayed to Ukko to endow his sword with magic powers, so that Untamo and all his people might be surely slain. And Ukko did as he had asked, and with the magic sword Kullervo slew, single-handed, all Untamo's people, and burned all their villages to ashes, leaving behind him only dead bodies and smoking ruins.

Then he hastened home, and found that it was only too true that all his family had died while he was away; and he went out to his mother's grave and wept over it. But as he wept, his mother spoke to him from the grave and bade him let their old dog lead him into the forest to the home of the wood-nymphs, who would care for him. So Kullervo set off, led by the faithful dog. But on the way they came to the grassy mound where Kullervo had met his long-lost sister, and there he found that even the grass and the flowers and the trees were weeping. Suddenly overcome with sorrow, he drew forth his magic sword from out its scabbard, and, bidding a last farewell to all the world, he thrust the handle firmly into the earth and threw himself upon the sword-point, so that it pierced his heart. Thus ended the evil life of Kullervo.

The Sister Of The Sun

Adapted by Andrew Lang in his Brown Fairy Book from an original by Josef Calasanz Poestion in Lapplandische Märchen. The Brown Fairy Book was published by Longman, Green & Co in 1904.

A LONG TIME AGO THERE LIVED a young prince whose favourite playfellow was the son of the gardener who lived in the grounds of the palace. The king would have preferred his choosing a friend from the pages who were brought up at court; but the prince would have nothing to say to them, and as he was a spoilt child, and allowed his way in all things, and the gardener's boy was quiet and well-behaved, he was suffered to be in the palace, morning, noon, and night.

The game the children loved the best was a match at archery, for the king had given them two bows exactly alike, and they would spend whole days in trying to see which could shoot the highest. This is always very dangerous, and it was a great wonder they did not put their eyes out; but somehow or other they managed to escape.

One morning, when the prince had done his lessons, he ran out to call his friend, and they both hurried off to the lawn which was their usual playground. They took their bows out of the little hut where their toys were kept, and began to see which could shoot the highest. At last they happened to let fly their arrows both together, and when they fell to earth again the tail feather of a golden hen was found sticking in one. Now the question began to arise whose was the lucky arrow, for they were both alike, and look as closely as you would you could see no difference between them. The prince declared that the arrow was his, and the gardener's boy was quite sure it was HIS - and on this occasion he was perfectly right; but, as they could not decide the matter, they went straight to the king.

When the king had heard the story, he decided that the feather belonged to his son; but the other boy would not listen to this and claimed the feather for himself. At length the king's patience gave way, and he said angrily:

"Very well; if you are so sure that the feather is yours, yours it shall be; only you will have to seek till you find a golden hen with a feather missing from her tail. And if you fail to find her your head will be the forfeit."

The boy had need of all his courage to listen silently to the king's words. He had no idea where the golden hen might be, or even, if he discovered that, how he was to get to her. But there was nothing for it but to do the king's bidding, and he felt that the sooner he left the palace the better. So he went home and put some food into a bag, and then set forth, hoping that some accident might show him which path to take.

After walking for several hours he met a fox, who seemed inclined to be friendly, and the boy was so glad to have anyone to talk to that he sat down and entered into conversation.

"Where are you going?" asked the fox.

"I have got to find a golden hen who has lost a feather out of her tail," answered the boy, "but I don't know where she lives or how I shall catch her!"

"Oh, I can show you the way!" said the fox, who was really very good-natured. "Far towards the east, in that direction, lives a beautiful maiden who is called "The Sister of the Sun." She has three golden hens in her house. Perhaps the feather belongs to one of them."

The boy was delighted at this news, and they walked on all day together, the fox in front, and the boy behind. When evening came they lay down to sleep, and put the knapsack under their heads for a pillow.

Suddenly, about midnight, the fox gave a low whine, and drew nearer to his bedfellow. "Cousin," he whispered very low, "there is someone coming who will take the knapsack away from me. Look over there!" And the boy, peeping through the bushes, saw a man.

"Oh, I don't think he will rob us!" said the boy; and when the man drew near, he told them his story, which so much interested the stranger that he asked leave to travel with them, as he might be of some use. So when the sun rose they set out again, the fox in front as before, the man and boy following.

After some hours they reached the castle of the Sister of the Sun, who kept the golden hens among her treasures. They halted before the gate and took counsel as to which of them should go in and see the lady herself.

"I think it would be best for me to enter and steal the hens," said the fox; but this did not please the boy at all.

"No, it is my business, so it is right that I should go," answered he.

"You will find it a very difficult matter to get hold of the hens," replied the fox.

"Oh, nothing is likely to happen to me," returned the boy.

"Well, go then," said the fox, "but be careful not to make any mistake. Steal only the hen which has the feather missing from her tail, and leave the others alone."

The man listened, but did not interfere, and the boy entered the court of the palace.

He soon spied the three hens strutting proudly about, though they were really anxiously wondering if there were not some grains lying on the ground that they might be glad to eat. And as the last one passed by him, he saw she had one feather missing from her tail.

At this sight the youth darted forward and seized the hen by the neck so that she could not struggle. Then, tucking her comfortably under his arm, he made straight for the gate. Unluckily, just as he was about to go through it he looked back and caught a glimpse of wonderful splendours from an open door of the palace. "After all, there is no hurry," he said to himself, "I may as well see something now I AM here," and turned back, forgetting all about the hen, which escaped from under his arm, and ran to join her sisters.

He was so much fascinated by the sight of all the beautiful things which peeped through the door that he scarcely noticed that he had lost the prize he had won; and he did not remember there was such a thing as a hen in the world when he beheld the Sister of the Sun sleeping on a bed before him.

For some time he stood staring; then he came to himself with a start, and feeling that he had no business there, softly stole away, and was fortunate enough to recapture the hen, which he took with him to the gate. On the threshold he stopped again. "Why should I not look at the Sister of the Sun?" he thought to himself, "she is asleep, and will never know." And he turned back for the second time and entered the chamber, while the hen wriggled herself free as before. When he had gazed his fill he went out into the courtyard and picked up his hen who was seeking for corn.

As he drew near the gate he paused. "Why did I not give her a kiss?" he said to himself, "I shall never kiss any woman so beautiful." And he wrung his hands with regret, so that the hen fell to the ground and ran away.

"But I can do it still!" he cried with delight, and he rushed back to the chamber and kissed the sleeping maiden on the forehead. But alas! when he came out again he found that the hen had grown so shy that she would not let him come near her. And, worse than that, her sisters began to cluck so loud that the Sister of the Sun was awakened by the noise. She jumped up in haste from her bed, and going to the door she said to the boy:

"You shall never, never, have my hen till you bring me back my sister who was carried off by a giant to his castle, which is a long way off."

Slowly and sadly the youth left the palace and told his story to his friends, who were waiting outside the gate, how he had actually held the hen three times in his arms and had lost her.

"I knew that we should not get off so easily," said the fox, shaking his head, "but there is no more time to waste. Let us set off at once in search of the sister. Luckily, I know the way."

They walked on for many days, till at length the fox, who, as usual, was going first, stopped suddenly.

"The giant's castle is not far now," he said, "but when we reach it you two must remain outside while I go and fetch the princess. Directly I bring her out you must both catch hold of her tight, and get away as fast as you can; while I return to the castle and talk to the giants - for there are many of them - so that they may not notice the escape of the princess."

A few minutes later they arrived at the castle, and the fox, who had often been there before, slipped in without difficulty. There were several giants, both young and old, in the hall, and they were all dancing round the princess. As soon as they saw the fox they cried out, "Come and dance too, old fox; it is a long time since we have seen you."

So the fox stood up, and did his steps with the best of them; but after a while he stopped and said, "I know a charming new dance that I should like to show you; but it can only be done by two people. If the princess honours me for a few minutes, you will soon see how it is done."

"Ah, that is delightful; we want something new," answered they, and placed the princess between the outstretched arms of the fox. In one instant he had knocked over the great stand of lights that lighted the hall, and in the darkness had borne the princess to the gate. His comrades seized hold of her, as they had been bidden, and the fox was back again in the hall before anyone had missed him.

He found the giants busy trying to kindle a fire and get some light; but after a bit someone cried out, "Where is the princess?"

"Here, in my arms," replied the fox. "Don't be afraid; she is quite safe." And he waited until he thought that his comrades had gained a good start, and put at least five or six mountains between themselves and the giants. Then he sprang through the door, calling, as he went, "The maiden is here; take her if you can!"

At these words the giants understood that their prize had escaped, and they ran after the fox as fast as their great legs could carry them, thinking that they should soon come up with the fox, who they supposed had the princess on his back. The fox, on his side, was far too clever to choose the same path that his friends had taken, but would in and out of the forest, till at last even HE was tired out, and fell fast asleep under a tree. Indeed, he was so exhausted with his day's work that he never heard the approach of the giants, and their hands were already stretched out to seize his tail when his eyes opened, and with a tremendous bound he was once more beyond their reach. All the rest of the night the fox ran and ran; but when bright red spread over the east, he stopped and waited till the giants were close upon him. Then he turned, and said quietly, "Look, there is the Sister of the Sun!"

The giants raised their eyes all at once, and were instantly turned into pillars of stone. The fox then made each pillar a low bow, and set off to join his friends.

He knew a great many short cuts across the hills, so it was not long before he came up with them, and all four travelled night and day till they reached the castle of the Sister of the Sun. What joy and feasting there was throughout the palace at the sight of the princess whom they had mourned as dead! and they could not make enough of the boy who had gone through such dangers in order to rescue her. The golden hen was given to him at once, and, more than that, the Sister of the Sun told him that, in a little time, when he was a few years older, she would herself pay a visit to his home and become his wife. The boy could hardly believe his ears when he heard what was in store for him, for his was the most beautiful princess in all the world; and however thick the darkness might be, it fled away at once from the light of a star on her forehead.

So the boy set forth on his journey home, with his friends for company; his heart full of gladness when he thought of the promise of the princess. But, one by one, his comrades dropped off at the places where they had first met him, and he was quite alone when he reached his native town and the gates of the palace. With the golden hen under his arm he presented himself before the king, and told his adventures, and how he was going to have for a wife a princess so wonderful and unlike all other princesses, that the star on her forehead could turn night into day. The king listened silently, and when the boy had done, he said quietly, "If I find that your story is not true I will have you thrown into a cask of pitch."

"It is true - every word of it," answered the boy; and went on to tell that the day and even the hour were fixed when his bride was to come and seek him.

But as the time drew near, and nothing was heard of the princess, the youth became anxious and uneasy, especially when it came to his ears that the great cask was being filled with pitch, and that sticks were laid underneath to make a fire to boil it with. All day long the boy stood at the window, looking over the sea by which the princess must travel; but there were no signs of her, not even the tiniest white sail. And, as he stood, soldiers came and laid hands on him, and led him up to the cask, where a big fire was blazing, and the horrid black pitch boiling and bubbling over the sides. He looked and shuddered, but there was no escape; so he shut his eyes to avoid seeing.

The word was given for him to mount the steps which led to the top of the cask, when, suddenly, some men were seen running with all their might, crying as they went that a large ship with its sails spread was making straight for the city. No one knew what the ship was, or from where it came; but the king declared that he would not have the boy burned before its arrival, there would always be time enough for that.

At length the vessel was safe in port, and a whisper went through the watching crowd that on board was the Sister of the Sun, who had come to marry the young peasant as she had promised. In a few moments more she had landed, and desired to be shown the way to the cottage which her bridegroom had so often described to her; and where he had been led back by the king's order at the first sign of the ship.

"Don't you know me?" asked the Sister of the Sun, bending over him where he lay, almost driven out of his senses with terror.

"No, no; I don't know you," answered the youth, without raising his eyes.

"Kiss me," said the Sister of the Sun; and the youth obeyed her, but still without looking up.

"Don't you know me NOW?" asked she.

"No, I don't know you - I don't know you," he replied, with the manner of a man whom fear had driven mad.

At this the Sister of the Sun grew rather frightened, and beginning at the beginning, she told him the story of his meeting with her, and how she had come a long way in order to marry him. And just as she had finished in walked the king, to see if what the boy had said was really true. But hardly had he opened the door of the cottage when he was almost blinded by the light that filled it; and he remembered what he had been told about the star on the forehead of the princess. He staggered back as if he had been struck, then a curious feeling took hold of him, which he had never felt before, and falling on his knees before the Sister of the Sun, he implored her to give up all thought of the peasant boy, and to share his throne. But she laughed, and said she had a finer throne of her own, if she wanted to sit on it, and that she was free to please herself, and would have no husband but the boy whom she would never have seen except for the king himself.

"I shall marry him to-morrow," ended she; and ordered the preparations to be set on foot at once.

When the next day came, however, the bridegroom's father informed the princess that, by the law of the land, the marriage must take place in the presence of the king; but he hoped his majesty would not long delay his arrival. An hour or two passed, and everyone was waiting and watching, when at last the sound of trumpets was heard and a grand procession was seen marching up the street. A chair covered with velvet had been made ready for the king, and he took his seat upon it, and, looking round upon the assembled company, he said, "I have no wish to forbid this marriage; but, before I can allow it to be celebrated, the bridegroom must prove himself worthy of such a bride by fulfilling three tasks. And the first is that in a single day he must cut down every tree in an entire forest.

The youth stood aghast as the king's words. He had never cut down a tree in his life, and had not the least idea how to begin. And as for a whole forest - ! But the princess saw what was passing in his mind, and whispered to him:

"Don"t be afraid. In my ship you will find an axe, which you must carry off to the forest. When you have cut down one tree with it just say, "So let the forest fall," and in an instant all the trees will be on the ground. But pick up three chips of the tree you felled, and put them in your pocket."

And the young man did exactly as he was bid, and soon returned with the three chips safe in his coat.

The following morning the princess declared that she had been thinking about the matter, and that, as she was not a subject of the king, she saw no reason why she should be bound by his laws; and she meant to be married that very day. But the bridegroom's father told her that it was all very well for her to talk like that, but it was quite different for his son, who would pay with his head for any disobedience to the king's commands. However, in consideration of what the youth had done the day before, he hoped his majesty's heart might be softened, especially as he had sent a message that they might expect him at once. With this the bridal pair had to be content, and be as patient as they could till the king's arrival.

He did not keep them long, but they saw by his face that nothing good awaited them.

"The marriage cannot take place," he said shortly, "till the youth has joined to their roots all the trees he cut down yesterday."

This sounded much more difficult than what he had done before, and he turned in despair to the Sister of the Sun.

"It is all right," she whispered encouragingly. "Take this water and sprinkle it on one of the fallen trees, and say to it, "So let all the trees of the forest stand upright," and in a moment they will be erect again."

And the young man did what he was told, and left the forest looking exactly as it had done before.

Now, surely, thought the princess, there was no longer any need to put off the wedding; and she gave orders that all should be ready for the following day. But again the old man interfered, and declared that without the king's permission no marriage could take place. For the third time his majesty was sent for, and for the third time he proclaimed that he could not give his consent until the bridegroom should have slain a serpent which dwelt in a broad river that flowed at the back of the castle. Everyone knew stories of this terrible serpent, though no one had actually seen it; but from time to time a child strayed from home and never came back, and then mothers would forbid the other children to go near the river, which had juicy fruits and lovely flowers growing along its banks.

So no wonder the youth trembled and turned pale when he heard what lay before him.

"You will succeed in this also," whispered the Sister of the Sun, pressing his hand, "for in my ship is a magic sword which will cut through everything. Go down to the river and unfasten a boat which lies moored there, and throw the chips into the water. When the serpent rears up its body you will cut off its three heads with one blow of your sword. Then take the tip of each tongue and go with it to-morrow morning into the king's kitchen. If the king himself should enter, just say to him, "Here are three gifts I offer you in return for the services you demanded of me!" and throw the tips of the serpent's tongues at him, and hasten to the ship as fast as your legs will carry you. But be sure you take great care never to look behind you."

The young man did exactly what the princess had told him. The three chips which he flung into the river became a boat, and, as he steered across the stream, the serpent put up its head and hissed loudly. The youth had his sword ready, and in another second the three heads were bobbing on the water. Guiding his boat till he was beside them, he stooped down and snipped off the ends of the tongues, and then rowed back to the other bank. Next morning he carried them into the royal kitchen, and when the king entered, as was his custom, to see what he was going to have for dinner, the bridegroom flung them in his face, saying, "Here is a gift for you in return for the services you asked of me." And, opening the kitchen door, he fled to the ship. Unluckily he missed the way, and in his excitement ran backwards and forwards, without knowing where he was going. At last, in despair, he looked round, and saw to his amazement that both the city and palace had vanished completely. Then he turned his eyes in the other direction, and, far, far away, he caught sight of the ship with her sails spread, and a fair wind behind her.

This dreadful spectacle seemed to take away his senses, and all day long he wandered about, without knowing where he was going, till, in the evening, he noticed some smoke from a little hut of turf nearby. He went straight up to it and cried, "O mother, let me come in for pity's sake!" The old woman who lived in the hut beckoned to him to enter, and hardly was he inside when he cried again, "O mother, can you tell me anything of the Sister of the Sun?"

But the woman only shook her head. "No, I know nothing of her," said she.

The young man turned to leave the hut, but the old woman stopped him, and, giving him a letter, begged him to carry it to her next eldest sister, saying, "If you should get tired on the way, take out the letter and rustle the paper."

This advice surprised the young man a good deal, as he did not see how it could help him; but he did not answer, and went down the road without knowing where he was going. At length he grew so tired he could walk no more; then he remembered what the old woman had said. After he had rustled the leaves only once all fatigue disappeared, and he strode over the grass till he came to another little turf hut.

"Let me in, I pray you, dear mother," cried he. And the door opened in front of him. "Your sister has sent you this letter," he said, and added quickly, "O mother! can you tell me anything of the Sister of the Sun?"

"No, I know nothing of her," answered she. But as he turned hopelessly away, she stopped him.

"If you happen to pass my eldest sister's house, will you give her this letter?" said she. "And if you should get tired on the road, just take it out of your pocket and rustle the paper."

So the young man put the letter in his pocket, and walked all day over the hills till he reached a little turf hut, exactly like the other two.

"Let me in, I pray you, dear mother," cried he. And as he entered he added, "Here is a letter from your sister and - can you tell me anything of the Sister of the Sun?"

"Yes, I can," answered the old woman. "She lives in the castle on the Banka. Her father lost a battle only a few days ago because you had stolen his sword from him, and the Sister of the Sun herself is almost dead of grief. But, when you see her, stick a pin into the palm of her hand, and suck the drops of blood that flow. Then she will grow calmer, and will know you again. Only, beware; for before you reach the castle on the Banka fearful things will happen."

He thanked the old woman with tears of gladness for the good news she had given him, and continued his journey. But he had not gone very far when, at a turn of the road, he met with two brothers, who were quarrelling over a piece of cloth.

"My good men, what are you fighting about?" said he. "That cloth does not look worth much!"

"Oh, it is ragged enough," answered they, "but it was left us by our father, and if any man wraps it round him no one can see him; and we each want it for our own."

"Let me put it round me for a moment," said the youth, "and then I will tell you who's it ought to be!"

The brothers were pleased with this idea, and gave him the stuff; but the moment he had thrown it over his shoulder he disappeared as completely as if he had never been there at all.

Meanwhile the young man walked briskly along, till he came up with two other men, who were disputing over a table-cloth.

"What is the matter?" asked he, stopping in front of them.

"If this cloth is spread on a table," answered they, "the table is instantly covered with the most delicious food; and we each want to have it."

"Let me try the table-cloth," said the youth, "and I will tell you who's it ought to be."

The two men were quite pleased with this idea, and handed him the cloth. He then hastily threw the first piece of stuff round his shoulders and vanished from sight, leaving the two men grieving over their own folly.

The young man had not walked far before he saw two more men standing by the road-side, both grasping the same stout staff, and sometimes one seemed on the point of getting it, and sometimes the other.

"What are you quarrelling about? You could cut a dozen sticks from the wood each just as good as that!" said the young man. And as he spoke the fighters both stopped and looked at him.

"Ah! you may think so," said one, "but a blow from one end of this stick will kill a man, while a touch from the other end will bring him back to life. You won't easily find another stick like that!"

"No; that is true," answered the young man. "Let me just look at it, and I will tell you who's it ought to be."

The men were pleased with the idea, and handed him the staff.

"It is very curious, certainly," said he, "but which end is it that restores people to life? After all, anyone can be killed by a blow from a stick if it is only hard enough!" But when he was shown the end he threw the stuff over his shoulders and vanished.

At last he saw another set of men, who were struggling for the possession of a pair of shoes.

"Why can't you leave that pair of old shoes alone?" said he. "Why, you could not walk a yard in them!"

"Yes, they are old enough," answered they, "but whoever puts them on and wishes himself at a particular place, gets there without going."

"That sounds very clever," said the youth. "Let me try them, and then I shall be able to tell you who's they ought to be."

The idea pleased the men, and they handed him the shoes; but the moment they were on his feet he cried:

"I wish to be in the castle on the Banka!" And before he knew it, he was there, and found the Sister of the Sun dying of grief. He knelt down by her side, and pulling a pin he stuck it into the palm of her hand, so that a drop of blood gushed out. This he sucked, as he had been told to do by the old woman, and immediately the princess came to herself, and flung her arms round his neck. Then she told him all her story, and what had happened since the ship had sailed away without him. "But the worst misfortune of all," she added, "was a battle which my father lost because you had vanished with his magic sword; and out of his whole army hardly one man was left."

"Show me the battle-field," said he. And she took him to a wild heath, where the dead were lying as they fell, waiting for burial. One by one he touched them with the end of his staff, till at length they all stood before him. Throughout the kingdom there was nothing but joy; and THIS time the wedding was REALLY celebrated. And the bridal pair lived happily in the castle on the Banka till they died.

Ilmarinen's Bride Of Gold

Adapted by R. Eivind in Finnish Legends for English Children, from the original Song of the Kervala. Finnish Legends for English Children was published in 1893 by T. fisher Unwin, London.

AFTER ILMARINEN'S WIFE HAD BEEN SO cruelly slain, he wept for three whole days and nights without ceasing. And after that for three months he did not go into his smithy nor even so much as lift his hammer from the ground. And as he mourned he cried, "Woe is me, for all is weariness and sorrow now that my dear wife is slain, and there is no more rest for me in my home."

But after the three months of mourning were past, Ilmarinen went out and dug up a great quantity of gold and silver and cut down thirty sledge-loads of birch-trees, which he burnt to charcoal. Then he put the charcoal in the bottom of his furnace and laid a large piece of gold and a still larger piece of silver on top, and closing the furnace, he started the fire and set the workmen to blowing the bellows; but the men were lazy and let the fire go out. So Ilmarinen drove them all away and began to blow the fire by magic spells alone. Three days he worked the bellows by his magic spells, and on the evening of the third day he looked inside the furnace, hoping to see an image rising from the melted gold and silver. And there came forth a lovely lamb all gold and silver, and everyone admired its beauty save Ilmarinen, who said, "Get back into the furnace, for I only desire a beauteous bride, born of the melted gold and silver."

So he threw the lamb back into the furnace and added still more gold and silver and other magic metals, and then set his workmen to blow the bellows again. But they proved lazy this time too, and he had once more to use his magic spells to blow the fire. Again he looked into the furnace, on the evening of the third day, and this time there arose a colt of gold and silver and with hoofs of shining copper. Everyone admired the beautiful colt save Ilmarinen, who threw it back into the furnace.

Once more he added gold and silver and set the workmen to blow the bellows, but they neglected their work this time too. Then he blew the fire by magic, and cast other magic spells over the furnace, so that the gold and silver should grow into a lovely maiden. When he looked into the furnace on the evening of the third day, he saw at last the figure of a maiden rising from the flames, but it had neither feet nor hands nor ears. So Ilmarinen took her from the fire and forged unceasingly until feet and hands and ears were all completed, and the maiden was now the most beautiful that any one had ever seen, but yet she could not walk, nor talk, nor see, nor hear.

But Ilmarinen carried the golden maiden out of the smithy and took her to the bath-room where he washed the golden and silver image and then took it and laid it in his couch, in his wife's place. That night he heaped up bear-skins and rugs of all kinds on top of the bed, hoping that the image would come to life from the warmth, but it was all in vain, and Ilmarinen was almost frozen himself when he rose next morning. Then he said to himself, "Surely this lovely maiden was not meant to be my bride. I will take her to Wainamoinen, and perhaps she may come to life for him."

So off he went and offered the beautiful image to Wainamoinen, telling him that he had brought a lovely maiden to be Wainamoinen's bride now in his old age. But Wainamoinen, after praising the image's beauty, said, "My dear brother Ilmarinen, it is better to throw this image back into your furnace, and to forge from the melted metal a thousand useful trinkets. For I will never wed an image made of gold and silver."

And then Wainamoinen turned to those of his people who were standing nearby, and said to them, "Never bow to any image made of gold or silver, for they cannot see, nor hear, nor speak, and they will only bring you sorrow."

Ilmarinen's Fruitless Wooing

Adapted by R. Eivind in Finnish Legends for English Children, from the original Song of the Kervala. Finnish Legends for English Children was published in 1893 by T. fisher Unwin, London.

SO ILMARINEN CAST THE MAID OF Gold into a corner of his smithy and harnessed up his sledge and drove off to the dismal Northland, to ask Louhi to give him another of her daughters in marriage. Three days he journeyed, and on the evening of the third he reached old Louhi's home.

Louhi asked him how her daughter, the Rainbow-maiden, fared, and Ilmarinen, with hanging head and sorrowful face, told how his poor wife had perished, and ended up his story by asking Louhi to give him her next fairest daughter to be his wife. But Louhi grew angry and upbraided him with not having guarded her other daughter, and thus being guilty of her death, and she scornfully refused to give him another of her daughters.

But Ilmarinen went into the house in great anger and there addressed Louhi's next fairest daughter, begging her to come to his home with him and become his wife. The maid replied, "I will never marry the man who has been the cause of my dear sister's death. And even if I were to marry I would wish a nobler suitor than a mere blacksmith." Then Ilmarinen grew pale with anger, and seizing the maiden in his mighty arms he rushed off to his sledge and drove off like the wind before anyone could stop him.

The poor maid wept and begged Ilmarinen to release her and to let her die by the roadside, rather than to take her thus to his home. "If you will not release me," she said, "I will change into a salmon and escape you." But Ilmarinen told her that he would pursue her in the shape of a pike. Then the maiden said, first, that she would become an ermine, but Ilmarinen told her he would turn into a snake and catch her; and then she said that she would become a swallow, but Ilmarinen threatened to become an eagle.

So they drove on and on, and the maiden wept the whole time, and begged Ilmarinen to let her go, even if it were only to die in the snow, but he refused and grew more and more angry at her obstinacy. At length they reached Ilmarinen's home and he took the maiden into the house. But here, seeing there was no hope of escape, she determined to make him so angry that he would kill her and thus she would be freed from him. So she began to make fun of him and to scorn him and laugh at him, until at length Ilmarinen was in such a rage that he scarcely knew what he was doing, and drew his sword to kill her.

But the sword refused to do this cruel deed, saying, "I was born to drink the blood of warriors, but not of such a pure and lovely maid as this." So Ilmarinen, being unable to kill her, began to weave a magic spell about her, and in a few minutes she changed all of a sudden into a seagull, and flew off screaming towards the sea-cliffs.

And when he had done this, Ilmarinen went out and got into his sledge and drove off to his brother Wainamoinen. When he arrived, Wainamoinen asked him why he was so sad, and whether all was well in Pohjola. To this Ilmarinen replied, "Why should not all be well in Pohjola? They have the Sampo there, and until it leaves them they will always prosper." And then Wainamoinen asked him of the maiden whom he had gone to woo. "I have turned that hateful maid into a seagull," Ilmarinen answered, frowning, "and now she flies shrieking above the rolling waves, and will never have another suitor."

Wainamoinen's Expedition And The Birth Of The Kantele

Adapted by R. Eivind in Finnish Legends for English Children, from the original Song of the Kervala. Finnish Legends for English Children was published in 1893 by T. fisher Unwin, London.

WAINAMOINEN REFLECTED ON WHAT ILMARINEN had said of the prosperity of the Northland, and at length proposed that they should go and capture the Sampo and bring it back to Kalevala. But Ilmarinen said, "It will be hard to carry off the Sampo, for Louhi has fastened it with nine great locks, and around it grow three roots, beneath the mountain and the waters and the sands."

Still Wainamoinen persuaded him to go, and Ilmarinen went to his smithy and began to forge a sword for Wainamoinen. And when it was finished, it was so strong, by the power of the magic spells that had been used in making it, that it would cut through the hardest flint stones.

Then the two heroes put on their armour and made their sledges ready, and drove off along the seashore northward. But they had not gone far before they heard a voice lamenting. They drove up to the spot from where the voice seemed to come, and there they found a ship lying deserted on the sands.

Wainamoinen asked the ship what it was lamenting over, and the ship replied, "Alas, I weep because I am obliged to remain here idle; for I was built to be a warship, and I long to sail filled with warriors against the foe, but I am left here to lie alone and rot to pieces." Then Wainamoinen said, "You shall lie here no longer, but we will sail in you against the men of Pohjola. But tell me whether you are a magic ship that can sail without wind, or oarsmen, or pilot." "Nay," the ship replied, "I cannot sail if the wind or oars do not help me on and someone guide me with the rudder. But give me these to help me, and I can sail faster than any other ship in the world."

Then they left their sledges and launched the ship and stepped aboard. And Wainamoinen began to sing his wondrous spells, and in an instant one side of the vessel was filled with bearded warriors, and the other with lovely maids, and in the middle came powerful grey-bearded heroes. First he set the young men at the oars, but however hard they strove they could not budge the ship. And next the maidens tried, but they too failed. Last of all the mighty grey-bearded heroes took the oars, but yet the vessel did not move. Then Ilmarinen himself grasped the oars, and in a moment the vessel was moving through the waters at full speed, with old Wainamoinen at the helm.

They had not gone far when they came to an island, and on the shore was a man working on a fishing-boat. As they drew nearer he looked up and hailed them, asking where they were bound. Wainamoinen answered, "Oh stupid Lemminkainen, do you not recognise us, and can you not guess where we are bound?" Then Lemminkainen, for it was really he, said, "I recognise you both now. It is Ilmarinen who is rowing, and you are Wainamoinen. But tell me where you are sailing?"

Then Wainamoinen told him that they were bound for Pohjola to capture the magic Sampo, and, on hearing this, Lemminkainen begged to go with them, saying that he would fight valiantly with them. So they took him on board, and the three great heroes sailed on their way. But before they had gone much farther, they came to a place where there were lovely maidens singing sweetly on the shore, but all around were hidden rocks and whirlpools, and their vessel was near sinking. But Lemminkainen knew the spell that would compel the maidens to calm the whirlpools, and to lead the ship in safety past all the hidden reefs out into open water again. And when Lemminkainen had sung this spell, old Wainamoinen was able to steer in safety through the foam-covered rocks and out into open water; but no sooner were they clear than the vessel stopped as suddenly as if she were anchored to the spot.

Ilmarinen and Lemminkainen then plunged a long pole to the bottom of the waters, and strove to push the ship ahead, but it was impossible. Then Wainamoinen bade Lemminkainen look beneath the vessel to see what it was that stopped them, and they found that it was no hidden reef or sand-bar, but a mighty pike on whose shoulders the vessel had stuck fast. At Wainamoinen's order, Lemminkainen drew his sword and aimed a mighty blow at the monster, but he missed it and fell overboard. He was drawn out all dripping, and the others consoled him for his failure. Next Ilmarinen drew his sword and struck at the monster, but at the first blow his sword broke in pieces. At last Wainamoinen, reproaching the others for their feebleness, drew his magic sword, and with one thrust he impaled the monster on it. Then lifting the monster out of the water he cut him into pieces and let them fall on the water, and float in towards land.

Thus the vessel was free at last. But the heroes were weary with their exertions, and so they rowed into land, and there gathered up the fragments of the fish that had floated to the shore. Wainamoinen handed these pieces to the maidens who were with them in the vessel, and they prepared the most delicious feast from the pike, having enough and to spare for all on board. And they piled the bones in a heap on the rocks.

Then Wainamoinen looked at the pile of bones, and after pondering deeply he said, "Wondrous things may be made from these bones, if only I can find a skilful workman to carry out my designs and make the kantele."[] But no workman could be found who was wise enough to understand Wainamoinen's directions, for no one had ever heard of a kantele before. At length old Wainamoinen saw that there was no one who could help him, and so he set to work himself. He made the arches of the harp from the pike's jawbones, and the pins that hold the strings he made from the teeth, and for the strings he took hairs from the tail of a magic steed.

And at last the first kantele was finished, and it was so beautiful that everyone crowded round to look at it. When it was ready Wainamoinen handed it to those around to try their skill, but they could only make discords whenever they touched it. Then Lemminkainen bade the others leave it to him, for he would show them how to play upon it. But when he touched the strings it sounded worse than when any of the others had tried it. And after one and all had tried it, and found that it only gave forth discords, they proposed to throw it into the sea. But the harp said, "I shall never perish in the sea, but will bring great joy to Kalevala. Put me in my maker's hands, and I will sing for him." So they took it and laid it at the aged Wainamoinen's feet.

Then the great magician took the wondrous kantele and rested it upon his knee. First he tuned it, tightening all the strings until they sounded sweetly together, and then he swept his hands across them, and a flood of wonderful melody poured forth from the kantele. And as the wondrous notes resounded in the air, every living thing that heard them stopped and listened. From the forests came the bears and ermines, and the wolves and lynxes. Even Tapio the forest-god drew near, with all his attendant spirits, enchanted by the magic sounds. From the sea the fishes came to the edge of the waters, and the sea-god Ahto with his water-spirits. The daughters of the Sun and Moon stopped their spinning on the clouds, and dropped their spindles, so that the threads were broken in two.

For three whole days the magic kantele poured forth its melody beneath Wainamoinen's skilful fingers, until everyone that heard it wept, and even the master-player himself was at last moved to tears by the power of his own playing. The bright teardrops flowed down his long beard and over his garments, and on over the earth in sparkling streams, until they were lost in the waters of the deep sea. And then the music ceased, and Wainamoinen laid the kantele aside and said, "Is there any one here who can gather up my teardrops from the sea?" But all were silent, for they could not do it.

But a raven came flying up and offered to attempt it, and Wainamoinen promised him the most beautiful plumage if he should succeed, but the raven tried and failed. Then came a duck, and Wainamoinen made it the same promise. And the duck swam off and dived down to the ocean's depths, and at length it had collected every teardrop and brought them to the great magician, but a wondrous change had taken place in them, for they were no longer tears, but the most beautiful pearls. Thus were pearls first created, and for this the blue duck received its lovely plumage.

The Six Hungry Beasts

Adapted by Andrew Lang in his Crimson Fairy Book from an original in Finnische Märchen. The Crimson Fairy Book was published by Longman, Green & Co in 1903.

ONCE UPON A TIME THERE LIVED a man who dwelt with his wife in a little hut, far away from any neighbours. But they did not mind being alone, and would have been quite happy, if it had not been for a marten, who came every night to their poultry yard, and carried off one of their fowls. The man laid all sorts of traps to catch the thief, but instead of capturing the foe, it happened that one day he got caught himself, and falling down, struck his head against a stone, and was killed.

Not long after the marten came by on the lookout for his supper. Seeing the dead man lying there, he said to himself, "That is a prize, this time I have done well"; and dragging the body with great difficulty to the sledge, which was waiting for him, drove off with his booty. He had not driven far when he met a squirrel, who bowed and said, "Good-morning, godfather! what have you got behind you?"

The marten laughed and answered, "Did you ever hear anything so strange? The old man that you see here set traps about his hen-house, thinking to catch me but he fell into his own trap, and broke his own neck. He is very heavy; I wish you would help me to draw the sledge." The squirrel did as he was asked, and the sledge moved slowly along.

By-and-by a hare came running across a field, but stopped to see what wonderful thing was coming. "What have you got there?" she asked, and the marten told his story and begged the hare to help them pull.

The hare pulled her hardest, and after a while they were joined by a fox, and then by a wolf, and at length a bear was added to the company, and he was of more use than all the other five beasts put together. Besides, when the whole six had supped off the man he was not so heavy to draw.

The worst of it was that they soon began to get hungry again, and the wolf, who was the hungriest of all, said to the rest:

"What shall we eat now, my friends, as there is no more man?"

"I suppose we shall have to eat the smallest of us," replied the bear, and the marten turned round to seize the squirrel who was much smaller than any of the rest. But the squirrel ran up a tree like lightning, and the marten remembering, just in time, that he was the next in size, slipped quick as thought into a hole in the rocks.

"What shall we eat now?" asked the wolf again when he had recovered from his surprise.

"We must eat the smallest of us," repeated the bear, stretching out a paw towards the hare; but the hare was not a hare for nothing, and before the paw had touched her, she had darted deep into the wood.

Now that the squirrel, the marten, and the hare had all gone, the fox was the smallest of the three who were left, and the wolf and the bear explained that they were very sorry, but they would have to eat him. Michael, the fox, did not run away as the others had done, but smiled in a friendly manner, and remarked, "Things taste so stale in a valley; one's appetite is so much better up on a mountain." The wolf and the bear agreed, and they turned out of the hollow where they had been walking, and chose a path that led up the mountain side. The fox trotted cheerfully by his two big companions, but on the way he managed to whisper to the wolf, "Tell me, Peter, when I am eaten, what will you have for your next dinner?"

This simple question seemed to put out the wolf very much. What would they have for their next dinner, and what was more important still, who would there be to eat it? They had made a rule always to dine off the smallest of the party, and when the fox was gone, why of course, he was smaller than the bear.

These thoughts flashed quickly through his head, and he said hastily, "Dear brothers, would it not be better for us to live together as comrades, and everyone to hunt for the common dinner? Is not my plan a good one?"

"It is the best thing I have ever heard," answered the fox; and as they were two to one the bear had to be content, though in his heart he would much have preferred a good dinner at once to any friendship.

For a few days all went well; there was plenty of game in the forest, and even the wolf had as much to eat as he could wish. One morning the fox as usual was going his rounds when he noticed a tall, slender tree, with a magpie's nest in one of the top branches.

Now the fox was particularly fond of young magpies, and he set about making a plan by which he could have one for dinner. At last he hit upon something which he thought would do, and accordingly he sat down near the tree and began to stare hard at it.

"What are you looking at, Michael?" asked the magpie, who was watching him from a bough.

"I'm looking at this tree. It has just struck me what a good tree it would be to cut my new snow-shoes out of." But at this answer the magpie screeched loudly, and exclaimed, "Oh, not this tree, dear brother, I implore you! I have built my nest on it, and my young ones are not yet old enough to fly."

"It will not be easy to find another tree that would make such good snow-shoes," answered the fox, cocking his head on one side, and gazing at the tree thoughtfully, "but I do not like to be ill-natured, so if you will give me one of your young ones I will seek my snow-shoes elsewhere."

Not knowing what to do the poor magpie had to agree, and flying back, with a heavy heart, he threw one of his young ones out of the nest. The fox seized it in his mouth and ran off in triumph, while the magpie, though deeply grieved for the loss of his little one, found some comfort in the thought that only a bird of extraordinary wisdom would have dreamed of saving the rest by the sacrifice of the one. But what do you think happened? Why, a few days later, Michael the fox might have been seen sitting under the very same tree, and a dreadful pang shot through the heart of the magpie as he peeped at him from a hole in the nest.

"What are you looking at?" he asked in a trembling voice.

"At this tree. I was just thinking what good snowshoes it would make," answered the fox in an absent voice, as if he was not thinking of what he was saying.

"Oh, my brother, my dear little brother, don't do that," cried the magpie, hopping about in his anguish. "You know you promised only a few days ago that you would get your snow-shoes elsewhere."

"So I did; but though I have searched through the whole forest, there is not a single tree that is as good as this. I am very sorry to put you out, but really it is not my fault. The only thing I can do for you is to offer to give up my snow-shoes altogether if you will throw me down one of your young ones in exchange."

And the poor magpie, in spite of his wisdom, was obliged to throw another of his little ones out of the nest; and this time he was not able to console himself with the thought that he had been much cleverer than other people.

He sat on the edge of his nest, his head drooping and his feathers all ruffled, looking the picture of misery. Indeed he was so different from the gay, jaunty magpie whom every creature in the forest knew, that a crow who was flying past, stopped to inquire what was the matter. "Where are the two young ones who are not in the nest?" asked he.

"I had to give them to the fox," replied the magpie in a quivering voice, "he has been here twice in the last week, and wanted to cut down my tree for the purpose of making snow-shoes out of it, and the only way I could buy him off was by giving him two of my young ones."

Oh, you fool," cried the crow, "the fox was only trying to frighten you. He could not have cut down the tree, for he has neither axe nor knife. Dear me, to think that you have sacrificed your young ones for nothing! Dear, dear! how could you be so very foolish!" And the crow flew away, leaving the magpie overcome with shame and sorrow.

The next morning the fox came to his usual place in front of the tree, for he was hungry, and a nice young magpie would have suited him very well for dinner. But this time there was no cowering, timid magpie to do his bidding, but a bird with his head erect and a determined voice.

"My good fox," said the magpie putting his head on one side and looking very wise - "my good fox, if you take my advice, you will go home as fast as you can. There is no use your talking about making snow-shoes out of this tree, when you have neither knife nor axe to cut it down with!"

"Who has been teaching you wisdom?" asked the fox, forgetting his manners in his surprise at this new turn of affairs.

"The crow, who paid me a visit yesterday," answered the magpie.

"The crow was it?" said the fox, "well, the crow had better not meet me for the future, or it may be the worse for him."

As Michael, the cunning beast, had no desire to continue the conversation, he left the forest; but when he came to the high road he laid himself at full length on the ground, stretching himself out, just as if he was dead. Very soon he noticed, out of the corner of his eye, that the crow was flying towards him, and he kept stiller and stiffer than ever, with his tongue hanging out of his mouth. The crow, who wanted her supper very badly, hopped quickly towards him, and was stooping forward to peck at his tongue when the fox gave a snap, and caught him by the wing. The crow knew that it was of no use struggling, so he said, "Ah, brother, if you are really going to eat me, do it, I beg of you, in good style. Throw me first over this precipice, so that my feathers may be strewn here and there, and that all who see them may know that your cunning is greater than mine." This idea pleased the fox, for he had not yet forgiven the crow for depriving him of the young magpies, so he carried the crow to the edge of the precipice and threw him over, intending to go round by a path he knew and pick him up at the bottom. But no sooner had the fox let the crow go than he soared up into the air, and hovering just out of reach of his enemy's jaws, he cried with a laugh, "Ah, fox! you know well how to catch, but you cannot keep."

With his tail between his legs, the fox slunk into the forest. He did not know where to look for a dinner, as he guessed that the crow would have flown back before him, and put everyone on their guard. The notion of going to bed without supper was very unpleasant to him, and he was wondering what in the world he should do, when he chanced to meet with his old friend the bear.

This poor animal had just lost his wife, and was going to get someone to mourn over her, for he felt her loss greatly. He had hardly left his comfortable cave when he had come across the wolf, who inquired where he was going. "I am going to find a mourner," answered the bear, and told his story.

"Oh, let me mourn for you," cried the wolf.

"Do you understand how to howl?" said the bear.

"Oh, certainly, godfather, certainly," replied the wolf; but the bear said he should like to have a specimen of his howling, to make sure that he knew his business. So the wolf broke forth in his song of lament, "Hu, hu, hu, hum, hoh," he shouted, and he made such a noise that the bear put up his paws to his ears, and begged him to stop.

"You have no idea how it is done. Be off with you," said he angrily.

A little further down the road the hare was resting in a ditch, but when she saw the bear, she came out and spoke to him, and inquired why he looked so sad. The bear told her of the loss of his wife, and of his search after a mourner that could lament over her in the proper style. The hare instantly offered her services, but the bear took care to ask her to give him a proof of her talents, before he accepted them. "Pu, pu, pu, pum, poh," piped the hare; but this time her voice was so small that the bear could hardly hear her. "That is not what I want," he said, "I will bid you good morning."

It was after this that the fox came up, and he also was struck with the bear's altered looks, and stopped. "What is the matter with you, godfather?" asked he, "and where are you going?"

"I am going to find a mourner for my wife," answered the bear.

"Oh, do choose me," cried the fox, and the bear looked at him thoughtfully.

"Can you howl well?" he said.

"Yes, beautifully, just listen," and the fox lifted up his voice and sang weeping, "Lou, lou, lou! the famous spinner, the baker of good cakes, the prudent housekeeper is torn from her husband! Lou, lou, lou! she is gone! she is gone!"

"Now at last I have found someone who knows the art of lamentation," exclaimed the bear, quite delighted; and he led the fox back to his cave, and bade him begin his lament over the dead wife who was lying stretched out on her bed of grey moss. But this did not suit the fox at all.

"One cannot wail properly in this cave," he said, "it is much too damp. You had better take the body to the storehouse. It will sound much finer there." So the bear carried his wife's body to the storehouse, while he himself went back to the cave to cook some pap for the mourner. From time to time he paused and listened for the sound of wailing, but he heard nothing. At last he went to the door of the storehouse, and called to the fox:

"Why don't you howl, godfather? What are you about?"

And the fox, who, instead of weeping over the dead bear, had been quietly eating her, answered:

"There only remain now her legs and the soles of her feet. Give me five minutes more and they will be gone also!"

When the bear heard that he ran back for the kitchen ladle, to give the traitor the beating he deserved. But as he opened the door of the storehouse, Michael was ready for him, and slipping between his legs, dashed straight off into the forest. The bear, seeing that the traitor had escaped, flung the ladle after him, and it just caught the tip of his tail, and that is how there comes to be a spot of white on the tails of all foxes.

The Capture Of The Sampo

Adapted by R. Eivind in Finnish Legends for English Children, from the original Song of the Kervala. Finnish Legends for English Children was published in 1893 by T. fisher Unwin, London.

AFTER THE MAGIC KANTELE WAS FINISHED, the three great heroes and magicians sailed away again towards the dismal Northland. Ilmarinen led the rowers on one side of the ship, and Lemminkainen on the other, and old Wainamoinen steered. They soon reached Pohjola and landed near Louhi's house.

When they had drawn their vessel up on land, they all went up to Louhi's house, and Wainamoinen told her that they were come for the Sampo; that if she would only give them the many-coloured lid they would go away content, but if not, they would take the whole Sampo by force. Then Louhi grew very angry and called together all the Northland warriors to slay them. But Wainamoinen began to play upon his kantele, and so wonderfully sweet were the tunes that he played, that the warriors forgot all about fighting and began to weep, and all the maidens of Pohjola began to dance. Still Wainamoinen played on and on, until a deep slumber came upon all the Northland folk. Then he ceased playing, and cast a powerful spell over them, so that they should not awake.

When all the Pohjola folk were sound asleep the three great heroes went to the mountains to seek the magic Sampo. And as they went Wainamoinen played such wonderful music that the great cliffs opened before them, and left them an open road to where the Sampo lay hid. When they had come near the cavern in which the Sampo lay, they sent Lemminkainen to enter the cave and bring it out. He, boasting of his strength, went into the cavern, and seizing hold of the magic Sampo, he put forth all his strength to lift it up, but it remained immovable, for the roots had grown deep into the earth, and bound it down tightly.

Then Lemminkainen remembered a huge ox that he had seen out in the fields, with horns seven fathoms long, and he went after it and hitched it to the biggest plough he could find, and began to plough all around the roots which held the Sampo down. And in a very short while the roots became loosened, and they were able to pick up the magic Sampo and carry it on board their vessel.

As soon as it was safely on board they sailed away, leaving all the Pohjola folk sleeping. On they flew towards their homes in Kalevala; but Lemminkainen grew weary of the silence, and asked Wainamoinen why he would not sing to cheer them. But Wainamoinen answered that song would only disturb the rowers, and that it was best never to rejoice until all danger was past. At length, when they had gone three days on their journey, Lemminkainen grew angry at Wainamoinen's silence, and began to sing himself. But his voice sounded harsh and unmelodious, and it made the very ship tremble.

Far off on the land a crane was standing amidst the rushes, amusing itself by counting its toes. But when it heard Lemminkainen's attempts at singing, it was so frightened that it flew off screaming over Pohjola, and by its screeching it awoke all the slumbering people. As soon as Louhi awoke she hurried off to her barns and cattle-pens to see if anything had been stolen, but she found everything all right. Next she hurried to the mountains, to the cavern where she had hidden the Sampo, but when she came there she found the cavern empty, and saw how her visitors had torn the Sampo loose from its fastenings.

Then Louhi returned to her house pale with anger and fear, for she knew that if the Sampo were lost that all the prosperity of the Northland would be lost with it. So she called up the goddess of the fogs, and sent her out to delay Wainamoinen's vessel. And then she called on Iko-Turso - a wicked monster living in the depths of the sea - to swim to the ship and sink it, and to eat the men in it, but to bring back the Sampo to Pohjola once more. And she prayed, moreover, to great Ukko that if the sea-monster should not succeed, that Ukko himself would send a fearful tempest to wreck the vessel.

First came the goddess of the fog, and wrapped them in such a thick mist that they could not move. Three days they lay so, and then Wainamoinen drew his sword, exclaiming, "We shall all perish here in the fog if no attempt is made to drive it away," and with these words he struck the waves with his sword. From the blade there flowed a stream of honey, and all at once the fog broke up, and left the way clear before them. But scarcely had the fog disappeared than they heard a mighty roaring sound, and the foam began to shoot up from the water alongside, and to cover the ship. Then Wainamoinen leaned over the vessel's side, and stretching out his arm he grasped something that he saw in the water, and pulled up the awful monster Iko-Turso. But the monster was so affrighted by being lifted out of the water that he promised to leave them in peace, and never to appear above the waters again if

Wainamoinen would only release him. So Wainamoinen let him go, and the second danger was past.

But now came the third and most terrible of all, for Ukko sent a mighty storm-wind, which lashed the waves into a fury, and stirred up the ocean to its very bottom. And at the very first pitch of the ship the magic kantele was swept overboard by the waves, and Ahto, the sea-god, caught it and carried it off to his home beneath the waves. Then Wainamoinen began to bewail the loss of his wonderful instrument; but as the storm grew worse, and tossed their ship about like a feather, all on board began to despair of ever reaching land alive. But Wainamoinen gave them comfort and courage, and he and Ilmarinen and Lemminkainen by their magic spells quietened the winds and the waves, and repaired the damage which the vessel had suffered from the storm. And then they went on their way in peace.

The Sampo Is Lost In The Sea

Adapted by R. Eivind in Finnish Legends for English Children, from the original Song of the Kervala. Finnish Legends for English Children was published in 1893 by T. fisher Unwin, London.

BUT WHEN LOUHI FOUND THAT ALL her magic had failed, she assembled all her warriors, and embarked them in her largest ship, and herself sailed off to recapture the Sampo by force of arms. Before long they came in sight of Wainamoinen's vessel, and when he saw that Louhi was pursuing him with such a mighty host of warriors, he cried out to Ilmarinen and Lemminkainen to row with all their might, in order to escape from their pursuers. So all the rowers rowed until the vessel fairly trembled, and the foam was tossed up from the bow as high as the clouds, but still they could not gain on their pursuers.

Then Wainamoinen saw that he must use some other means, so he took out a piece of flint from his tinder-box and dropped it into the water, saying as he did so, "Rise up from the bottom of the sea into a mighty mountain, so that Louhi's ship may be dashed to pieces." And suddenly a mountain of rock sprang up out of the water, and before Louhi could stop her ship it had hit upon the rocks and was wrecked.

But Louhi was not to be outdone in magic, so she took the timbers of the ship and made from them a magic eagle, using the rudder for its tail and five sharp iron scythes for its talons. And on his wings and back she posted all her warriors, and then the magic eagle rose up into the air. It made one circle round the heavens, and then lit upon the mast of Wainamoinen's vessel, almost overturning it by its weight. Wainamoinen first prayed to Ukko for aid, and then he asked Louhi if she would consent now to divide the Sampo between them. But she scorned his offer, and the eagle made a swoop downward to pick up the Sampo in its talons. But Lemminkainen raised his sword, and no sooner had the eagle grasped the Sampo than he brought down his sword with such force that every talon was cut off but one.

Then the eagle flew up on to the mast once more, and upbraided Lemminkainen because he had broken his promise to his mother that he would not go to war for sixty years. But Wainamoinen, believing that his last hour was come, took the rudder in his hand and struck the eagle such a mighty blow that all the warriors fell from its wings and back into the water. Then the eagle made one more swoop down upon the vessel, and, with the one talon it had left, it dragged the Sampo over the side of the ship so that it fell to the bottom of the ocean and was broken to pieces. And it is this that has brought so much wealth to the sea, for where the Sampo is there will always be wealth also. But a few pieces of the lid floated ashore to Kalevala, and it is therefore that our country has now the harvests that before that grew in the dismal Northland.

But Louhi threatened Wainamoinen, saying, "I will steal away your silver moonlight and your golden sunlight. I will send the frost and hail to kill your crops, and will send the bear - Otso - from the forests to kill your cattle and sheep. I will send upon your people nine diseases, each one of them more fatal than the one before." Then Wainamoinen replied, "No one from dismal Northland can harm us of Kalevala, Only Ukko rules the fate of peoples, and he will guard my crops from frost and hail, and my cattle from the bear, Otso. You may hide evil people in your Northland caverns, but you can never steal the Sun and Moon, and all your frosts and plagues and bears may turn against yourself."

And then Louhi departed to her home, weeping for the loss of the magic Sampo, and ever since that time there have been famines and poverty in gloomy Pohjola. But Wainamoinen and the other heroes returned home rejoicing, and on the shore they found fragments of the Sampo's lid. Then Wainamoinen prayed to Ukko to be merciful and kind to them, and to protect them from frost and hail and bears, and to let the golden light of the Moon and Sunshine for ever on the plains of Kalevala.

The Birth Of The Second Kantele

*Adapted by R. Eivind in Finnish Legends for English Children,
from the original Song of the Kervala. Finnish Legends for English
Children was published in 1893 by T. fisher Unwin, London.*

WHEN THE HEROES HAD RETURNED HOME, and found the fragments of the Sampo on the shore, they wished to make merry over the good fortune which even these fragments were sure to bring, but Wainamoinen could not give them music, since the wondrous kantele had been lost in the sea. Then he bade Ilmarinen make a huge rake with copper teeth a hundred fathoms long and the handle a thousand fathoms, and when the rake was ready, Wainamoinen took it, and sailing out over the sea in a magic vessel that needed neither sails nor oars to move it, he raked over the whole bottom of the ocean. But he only raked up shells and seaweed, and found no trace of the kantele.

Then Wainamoinen returned sadly home, saying, "Never again shall I pour forth floods of music to the people of Kalevala from the magic strings of my kantele." And driven on by his grief he left his house and went far off into the forest. As he wandered there he heard the birch-tree lamenting, and Wainamoinen asked the tree why it was unhappy when it had such lovely silver leaves and tassels. To this the birch-tree replied, "You think that I am always happy, and that my leaves and tassels must always be whispering joy. But alas! I am so weak and feeble, and must always stand alone without a word of sympathy. Others rejoice at the coming of the spring, but I am robbed of bark and tassels and tender twigs, and am cut up for firewood, and then in the wintertime the frost and the cold biting winds kill my young shoots and strip me of my silver leaves and leave me cold and naked."

While the birch-tree was speaking, Wainamoinen's face began to brighten, and he finally exclaimed, "Weep no more, good birch-tree, for I will turn your grief into joy and make you sing the most marvellous songs." Having said this he set to work to make a new kantele, taking birch-wood for the framework. At length the frame was already, but he did not know of what to make the pegs. Suddenly he came upon a great oak-tree on which grew golden-coloured acorns, and on each acorn sat a sacred cuckoo singing its melody. So Wainamoinen took a piece of the oak and made the pegs from it.

But the harp was not yet finished, for the five strings were still lacking. Then Wainamoinen journeyed on through the forest, until at length he came to where a forest-maiden was sitting on a mound and singing, and her long golden hair was falling loose over her shoulders. So Wainamoinen went up to her and begged her to give him some of her golden tresses, from which to weave the five strings for the kantele. And the maiden willingly gave up a portion of her golden hair, and from it Wainamoinen wove five strings, and at last the second kantele was complete. Then Wainamoinen sat down upon a rock and placed the kantele upon his knees, and after putting all the strings in tune he began to play. The fairy music resounded over hill and dale, until at length the very mountains began to dance with delight, and the rocks were rent in sunder and floated on the surface of the ocean. The trees of the forest, too, laughed with joy and began to dance about like children. The young men and maidens rejoiced as they listened to the music, and the grey-haired men and women were amazed, while the babies tried to crawl to where the sweet sounds came from.

The magic music resounded far and wide over Kalevala, and all the wild beasts of the forest fell upon their knees in wonder, while the birds perched upon the trees about him and accompanied the music with their singing. The fish left their homes beneath the waters and crowded to the shore to listen. And everything in nature, from earth and air and water, came to listen to the magic sweetness of Wainamoinen's playing.

Three days and more he played unceasing; playing in the houses of his people until their very beams rejoiced, and wandering through the forest, where the trees all bent in homage to him and waved their branches to his music. Then over the meadows, still playing, until the very ferns and flowers laughed with delight and the bushes chimed in in unison with the magic music of the kantele.

The White Slipper

Adapted by Andrew Lang in his Orange Fairy Book, 1906, from an original by Josef Calasanz Poestion in Lapplandische Märchen. The Orange Fairy Book was published by Longman, Green & Co in 1906.

ONCE UPON A TIME THERE LIVED a king who had a daughter just fifteen years old. And what a daughter!

Even the mothers who had daughters of their own could not help allowing that the princess was much more beautiful and graceful than any of them; and, as for the fathers, if one of them ever beheld her by accident he could talk of nothing else for a whole day afterwards.

Of course the king, whose name was Balancin, was the complete slave of his little girl from the moment he lifted her from the arms of her dead mother; indeed, he did not seem to know that there was anyone else in the world to love.

Now Diamantina, for that was her name, did not reach her fifteenth birthday without proposals for marriage from every country under heaven; but be the suitor who he might, the king always said him nay.

Behind the palace a large garden stretched away to the foot of some hills, and more than one river flowed through. Here the princess would come each evening towards sunset, attended by her ladies, and gather herself the flowers that were to adorn her rooms. She also brought with her a pair of scissors to cut off the dead blooms, and a basket to put them in, so that when the sun rose next morning he might see nothing unsightly. When she had finished this task she would take a walk through the town, so that the poor people might have a chance of speaking with her, and telling her of their troubles; and then she would seek out her father, and together they would consult over the best means of giving help to those who needed it.

But what has all this to do with the White Slipper? my readers will ask.

Have patience, and you will see.

Next to his daughter, Balancin loved hunting, and it was his custom to spend several mornings every week chasing the boars which abounded in the mountains a few miles from the city. One day, rushing downhill as fast as he could go, he put his foot into a hole and fell, rolling into a rocky pit of brambles. The king's wounds were not very severe, but his face and hands were cut and torn, while his feet were in a worse plight still, for, instead of proper hunting boots, he only wore sandals, to enable him to run more swiftly.

In a few days the king was as well as ever, and the signs of the scratches were almost gone; but one foot still remained very sore, where a thorn had pierced deeply and had festered. The best doctors in the kingdom treated it with all their skill; they bathed, and poulticed, and bandaged, but it was in vain. The foot only grew worse and worse, and became daily more swollen and painful.

After everyone had tried his own particular cure, and found it fail, there came news of a wonderful doctor in some distant land who had healed the most astonishing diseases. On inquiring, it was found that he never left the walls of his own city, and expected his patients to come to see him; but, by dint of offering a large sum of money, the king persuaded the famous physician to undertake the journey to his own court.

On his arrival the doctor was led at once into the king's presence, and made a careful examination of his foot.

"Alas! your majesty," he said, when he had finished, "the wound is beyond the power of man to heal; but though I cannot cure it, I can at least deaden the pain, and enable you to walk without so much suffering."

"Oh, if you can only do that," cried the king, "I shall be grateful to you for life! Give your own orders; they shall be obeyed."

"Then let your majesty bid the royal shoemaker make you a shoe of goat-skin very loose and comfortable, while I prepare a varnish to paint over it of which I alone have the secret!" So saying, the doctor bowed himself out, leaving the king more cheerful and hopeful than he had been for long.

The days passed very slowly with him during the making of the shoe and the preparation of the varnish, but on the eighth morning the physician appeared, bringing with him the shoe in a case. He drew it out to slip on the king's foot, and over the goat-skin he had rubbed a polish so white that the snow itself was not more dazzling.

"While you wear this shoe you will not feel the slightest pain," said the doctor. "For the balsam with which I have rubbed it inside and out has, besides its healing balm, the quality of strengthening the material it touches, so that, even were your majesty to live a thousand years, you would find the slipper just as fresh at the end of that time as it is now."

The king was so eager to put it on that he hardly gave the physician time to finish. He snatched it from the case and thrust his foot into it, nearly weeping for joy when he found he could walk and run as easily as any beggar boy.

"What can I give you?" he cried, holding out both hands to the man who had worked this wonder. "Stay with me, and I will heap on you riches greater than ever you dreamed of." But the doctor said he would accept nothing more than had been agreed on, and must return at once to his own country, where many sick people were awaiting him. So king Balancin had to content himself with ordering the physician to be treated with royal honours, and desiring that an escort should attend him on his journey home.

For two years everything went smoothly at court, and to king Balancin and his daughter the sun no sooner rose than it seemed time for it to set. Now, the king's birthday fell in the month of June, and as the weather happened to be unusually fine, he told the princess to celebrate it in any way that pleased her. Diamantina was very fond of being on the river, and she was delighted at this chance of delighting her tastes. She would have a merry-making such as never had been seen before, and in the evening, when they were tired of sailing and rowing, there should be music and dancing, plays and fireworks. At the very end, before the people went home, every poor person should be given a loaf of bread and every girl who was to be married within the year a new dress.

The great day appeared to Diamantina to be long in coming, but, like other days, it came at last. Before the sun was fairly up in the heavens the princess, too full of excitement to stay in the palace, was walking about the streets so covered with precious stones that you had to shade your eyes before you could look at her. By-and-by a trumpet sounded, and she hurried home, only to appear again in a few moments walking by the side of her father down to the river. Here a splendid barge was waiting for them, and from it they watched all sorts of races and feats of swimming and diving. When these were over the barge proceeded up the river to the field where the dancing and concerts were to take place, and after the prizes had been given away to the winners, and the loaves and the dresses had been distributed by the princess, they bade farewell to their guests, and turned to step into the barge which was to carry them back to the palace.

Then a dreadful thing happened. As the king stepped on board the boat one of the sandals of the white slipper, which had got loose, caught in a nail that was sticking out, and caused the king to stumble. The pain was great, and unconsciously he turned and shook his foot, so that the sandals gave way, and in a moment the precious shoe was in the river.

It had all occurred so quickly that nobody had noticed the loss of the slipper, not even the princess, whom the king's cries speedily brought to his side.

"What is the matter, dear father?" asked she. But the king could not tell her; and only managed to gasp out, "My shoe! my shoe!" While the sailors stood round staring, thinking that his majesty had suddenly gone mad.

Seeing her father's eyes fixed on the stream, Diamantina looked hastily in that direction. There, dancing on the current, was the point of something white, which became more and more distant the longer they watched it. The king could bear the sight no more, and, besides, now that the healing ointment in the shoe had been removed the pain in his foot was as bad as ever; he gave a sudden cry, staggered, and fell over the bulwarks into the water.

In an instant the river was covered with bobbing heads all swimming their fastest towards the king, who had been carried far down by the swift current. At length one swimmer, stronger than the rest, seized hold of his tunic, and drew him to the bank, where a thousand eager hands were ready to haul him out. He was carried, unconscious, to the side of his daughter, who had fainted with terror on seeing her father disappear below the surface, and together they were place in a coach and driven to the palace, where the best doctors in the city were awaiting their arrival.

In a few hours the princess was as well as ever; but the pain, the wetting, and the shock of the accident, all told severely on the king, and for three days he lay in a high fever. Meanwhile, his daughter, herself nearly mad with grief, gave orders that the white slipper should be sought for far and wide; and so it was, but even the cleverest divers could find no trace of it at the bottom of the river.

When it became clear that the slipper must have been carried out to sea by the current, Diamantina turned her thoughts elsewhere, and sent messengers in search of the doctor who had brought relief to her father, begging him to make another slipper as fast as possible, to supply the place of the one which was lost. But the messengers returned with the sad news that the doctor had died some weeks before, and what was worse, his secret had died with him.

In his weakness this intelligence had such an effect on the king that the physicians feared he would become as ill as before. He could hardly be persuaded to touch food, and all night long he lay moaning, partly with pain, and partly over his own folly in not having begged the doctor to make him several dozens of white slippers, so that in case of accidents he might always have one to put on. However, by-and-by he saw that it was no use weeping and wailing, and commanded that they should search for his lost treasure more diligently than ever.

What a sight the riverbanks presented in those days! It seemed as if all the people in the country were gathered on them. But this second search was no more fortunate than the first, and at last the king issued a proclamation that whoever found the missing slipper should be made heir to the crown, and should marry the princess.

Now many daughters would have rebelled at being disposed of in the manner; and it must be admitted that Diamantina's heart sank when she heard what the king had done. Still, she loved her father so much that she desired his comfort more than anything else in the world, so she said nothing, and only bowed her head.

Of course the result of the proclamation was that the riverbanks became more crowded than before; for all the princess's suitors from distant lands flocked to the spot, each hoping that he might be the lucky finder. Many times a shining stone at the bottom of the stream was taken for the slipper itself, and every evening saw a band of dripping downcast men returning homewards. But one youth always lingered longer than the rest, and night would still see him engaged in the search, though his clothes stuck to his skin and his teeth chattered.

One day, when the king was lying on his bed racked with pain, he heard the noise of a scuffle going on in his antechamber, and rang a golden bell that stood by his side to summon one of his servants.

"Sire," answered the attendant, when the king inquired what was the matter, "the noise you heard was caused by a young man from the town, who has had the impudence to come here to ask if he may measure your majesty's foot, so as to make you another slipper in place of the lost one."

"And what have you done to the youth?" said the king.

"The servants pushed him out of the palace, and, added a few blows to teach him not to be insolent," replied the man.

"Then they did very ill," answered the king, with a frown. "He came here from kindness, and there was no reason to maltreat him."

"Oh, my lord, he had the audacity to wish to touch your majesty's sacred person - he, a good-for-nothing boy, a mere shoemaker's apprentice, perhaps! And even if he could make shoes to perfection they would be no use without the soothing balsam."

The king remained silent for a few moments, then he said, "Never mind. Go and fetch the youth and bring him to me. I would gladly try any remedy that may relieve my pain."

So, soon afterwards, the youth, who had not gone far from the palace, was caught and ushered into the king's presence.

He was tall and handsome and, though he professed to make shoes, his manners were good and modest, and he bowed low as he begged the king not only to allow him to take the measure of his foot, but also to suffer him to place a healing plaster over the wound.

Balancin was pleased with the young man's voice and appearance, and thought that he looked as if he knew what he was doing. So he stretched out his bad foot which the youth examined with great attention, and then gently laid on the plaster.

Very shortly the ointment began to soothe the sharp pain, and the king, whose confidence increased every moment, begged the young man to tell him his name.

"I have no parents; they died when I was six, sire," replied the youth, modestly. "Everyone in the town calls me Gilguerillo, because, when I was little, I went singing through the world in spite of my misfortunes. Luckily for me I was born to be happy."

"And you really think you can cure me?" asked the king.

"Completely, my lord," answered Gilguerillo.

"And how long do you think it will take?"

"It is not an easy task; but I will try to finish it in a fortnight," replied the youth.

A fortnight seemed to the king a long time to make one slipper. But he only said, "Do you need anything to help you?"

"Only a good horse, if your majesty will be kind enough to give me one," answered Gilguerillo. And the reply was so unexpected that the courtiers could hardly restrain their smiles, while the king stared silently.

"You shall have the horse," he said at last, "and I shall expect you back in a fortnight. If you fulfil your promise you know your reward; if not, I will have you flogged for your impudence."

Gilguerillo bowed, and turned to leave the palace, followed by the jeers and scoffs of everyone he met. But he paid no heed, for he had got what he wanted.

He waited in front of the gates till a magnificent horse was led up to him, and vaulting into the saddle with an ease which rather surprised the attendant, rode quickly out of the town amidst the jests of the assembled crowd, who had heard of his audacious proposal. And while he is on his way let us pause for a moment and tell who he is.

Both father and mother had died before the boy was six years old; and he had lived for many years with his uncle, whose life had been passed in the study of chemistry. He could leave no money to his nephew, as he had a son of his own; but he taught him all he knew, and at his dead Gilguerillo entered an office, where he worked for many hours daily. In his spare time, instead of playing with the other boys, he passed hours poring over books, and because he was timid and liked to be alone he was held by everyone to be a little mad. Therefore, when it became known that he had promised to cure the king's foot, and had ridden away - no one knew where - a roar of laughter and mockery rang through the town, and jeers and scoffing words were sent after him.

But if they had only known what Gilguerillo's thoughts were they would have thought him madder than ever.

The real truth was that, on the morning when the princess had walked through the streets before making holiday on the river Gilguerillo had seen her from his window, and had straightway fallen in love with her. Of course he felt quite hopeless. It was absurd to imagine that the apothecary's nephew could ever marry the king's daughter; so he did his best to forget her, and study harder than before, till the royal proclamation suddenly filled him with hope. When he was free he no longer spent the precious moments poring over books, but, like the rest, he might have been seen wandering along the banks of the river, or diving into the stream after something that lay glistening in the clear water, but which turned out to be a white pebble or a bit of glass.

And at the end he understood that it was not by the river that he would win the princess; and, turning to his books for comfort, he studied harder than ever.

There is an old proverb which says, "Everything comes to him who knows how to wait." It is not all men who know how to wait, any more than it is all men who can learn by experience; but Gilguerillo was one of the few and instead of thinking his life wasted because he could not have the thing he wanted most, he tried to busy himself in other directions. So, one day, when he expected it least, his reward came to him.

He happened to be reading a book many hundreds of years old, which told of remedies for all kinds of diseases. Most of them, he knew, were merely invented by old women, who sought to prove themselves wiser than other people; but at length he came to something which caused him to sit up straight in his chair, and made his eyes brighten. This was the description of a balsam - which would cure every kind of sore or wound - distilled from a plant only to be found in a country so distant that it would take a man on foot two months to go and come back again.

When I say that the book declared that the balsam could heal every sort of sore or wound, there were a few against which it was powerless, and it gave certain signs by which these might be known. This was the reason why Gilguerillo demanded to see the king's foot before he would undertake to cure it; and to obtain admittance he gave out that he was a shoemaker. However, the dreaded signs were absent, and his heart bounded at the thought that the princess was within his reach.

Perhaps she was; but a great deal had to be accomplished yet, and he had allowed himself a very short time in which to do it.

He spared his horse only so much as was needful, yet it took him six days to reach the spot where the plant grew. A thick wood lay in front of him, and, fastening the bridle tightly to a tree, he flung himself on his hands and knees and began to hunt for the treasure. Many time he fancied it was close to him, and many times it turned out to be something else; but, at last, when light was fading, and he had almost given up hope, he came upon a large bed of the plant, right under his feet! Trembling with joy, he picked every scrap he could see, and placed it in his wallet. Then, mounting his horse, he galloped quickly back towards the city.

It was night when he entered the gates, and the fifteen days allotted were not up till the next day. His eyes were heavy with sleep, and his body ached with the long strain, but, without pausing to rest, he kindled a fire on is hearth, and quickly filling a pot with water, threw in the herbs and left them to boil. After that he lay down and slept soundly.

The sun was shining when he awoke, and he jumped up and ran to the pot. The plant had disappeared and in its stead was a thick syrup, just as the book had said there would be. He lifted the syrup out with a spoon, and after spreading it in the sun till it was partly dry, poured it into a small flask of crystal. He next washed himself thoroughly, and dressed himself, in his best clothes, and putting the flask in his pocket, set out for the palace, and begged to see the king without delay.

Now Balancin, whose foot had been much less painful since Gilguerillo had wrapped it in the plaster, was counting the days to the young man's return; and when he was told Gilguerillo was there, ordered him to be admitted at once. As he entered, the king raised himself eagerly on his pillows, but his face fell when he saw no signs of a slipper.

"You have failed, then?" he said, throwing up his hands in despair.

"I hope not, your majesty; I think not," answered the youth. And drawing the flask from his pocket, he poured two or three drops on the wound.

"Repeat this for three nights, and you will find yourself cured," said he. And before the king had time to thank him he had bowed himself out.

Of course the news soon spread through the city, and men and women never tired of calling Gilguerillo an impostor, and prophesying that the end of the three days would see him in prison, if not on the scaffold. But Gilguerillo paid no heed to their hard words, and no more did the king, who took care that no hand but his own should put on the healing balsam.

On the fourth morning the king awoke and instantly stretched out his wounded foot that he might prove the truth or falsehood of Gilguerillo"s remedy. The wound was certainly cured on that side, but how about the other? Yes, that was cured also; and not even a scar was left to show where it had been!

Was ever any king so happy as Balancin when he satisfied himself of this?

Lightly as a deer he jumped from his bed, and began to turn head over heels and to perform all sorts of antics, so as to make sure that his foot was in truth as well as it looked. And when he was quite tired he sent for his daughter, and bade the courtiers bring the lucky young man to his room.

"He is really young and handsome," said the princess to herself, heaving a sigh of relief that it was not some dreadful old man who had healed her father; and while the king was announcing to his courtiers the wonderful cure that had been made, Diamantina was thinking that if Gilguerillo looked so well in his common dress, how much improved by the splendid garments of a king" son. However, she held her peace, and only watched with amusement when the courtiers, knowing there was no help for it, did homage and obeisance to the chemist's boy.

Then they brought to Gilguerillo a magnificent tunic of green velvet bordered with gold, and a cap with three white plumes stuck in it; and at the sight of him so arrayed, the princess fell in love with him in a moment. The wedding was fixed to take place in eight days, and at the ball afterwards nobody danced so long or so lightly as king Balancin.

Louhi Attempts Revenge

Adapted by R. Eivind in Finnish Legends for English Children, from the original Song of the Kervala. Finnish Legends for English Children was published in 1893 by T. fisher Unwin, London.

LOUHI GREW MORE AND MORE ANGRY and envious when she heard how prosperous and happy all the folk of Kalevala were, since the fragments of the Sampo had floated to their shore. So she pondered long in her evil heart, how she might send them sorrow and misfortune. Now just at that time the old witch Lowjatar, Tuoni's daughter, came to Louhi and asked for shelter from the storms and cold, and Louhi took her in and treated her like an honoured guest. And while Lowjatar was there, nine children were born to her, all horrible diseases, and she named them Colic, Fever, Plague, Pleurisy, Ulcer, Consumption, Gout, Sterility, and Cancer. And then Louhi's evil heart rejoiced, and she took the nine diseases and sent them into Kalevala, there to harass and kill Wainamoinen's people.

And when the diseases came, everyone in Kalevala, both young and old, fell ill of all sorts of illnesses, and Wainamoinen at first did not know from where all this evil had come. But soon by his magic power he learned that it came from the children of Tuoni's daughter, Lowjatar, and then he set to work to drive them away. First he took all those that were ill to the bath-houses, and then he brought buckets of water and heated blocks of stone until he had filled the whole room with warm steam. Then he prayed to Ukko to drive away all these diseases from them, and to send these evil spirits to Tuoni's kingdom, where they belonged.

After Wainamoinen had prayed thus to Ukko, he took a magic balsam and rubbed it over all those that were ill, and sang magic spells over them, and then prayed once more to Ukko for success, and at length he drove out the nine diseases and saved his people from dying.

When the nine diseases had been driven out of Kalevala, the news of Wainamoinen's victory over them came at length to the old witch Louhi, and she grew angrier than ever that her revenge had failed. But she pondered over what means of revenge she should try next, and at length she hit upon another plan. She went out into the forest and cast a magic spell upon the hugest bear in all the Northland - the great bear, Otso - and he hastened from his Pohjola home and began to kill the flocks and herds in Kalevala.

Then Wainamoinen hastened to Ilmarinen, and bade him make a triple-pointed spear with which to kill Otso. And when the spear was ready, Wainamoinen hastened off to the forest to find the bear, singing as he went, and calling upon the forest-god Tapio and his wife to grant him success in his hunt. He had not gone far before he heard his dog bark, and hurrying up to the spot he found Otso standing facing the dog and trying to snap him up, and before the bear perceived him, Wainamoinen was able to end Otso's life with a single thrust of his magic spear.

When Otso was dead, Wainamoinen threw the body across his shoulder and hastened off home, singing songs of rejoicing as he went. And when he reached his house there was great rejoicing, and everyone came out to welcome the dead bear, addressing it as if Otso were some honoured guest come to see them. First Wainamoinen sang a song of praise to the dead Otso, and bade his people welcome him with all due honour. And then the people answered with the most extravagant expressions of pleasure and welcome and admiration for Otso, and offered him all the best things in the house, and when all this ceremony was over they took off the fur and cut the body up ready for cooking, and prepared the steaks and joints to make a grand feast.

At length the whole of the bear was cooked, and a great feast was spread in Wainamoinen's house on golden dishes, and with sparkling beer in copper beakers. And when all were seated at the table, Wainamoinen rose and sang the story of Otso's birth and life. And this is the story which he sang, "Long ago a maiden walked in the ether on the edges of the clouds, and as she walked she threw down wool and hair upon the waters from two boxes that she carried. The wool and hair were floated into the shore, and there Mielikki, wife of the forest-god, found them and joined the wool and hair together by magic spells. Then she laid the bundle in a birch-bark basket and bound it in the top of the lofty pine, and there the young bear was rocked into life.

"Otso grew quickly and became graceful in his movements, although his feet were clumsy and his ankles crooked, his mouth large and forehead broad; but he still had no teeth or claws. Then Mielikki said, 'I would give you claws and teeth, Otso, but I fear that you will use them to harm people with.' But Otso fell on his knees and swore that he would never harm the good. So Mielikki took the hardest knots from all the trees to make him teeth and claws, but all of them were too weak. Then she went to a magic fir that grew in Tapio's kingdom, and which had silver branches and golden cones, and from these she made Otso's claws and teeth. Thus was Otso born and reared."

So they feasted and made merry, and when the feast was over they all tried to see which could pull out Otso's teeth and claws, in order to preserve them for their magic power. And of all the men there only the aged Wainamoinen could draw them out. When this was done, Wainamoinen called for his kantele and bade them light torches, as it was already dark. Then he sang sweet songs and played lovely music, so that the long evening passed away like magic, and he sang of the hunter's victory and prayed to Ukko always to give good fortune to the hunters of Kalevala.

Thus were Louhi's two first attempts at revenge unsuccessful.

Louhi Steals The Sun, The Moon, And Fire

Adapted by R. Eivind in Finnish Legends for English Children, from the original Song of the Kervala. Finnish Legends for English Children was published in 1893 by T. fisher Unwin, London.

WHEN THESE TWO DANGERS WERE OVERCOME, Wainamoinen played upon his kantele so sweetly that the Sun and Moon came down from their stations in the sky to listen to his music. But evil Louhi crept upon them unawares and made both Sun and Moon her captives, and carried them off to the dismal Northland, and there she hid them both in caverns in the mountains, that they might never again shine upon Kalevala. Next Louhi crept back to Kalevala and stole all the fire from the hearths, and left all their homes cold and cheerless. Then there was nothing but black night in the world, and great Ukko himself did not know what to do without the light of the Sun and Moon.

Ukko wandered all over the clouds to find out what had become of the Sun and Moon, and at last he whirled his fire-sword round his head so that the lightning flashed over the whole sky. From this lightning he kindled a little fire, and putting it in a gold and silver cradle, he gave it to the Ether-maidens to rock and care for, until it grew into a second Sun. So the Fire-child was cared for tenderly, and he grew fast; but one day the maidens were not watching him closely, and he escaped from them, and bursting through the clouds with a noise like a thunder-clap, he shot across the heavens like a red fire-ball.

Then Wainamoinen said to Ilmarinen, "Come, let us see what this fire is that is fallen from the heavens." And so they set out towards the spot where the ball of fire had seemed to fall. Soon they came to a wide river and set to work to make a magic boat to cross it, and in a very short time the boat was made, and they rowed over. On the other bank they were met by the oldest of the Ether-maidens, who asked them where they were going.

So they told her who they were, and that they had lost all fire and light in Kalevala, so that they were come to seek the fire that they had seen fall from the heavens. Then the Ether-maiden told them what had happened, saying, "After the Fire-child had begun to grow, he escaped from us one day and bursting through the clouds he came down to Pohjola. There he killed youths and babes and old people, until he was driven away by a magic spell. He fled then, burning fields and forests on his way, until at length he plunged into a great lake, and made the waters boil and rage. Then the fish held a council how to get rid of him, and it was decided that one of them must swallow him. First the salmon tried, but failed, and then the bold whiting made a dash and succeeded in swallowing the evil Fire-child. After this the waters of the lake grew quiet, and all went on as before.

But soon the whiting was seized with terrible pains and began to swim round in agony, begging for someone to kill him and put him out of his sufferings. For a long time he swam about unheeded, but at last a trout seized the whiting and swallowed him. For a while all was quiet again, but then the trout began to suffer in his turn. Still every fish was afraid to swallow him, until a pike darted up and ate up the trout. But then the pike was seized with the same pains, and he is now swimming about in great agony, but none will help him.

When the Ether-maiden had finished her account of what had happened, Wainamoinen and Ilmarinen wove a great net from seaweed, and hurrying to the lake they began to draw the net all through it in order to catch the Fire-fish. But the net was a poor one, and they failed to catch the pike that had swallowed the other fish and the Fire-child.

Then the two magicians gave up their useless net, and, choosing an island nearby, they resolved to plant flax that they might make a stronger and better net. They went to Tuoni's kingdom before they could find the proper seed, and found it there under the care of a tiny insect. When they had brought the seed from the Deathland, they planted it on the shore, in the ashes of a ship that had been burnt there, and in a single night the flax had grown up and ripened. Then they pulled it, and washed and dried and combed it, and took it to the Kalevala maidens to spin. Soon the spinning was done and the net was woven.

So the two great heroes took the flaxen net and hastened back to the lake and began to drag for the Fire-fish. But they only caught common fish, and the pike remained hidden in the deep caverns. Then Wainamoinen made the net longer and wider and they tried again, but though they caught fish of every species, the Fire-fish was not amongst them. Wainamoinen then prayed to Ahto, god of the ocean, and his wife, Wellamo, that they would drive the Fire-fish into his nets. Scarcely had Wainamoinen finished speaking, when a little dwarf rose from the waters and offered to help them. They accepted the tiny man's aid, and while they drew their nets, the dwarf beat the waters with a magic pole and scared all the fish toward them. And as they drew, Wainamoinen sang a magic charm to bring the fish in still greater numbers.

This time the net was full of pike, and they dragged it to the shore rejoicing, and among them they found the Fire-fish. So they threw the other fish back into the water, and Wainamoinen drew his knife and began to cut up the Fire-fish. Inside of the pike he found the trout, and inside of the trout the whiting, and on opening the whiting he came upon a ball of blue yarn. Wainamoinen quickly unwound the blue ball, and within that found a red ball, and when he had opened the red ball he came to the ball of fire in the middle.

They pondered how they should get the fire to Kalevala, and at last Ilmarinen seized it in his hands to carry it off. But it singed Wainamoinen's beard and burned Ilmarinen's hands dreadfully, and then it jumped out of their reach and rolled off over field and forest, burning everything in its course. Wainamoinen hastened after it, and at length caught it hidden in a mass of punk-wood. Then he took it and put it, wood and all, in a copper box and hastened off home. Thus the fire returned to Kalevala.

But Ilmarinen, suffering great agony from his burnt hands, hastened to the sea to lave them in the cool water. And he called up the ice and frost and snow to come and cool his parched hands, and, when all these proved insufficient, he called on great Ukko to send him some healing balm to take away the cruel torture. And Ukko granted his prayer and his hands were healed. Then Ilmarinen returned home and rejoiced to find that Wainamoinen had already brought the fire there.

The Restoration Of The Sun And Moon

Adapted by R. Eivind in Finnish Legends for English Children, from the original Song of the Kervala. Finnish Legends for English Children was published in 1893 by T. fisher Unwin, London.

THOUGH THE FIRE HAD BEEN RESTORED to Kalevala, still the golden Moon and the silver Sun were lost, and the frost came and killed the crops, and the cattle began to die of hunger. Every living thing felt sick and faint in the dark, dreary world. Then one of the maidens of Kalevala suggested to Ilmarinen to make a moon of gold and a sun of silver, and to hang them up in the heavens; so Ilmarinen set to work. While he was forging them, Wainamoinen came and asked what he was working at, and so Ilmarinen told him that he was going to make a new sun and moon. But Wainamoinen said, "This is mere folly, for silver and gold will not shine like the sun and moon." Still Ilmarinen worked on, and at length he had forged a moon of gold and a sun of silver, and hung them in their places in the sky. But they gave no light, as Wainamoinen had said.

Then Wainamoinen determined to find out where the sun and moon had gone. So he cut three chips from an alder-tree, and laying them on the ground before him, he cast many magic spells over them. Then when all was ready, he asked the alder-chips to tell him truly where the sun and moon were hidden. The alder-chips then answered that they were hidden in the caverns of the mountains of Pohjola.

No sooner had Wainamoinen heard this, than he made ready for a journey and started off for the dismal Northland. When he had travelled three days and was come to the borders of Pohjola, he found a wide river in the road and no boat to cross over in. So he built a huge fire on the shore, and soon such a dense column of smoke arose that Louhi sent someone to see what the matter was. But when Wainamoinen called to the messenger to bring him a boat, the man made no reply, but hurried back to Louhi and told her that it was Wainamoinen, who was coming to her house.

Then Wainamoinen saw that he could never get across in that way, so he changed himself into a pike and swam over very easily, and then changed back to his own shape when he had reached the opposite shore. He hastened on with mighty strides, and soon reached Louhi's dwelling. There he was met as if he were a most honoured guest, and they invited him into the hall. Wainamoinen went in unsuspectingly, but no sooner was he inside than he found himself surrounded by crowds of armed warriors.

The warriors asked him in a threatening tone why he had come there. But Wainamoinen was not frightened, but answered boldly that he had come to seek the Sun and the Moon. Then the chief of the warriors replied, "We have the Sun and Moon safe in a mountain cavern, and you shall never get them back, nor shall you leave this hall alive." No sooner had he finished speaking than Wainamoinen drew his magic sword, and fell upon those that stood between him and the door. They gave way before him, and in a moment he was out in the courtyard, where he could have room to fight fairly. All the warriors rushed at him with drawn swords and lifted spears, and the fire flashed from their weapons. But Wainamoinen was more than a match for all of them, and in a very short time he had stretched them all lifeless on the ground.

Then he left the court and hastened on to find the Sun and Moon. Soon he came to a solitary birch-tree, and beside the tree stood a carved pillar of stone, which concealed an opening in the rocks. Wainamoinen gave three blows with his magic sword, and the pillar broke in pieces, showing behind it an entrance into the rock; but the entrance was shut by a massive door, and there was only a little crack through which he could peep. Inside he saw the Sun and Moon prisoners, but though he tried with all his strength and all his magic spells to open the door, it still remained tightly shut, and he could not budge it so much as an inch.

Wainamoinen despaired of ever succeeding in liberating the Sun and Moon, and he hastened home to ask for Ilmarinen's help. He told him to forge a set of skeleton-keys, so that one of them would fit the lock of the door to the Sun's prison. Ilmarinen went to work and soon his anvil was ringing merrily to the blows of his hammer.

Now Louhi had grown very much alarmed after Wainamoinen had slain all her warriors, and so she assumed the shape of an eagle and flew away to Kalevala to see what was going on there. She heard the merry ring of Ilmarinen's work and flew down and lit in the window of the smithy. There she asked what he was doing, and the cunning Ilmarinen replied, "I am forging a collar of steel for the neck of evil Louhi, and with it I shall bind her fast to the rocks."

Louhi was terribly alarmed at this, so she flew to Pohjola and released the Sun and Moon from prison immediately, and sent them to their places in the heavens. Then the silver sunlight and the golden moonlight returned once more to Kalevala, and Ilmarinen, and Wainamoinen, and all the people offered up a prayer that they might never again be deprived of the blessed Sun and Moon.

Mariatta And Wainamoinen's Departure

Adapted by R. Eivind in Finnish Legends for English Children, from the original Song of the Kervala. Finnish Legends for English Children was published in 1893 by T. fisher Unwin, London.

THERE LIVED A FAIR AND LOVELY maiden in Kalevala, called Mariatta. She was the loveliest and purest of virgins, and tended her parents" flocks upon the mountain sides. Here one day, as she was watching the sheep, she heard a voice calling to her, and on looking round she found that it was a bright red berry calling to her, and asking her to pluck it. Mariatta did not know that this was a magic berry, so she picked it and put it to her lips to eat it. But the berry rolled from her lips down into her bosom, and said to her, "You shall have a son, and he shall become a mighty man and drive forth the old magician Wainamoinen."

Then Mariatta took the flocks home and was so silent and still that her parents noticed it and asked her what the matter was. So she told them what had happened, but they grew angry and would not keep her in their house, for they did not believe the story about the berry.

Poor Mariatta was now obliged to wander about without a shelter from the cold winds. At length she sent a servant, who had remained faithful to her and had accompanied her, to a village of Pohjola to ask for shelter from an old man named Ruotus. The maid, Piltti, went to Ruotus and told him of Mariatta's hard lot, but Ruotus and his wife would not have her in their house, but only grudgingly consented to let her go to a stable in the forest, where the Fire-horse of Hisi was kept.

So Mariatta was obliged to go to the stable in the dense forest far off from every human being, and there she begged the Hisi-horse to keep her warm by his fiery breath. The Hisi-horse was kinder to her than men had been, for he let her lie down comfortably in his manger, and kept her warm with his fiery breath. There the babe was born, and his mother grew happy once more, in spite of her sorrowful circumstances. But one night, while she slept, the babe disappeared, and the poor mother was overwhelmed with grief.

Then she wandered forth and looked everywhere for him, but in vain. So she asked the North-star if he had seen her son. But the North-star answered, "I would not tell you even if I knew. For it is your son who has made me and set me here in the bitter cold." And next Mariatta asked the Moon, and received the same answer as the North-star had given. Then she went to the Sun and asked him. And the Sun said, "I know very well where your son is hidden, for he made me and put me here to shine with my silver light. He lies sleeping yonder in the Swampland." So Mariatta hastened to the spot that the Sun had pointed out and there found her babe sleeping peacefully in the water among the rushes.

Then she returned with the babe to her father's house, and this time he received her and allowed her to live there in peace. And the child grew in beauty and wisdom, and his mother called him

Flower, but others called him Son-of-Sorrow. Then his mother called in an old man, Wirokannas, to baptize the child, but Wirokannas said, "First must someone see if the child shall become an honest man, or a wicked wizard, for if he be not honest I will not baptize him."

So Wainamoinen was called to examine the child - it was only two weeks old then - and see if it would grow up a noble man or not. Wainamoinen came and saw the child, and then said, "Since this child is only a poor outcast, born in a manger, and having no father save a berry, let him be cast out on to the hillsides or into the marshes to perish."

But all at once the babe himself began to speak, saying, "Oh aged Wainamoinen, foolish hero, you have given a false decision. You yourself have done great wrongs, yet have not been punished. You gave your own brother Ilmarinen to ransom your poor life. You persecuted the lovely Aino so that she perished in the deep sea, yet you were not killed for all this."

Then Wirokannas saw that this was truly a magic babe, and he baptized him to become a mighty hero, and a ruler and king over Kalevala.

Years passed by after this, and Wainamoinen felt his power gradually leaving him and going over to Mariatta's child. So the ancient hero, with a sad heart, sang his last magic spell in Kalevala, and made a magic boat of copper to sail away in. Then he cast loose from the shore and sailed off towards the west, singing as he went, "Fare you well, my people. Many suns shall rise and set on Kalevala until the people shall at length regret my absence and shall call upon me to come back with my magic songs and wisdom. Fare you well."

Thus Wainamoinen, in his magic boat of copper, left Kalevala. On he sailed to the land of the setting sun, and at length he reached the haven and anchored his boat, never again to return to Kalevala. But the wondrous kantele and all his songs and wisdom remain among us to this day.

Historical Notes

This section contains some brief biographical notes about the original collectors and their books featured in this collection. These notes have been adapted from those primarily on Wikipedia along with other supporting sources and notes.

R. Eivind

Little seems to be known about R. Eivind. Research on the internet and in biographical dictionaries has produced little other than that this person was the author of *Finnish Legends for English Children*.

The book contains thirty-eight Finnish children's stories that cover almost all of the songs and runes contained in the Kalevala, the epic of the Finnish people. These stories lead English speaking children into a hitherto unexplored region of the fairy world, for the folklore of Finland is probably the least known in the West.

As an introduction "Father Mikko" has been chosen as the story-teller, and we find stories like *Illmarinen Forges the Sampo*, a classic Finnish tale, alongside stories like *The Isle of Refuge, Wainamoinen And Youkahainen, Aino's Fate, Wainamoinen's Search For Aino, The Rainbow-Maiden* and *Ilmarinen's Bride Of Gold*".

While some of the characters' names are, at first, unfamiliar to us compared with other northern tales, by the end of the book they become as familiar as old friends.

The first version of The Kalevala (called The Old Kalevala) was published in 1835 by Elias Lönnrot. The version most commonly known today was first published in 1849 and consists of 22,795 verses, divided into fifty folk stories .

Of the five complete translations into English, it is only the older translations by John Martin Crawford (1888) and William Forsell Kirby (1907) which attempt to strictly follow the original (Kalevala metre) of the poems. Eino Friberg's 1988 translation uses it selectively but in general is more attuned to pleasing the ear than being an exact metrical translation. and also often reduces the length of songs for aesthetic reasons.

Andrew Lang

Andrew Lang FBA was a Scottish poet, novelist, literary critic, and contributor to the field of anthropology. He is best known as a collector of folk and fairy tales. The Andrew Lang lectures at the University of St Andrews are named after him.

Lang was born on 31st March 1844 in Selkirk. He was the eldest of the eight children born to John Lang, the town clerk, and his wife Jane Plenderleath Sellar, who was the daughter of Patrick Sellar, factor to the first duke of Sutherland. On 17th April 1875, he married Leonora Blanche Alleyne, youngest daughter of C. T. Alleyne of Clifton and Barbados. She was (or should have been) variously credited as author, collaborator, or translator of Lang's Colour / Rainbow Fairy Books, which he edited.

He was educated at Selkirk Grammar School, Loretto School, and the Edinburgh Academy, as well as the University of St Andrews and Balliol College, Oxford, where he took a first class in the final classical schools in 1868, becoming a fellow and subsequently honorary fellow of Merton College. He soon made a reputation as one of the most able and versatile writers of the day as a journalist, poet, critic, and historian. In 1906, he was elected FBA.

He died of angina pectoris on 20th July 1912 at the Tor-na-Coille Hotel in Banchory, survived by his wife. He was buried in the cathedral precincts at St Andrews, where a monument can be visited in the south-east corner of the 19th century section.

Lang is now chiefly known for his publications on folklore, mythology, and religion. The earliest of his publications is *Custom and Myth* (1884). In *Myth, Ritual and Religion* (1887) he explained the "irrational" elements of mythology as survivals from more primitive forms. Lang's *Making of Religion* was heavily influenced by the 18th century idea of the "noble savage", in it, he maintained the existence of high spiritual ideas among so-called "savage" races, drawing parallels with the contemporary interest in occult phenomena in England.

His *Blue Fairy Book* (1889) was a beautifully produced and illustrated edition of fairy tales that has become a classic. This was followed by many other collections of fairy tales, collectively known as *Andrew Lang's Fairy Books*. In the preface of the *Lilac Fairy Book* he credits his wife with translating and transcribing most of the stories in the collections.

Lang was one of the founders of "psychical research" and his other writings on anthropology include *The Book of Dreams and Ghosts* (1897), *Magic and Religion* (1901) and *The Secret of the Totem* (1905). He served as President of the Society for Psychical Research in 1911.

He collaborated with S. H. Butcher in a prose translation (1879) of Homer's *Odyssey*, and with E. Myers and Walter Leaf in a prose version (1883) of the *Iliad*, both still noted for their archaic but attractive style.

Lang's writings on Scottish history are characterised by a scholarly care for detail, a piquant literary style, and a gift for disentangling complicated questions. *The Mystery of Mary Stuart* (1901) was a consideration of the fresh light thrown on Mary, Queen of Scots, by the Lennox manuscripts in the University Library, Cambridge, approving of her and criticising her accusers.

Lang was active as a journalist in various ways, ranging from sparkling "leaders" for the Daily News to miscellaneous articles for the Morning Post, and for many years he was literary editor of Longman's Magazine.

Zacharias Topelius

Zacharias Topelius, 1818 –1898, was a Swedish-speaking Finnish author, poet, journalist, historian, and rector of the University of Helsinki who wrote novels related to Finnish history in Swedish.

The original name of the Topelius family was the Finnish name Toppila which had been Latinized to Toppelius by the author's great-great-grandfather and later changed to Topelius.

Topelius was born at Kuddnäs, near Nykarleby in Ostrobothnia, the son of a physician of the same name (Zacharias Topelius the Elder), who was distinguished as the earliest collector of Finnish folk-songs. As a child he heard his mother, Katarina Sofia Calamnius, sing the songs of the Finnish-Swedish poet Franzén. At the age of eleven, he was sent to school in Oulu and boarded with relatives who managed a lending library, where he nurtured his love of literature and fantasy.

Topelius arrived in Helsinki in 1831 and became a member of the circle of young nationalist men surrounding Johan Ludvig Runeberg, in whose home he stayed for some time. Topelius became a student at the Imperial Alexander University of Finland in 1833, received his master's degree in 1840, the Licentiate degree in history in 1844 and his PhD in 1847, having defended a dissertation titled *De modo matrimonia jungendi apud fennos quondam vigente* ("About the custom of marriage among the ancient Finns"). Besides history, his academic studies included Theology and Medicine. He was secretary of Societas pro fauna et flora fennica from 1842 until 1846, was employed by the university library between 1846 and 1861, and taught History, Statistics and Swedish at Helsingfors lyceum during the same period.

Through the intervention of a friend, Fredrik Cygnæus, Topelius was named professor extraordinary of the History of Finland at the University in 1854. He was made first ordinary professor of Finnish, Russian and Nordic history in 1863, and exchanged this chair for the one in general history in 1876. He was rector of the university from 1875 until 1878, when he retired as Emeritus Professor and received the title of verkligt statsråd, or "state councillor", a Russian honorary title.

Quite early in his career he began to distinguish himself as a lyric poet, with the three successive volumes of his *Heather Blossoms* (1845–54). The earliest of his historical romances was *The Duchess of Finland*, published in 1850. He was also editor-in-chief of the *Helsingfors Gazette* from 1841 to 1860.

In 1878, Topelius was allowed to withdraw from his professional duties, but this did not sever his connection with the university. It gave him, however, more leisure for his abundant and various literary enterprises. Of all the multifarious writings of Topelius, in prose and verse, that which has enjoyed the greatest popularity is his *Tales of a Barber-Surgeon*, episodes of historical fiction from the days of Gustavus II. Adolphus to those of Gustavus III., treated in the manner of Sir Walter Scott. The five volumes of this work appeared at intervals between 1853 and 1867. Topelius attempted to write plays as well, finding success in his tragedy, *Regina von Emmeritz* (1854). Topelius aimed at the cultivation of a strong Finnish patriotism. He wrote a poem which Jean Sibelius used for a composition with a political statement, *Islossningen i Uleå älv*.

Together with the composer Friedrich Pacius he wrote the libretto in the style of Romantic nationalism to the first Finnish opera: *Kung Karls jakt*. Topelius initially thought of writing a trivial entertainment, but having heard extracts from the opera project at a concert in 1851, he realized that Pacius was writing a grand opera on the theme of salvation, following the early Romantic style of Carl Maria von Weber's *Der Freischütz* (1821) and *Oberon* (1826). Topelius wrote the libretto in Swedish, though it was translated later by others, but its subject is emphatically Finnish. He also wrote the libretto for *Prinsessan av Cypern*, set by Fredrik Pacius and Lars-Erik Larsson.

Many of his works employed esoterical allegories harking back to ancient mysteries and perhaps Rosicrucian and alchemical themes, but on the other hand some of his short works examined the effects of industrialisation on Finnish society.

Topelius died in his manor house of Koivuniemi, in Sipoo, Finland, where he wrote his greatest works. He is buried in the Hietaniemi Cemetery in Helsinki. There was a small Finnish American village named after Topelius, founded in 1901 in Otter Tail County, Minnesota, USA.

About The Editor

I was born in 1962 into a predominantly sporting household – Dad being a good footballer, playing senior amateur and lower league professional football in England, as well as running a series of private businesses in partnership with mum, herself an accomplished and medal winning dancer.

I obtained a degree in History from Leeds University before wandering rather haphazardly into the emerging world of business computing in the late nineteen-eighties.

A little like my sporting father, I followed a succession of amateur writing paths alongside my career in technology, including working as a freelance journalist and book reviewer, my one claim to fame being a by-line in a national newspaper in the UK, The Sunday People.

I also spent 10 years treading the boards, appearing all over the south of the UK in pantos and plays, in village halls and occasionally on the stage of a professional theatre or two.

Following the sporting theme, and a while after I hung up my own boots, I worked on live TV broadcasts for the BBC, ITV, TVNZ, EuroSport and others as a rugby "Stato", covering Heineken Cups,

Six Nations, IRB World Sevens and IRB World Cups in the late '90's and early '00's.

You can find out more at: www.clivegilson.com

287

www.ingramcontent.com/pod-product-compliance
Lightning Source LLC
Chambersburg PA
CBHW060909190726

48286CB00002B/432